THE SHADOWS OF MIGHT

A SAM ABEL NOVEL

CLARKE MAYER

To Dale, who said, "You should write a book."

1

———

The long shadows formed by a broken window's glass remnants reached for Sigrid Lang. Each sharp, pointed edge emulated the claws of an angry specter. Behind a rotted, paint-stripped door at the end of the corridor, the sound of muffled voices and strained whispers in heated debate echoed through the hall. Each hissing consonant bounced from wall to wall like dueling snakes. The only other source of light came through a pinhole in the window beside her. Much of it had been boarded up with wooden planks, and where one chunk been broken off, only a meager helping of light punched through. With each soft step she took, she grew closer to the door and further plunged into absolute darkness.

She was tall—six feet and two inches, to be exact. The only color that produced any evidence of life in the room belonged to the blonde, curled hair that fell chin-length. Her uniform, a dark-grey khaki skirt that met a similar jacket at the waist, acted as a sort of camouflage in the dark tunnel. Her cool, pale skin shuddered with goose bumps in the frigid room, and each hair stood at attention on the back of her neck—not just because of the temperature, but because of the action she was about to take.

The building, which was in the city of Pforzheim in Germany—specifically the intersection of Leopoldstraße and Zerrennerstraße—was now empty save for the men that had taken up residence directly ahead of her. It was that residency that had tipped her off in the first place. She'd first spotted them coming and going in the night through a makeshift entrance at the back of the building. They used a door that *looked* like it had been sealed shut, but was quite operable for those that knew it was there. Only a slight push had been needed to open it. Any citizen who'd had adequate housing wouldn't dare live in a building that looked ready to be condemned. It was all the more strange that the two souls coming and going were dressed in the clothing of patrol officers.

The men behind the door, both of whom limited their voices to low hisses, were, to the best of her knowledge, unaware they were being overheard. Sigrid retrieved a Luger from its holster inside her blouse and let it fall to her side before she ventured any further. She stepped quietly, each movement slow and calculated, until finally she had fallen into complete shadow.

When she arrived at the door, she pressed her ear close to the splintered wooden surface and listened closely, silencing her own breath. The subtle whispers had been hard to decipher, and there was little evidence of just *what* exactly they were saying or what language they were speaking. She had hoped, for her sake, that her assumptions had been correct. The two men could be her ticket to safety, and the risk of what she was about to do was far outweighed by the reward.

She composed herself, closing her eyes for a moment, preparing herself for what she was about to do. She'd relied on her instinct to work up the guts to get this far, and now all she could do was pray she had been right. Sigrid breathed deeply, exhaled, and gripped the Luger tightly in her black-gloved hand. She then grabbed the door handle and twisted before pushing the door open and drawing her weapon in one fluid motion.

Both men, bewildered at the surprising entry, were half-dressed in olive green *Ordnungspolizei* uniforms, and they sat over a table with a small radio pinning down a map of Pforzheim. They stared back at Sigrid slack-jawed, and neither moved when they recognized the weapon pointed at them. The man to her left was slim and blonde-haired. His blue eyes reflected vibrantly off the light pouring in through the window on the opposite side of the room, and he held a sandwich in his hand that was only partly eaten. With each breath he took, plumes of moisture exited his mouth. The other was a brawny, brown-haired man with a stubble-kissed face that hadn't seen a razor in days.

"*Was ist das?*" the larger man asked.

Sigrid searched the room for evidence to support her cause. For a moment she was concerned she had gathered flawed information and stumbled upon an operation that she had either compromised or foolishly entered. Her assumptions were confirmed, though, after quickly scrutinizing the details of this hidden outfit.

"*Was wird hier für Arbeit geleistet?*" Sigrid demanded to know.

"*Wer will das wissen?*" the blonde man asked. He

resumed eating his sandwich, and Sigrid pointed the gun at him.

"Hands up!" Neither of the men responded to her English instruction. She repeated in her mother tongue, *"Hände hoch!"* Both men followed the order, but Sigrid was not convinced they hadn't understood her initial instruction. "Don't act foolish with me, I know that both of you can understand what I'm saying."

"Wir sprechen kein Englisch. Warum bist du?" the thin man replied, but Sigrid was not fooled.

She craned her neck to get a look at the notes the men had scribbled across the map and kept the gun drawn on the larger man. "You don't speak English, you say? Then why are all of your notes in English?" Neither man replied. The blonde man's eyes narrowed to form thin, suspicious slits where they had previously been bold and full of surprise. She had *caught* them.

"You might fool the people in the streets, even the lesser officials," Sigrid said, waving the gun between the two, "but you don't fool me. Neither of your uniforms would pass an amateur inspection." Both men's eyes fell to their uniforms. "And you," she said, pointing to the man with the neat blonde hair. "When I entered I could see the vertical collar slit at your back. You'll need to do better than that. I suppose you took the uniforms off of two dead officers, or you killed them both yourselves. If my guess is correct, then perhaps a little searching in this building would yield the bodies." Sigrid aimed the gun toward the man with the brown hair, pointing it directly at his chest. "And this one! This one has day-old stubble from his cheeks to his chin. You are *asking* to be caught."

The blonde man's eyes fell to the small table at his shoulder. Sigrid quickly redirected the barrel of her gun toward him. "Don't even think about it!" she hissed. "An Astra, no less. That's a *Luftwaffe*-issued weapon. No *Wehrmacht* or *Grüne Polizei* soldier would carry that type of pistol."

"*Wer ist Ihr Kommandant?*" the blonde-haired man barked. "*Ich möchte jetzt mit ihm sprechen.*"

Sigrid scoffed. "Who is *your* commanding officer?"

The other man stood, his chest pumped and proud. "*Sie laufen Gefahr, eine sehr wichtige Mission zu gefährden.*"

"A very important mission for *whom*?" Sigrid asked. "You can stop attempting to speak in the *Muttersprache*, by the way, since you are not doing a good job. Any citizen from the street would have quickly seen through your attempts, and I'm surprised you haven't already been caught. I suppose that is because you have kept your actions limited thus far." Sigrid turned to the man standing. "*Sitzen!*"

The gun in her hand shook, and the trembling traveled up and toward her shoulders. She clasped another hand on the pistol's grip, interlocking her fingers around each other in an attempt to steady the weapon. "Who are you working for? Are you Americans?"

Neither man responded—they had been caught in a lie. Sigrid wagged the gun between them once more before saying, "There is only one way out of this building. I know, because I have seen both of you using it. I have followed you. If you don't answer my questions, I will see to it that I find a *real* officer below and make him aware of just what it is the two of you are doing up here. Then we will know the truth, won't we?"

Despite the low temperature, a bead of sweat began to run down the large man's temple. Even in the shadowy room, Sigrid could see the nervousness in both of their rapidly moving eyes. Her hunch had been right, and now she was going to leverage it in her favor. "Or, you can listen to what I have to say, and I will be on my way—because you see, *friends*, I am not here to oust either of you. I am here to protect my own interests, and if the two of you can help me, then you would not only see another day, you would be doing a great service to your country."

Sigrid removed one hand from the pistol slowly. She let the other hand ease up and placed her finger loosely against the trigger guard, then raised her free hand and showed them her palm. Once satisfied she'd deescalated the situation, she placed the gun back inside its holster.

"Blimey," the blonde-haired man said with a sigh of relief.

Sigrid smiled. "Ah, British. You're going to need to blend in better if you're going to hide in plain sight. Your disguises are inadequate, and your German is lacking."

"Who are *you* with?" the larger man asked. His voice had changed from the gruff delivery he had been faking and now emulated a smooth, soft purr that was indicative of his native tongue.

"I am with no one," Sigrid replied. "I am just a woman with information—*valuable* information. I need to see to it that the information I provide you with gets to your people, and furthermore, America."

The blonde-haired man rose from his seat and began to pace, cracking his knuckles nervously after tossing his half-finished sandwich on to the table. He paused, then turned to his partner. "I told you the uniforms would be the thing to do us in. We'd have been better off dressing in plain clothes."

"That would have been ill-advised," Sigrid replied. "There's a chance you would have been harassed for your papers or documentation, and that really would have left you in trouble. I think the service uniforms were a wise choice, but of course, one who is *in* the service is more apt to notice the inconsistencies."

"Pretty good English you've got there," the brunette man said. "Where'd you learn?"

"My career requires that I can speak a few languages," Sigrid relied. "English is one in particular that I have learned rather quickly."

"How do we know your word is good?" he replied. "How do we know you're not going to walk out that door and have a battalion on our backs as soon as you leave?"

Sigrid removed a series of folded documents that she had tucked into her coat. "Because someone you couldn't trust would never provide you with documents as important as these," Sigrid replied. "London is in grave danger, friends, and so am I. I am in possession of precious information, and my time is limited. I have just delivered these documents for review by Herr Speer in Berlin. Do you know who that is?"

"Of course," they both replied. The larger man pulled a cigarette from his pocket and lit it. "That's the bloke who's the new Minister of Armaments."

"He is the reason you are both able to occupy this space currently," Sigrid said as she unfolded the papers. "And more importantly, perhaps the Führer's greatest ally." Sigrid placed the large document on the table where the men had been working.

On the paper were the designs for a massive tank, complete with descriptions of its parts and functions. At the top of the paper, the word *Erdschlag* had been printed in bold lettering. The brawny man's cigarette almost fell from his lips, but he quickly caught it, inhaling deeply, filling his eyes with a brilliant orange glow.

"I am going to ask for your help in exchange, but right now we must get to work. If I am not back at the location where the documents came from shortly, then I only endanger myself further. So let's not waste time discussing what it is I am giving you, and instead grab those pencils you have on that map over there and start tracing."

2

———

S am Abel felt a throbbing sensation in his ears as his heart pumped blood to his extremities. Every painful pump was a vicious reminder of each of the drinks he had the night before—he'd lost count how many that was. As if that weren't enough, an argument had broken out in the street below his bedroom window. There was a small produce market on the corner, and its customers were apt to haggle with its owner, who was rarely in the mood to barter. His product was sub-par, though, and that usually led to disappointment from his customers. The noise at street level always served as Sam's alarm when he overslept.

He turned over on his side, unwilling to begin his day just yet, and was perplexed to find the smooth curve of a woman's lower back staring back at him. Long, black curls fell down the side of her shoulder, and the dimples near the lower spine that met the top of her rear end only enticed him to stay in bed even longer. Her skin was a dark olive, and the bed sheet wrapped just around her bottom half hugged her long legs in a contour that made her look statuesque. Despite her almost celebrity-like beauty, he had no idea what her name was. There was a small purse resting on the table on her side of the bed, and next to that, a wrinkled dress had been sloppily draped. He didn't dare check the purse for her identity; his fear of waking her up and having to *talk* was too great.

He'd become accustomed to sleeping in ever since the burned man had sent him on his last mission. After he'd foiled the plot of Lothar Eichler and put a dent in his efforts to recruit some particular American business-men, he hadn't been up to very much at all. He had no need to go back to the bakery that had been supporting him until he'd been found, and the burned man had seen to it that he wanted for nothing until he was called on again. Sam was sure of one thing: he *would* be called on again. The burned man had made that clear, not only because Sam had done a damn good job, but because things had heated up since that night. The Japanese attack on Pearl Harbor had surprised everyone—himself included—and now Sam was waiting for the next time the man with the charred face would show up unannounced and send him into the lion's mouth.

Sam shifted quietly, grabbed a cigarette, and climbed from the bed. He walked softly on the groaning hardwood floor of the Brooklyn apartment as he searched for a match. Though water might have been the best cure for his current predicament, he'd decided to smoke instead. When a man wanted a cigarette, he had one. He too was nude, which confirmed his suspicions that he hadn't been a gentleman and just kept the woman company.

On any normal day, he might have gotten the sleep out of his eyes with a series of exercises, but he didn't dare wake the woman just yet. He found the matches, then struck one with a precise flick that was nearly silent save for the quick crack. A spy trains just as well for sneaking around a girl in his own bed as he does lurking in the dark corners of enemy strongholds.

He was a tall man, muscular and fit, but not bulky. Sneaking requires one to be nimble and not cumbersome. He had a thin carpet of black curls on his chest and his hair fell sloppily from the top of his head. He'd normally kept it presentable, but the sleep had displaced it. The light pouring through the window hit his blue eyes in such a way that they glimmered like precious gems. His jaw-line was firm, and the edge sharpened in a callous nature when he became serious or stoic. The face was soft and the skin clear and classic.

If he didn't spend his time crouching in the shadows, he might have had a career in Los Angeles. There was always room for men like him that had the dream-like quality. He'd once been approached on the street to pose for the cover of a dime detective novel, but declined so he could maintain his secrecy—after all, no one really knew *who* Sam Abel was. No one, that is, except the burned man.

The burned man knew a lot about Sam; enough, in fact, to convince him to participate in the shadowy dealings of American interests. Sam had planned to leave that life behind. He was good at it, perhaps *too* good, although even the best wind up with a bullet in the back of their head at some point or another. No spy lasts forever—they either die in the field or get out and hide in perpetuity.

Sam wasn't like *every* other spy. He would be lying if he said he didn't enjoy it. He had an affinity for it—the decisive actions it required, the ability to make quick decisions, the stomach for the risk that one might be killed, captured, or tortured. It also required that a person have no life, no *real* life. Sam was okay with that part. He hadn't lived what one would call a normal life —even as a child.

What made the deal all the more enticing was that unlike some of Sam's previous recruitments, the burned man was giving him a say in just how he was going to run the operation. For all intents and purposes, Sam operated outside the lines, and the boundaries, of acceptable engagement in regard to war and espionage. What type of espionage doesn't, though? The nature of the job is inherently deceitful, and as long as the checks came in and someone pointed his gun in a direction, he was game.

The woman in Sam's bed shifted with a soft groan. His lips hung puckered on his cigarette, his hand frozen. After a moment of pause, he was confident she had not woken yet. He was liable to go downstairs and give the men below a piece of his mind, but after he exhaled the smoke lingering in his mouth the ruckus died down. Why was he so scared she would wake? Perhaps because he'd gone from living one lie to another. Truthfully, he'd gone from living a false identity to digging himself in even deeper—and now for the Americans no less. If the nude woman under his sheets asked him what he did for a living, or who he was, or what made him tick, he'd hardly have a straight answer for her. For now, he'd convinced himself he was a traveling salesman—if only because he'd told himself the lie enough that he believed it. Why should he, a foreigner, even be granted access to the secret comings and goings and espionage of American interests? Surely there was a man who could do the job better than him—a man who was more patriotic.

As he maneuvered around the apartment seeking a glass of water, sticking to the floorboards that didn't creak under the pressure of his feet, he was quickly reminded of his inherent skill. Sam Abel moved unlike other men: he moved with cunning, purpose, and stealth—even if it meant avoiding a woman he'd slept with the night before to avoid dull conversation. He'd always admired the calculated, purposeful movements of cats—the way their paws struck surfaces softly and delicately, and the way their eyes searched with razor-like precision.

The knock that rapped against the door called upon those special talents yet again, and Sam bounded toward the bedside table with lightning-fast speed. The woman stirred, but this time Sam saw her face, and as he retrieved and loaded the pistol he'd removed from the drawer, her eyes widened into glistening spheres of panic. Time moved slowly for a moment, and Sam took note of the eyes—they were probably what had drawn him to her in the first place. He hadn't remembered meeting her, let alone learning her name.

She pulled the bed sheet above her chest, sat up in the bed, and wiped the hair out of her face. Sam pressed an index finger to his lips, instructing her to stay quiet, and mashed the cigarette into an ash tray. He loaded the last bullet into the revolver before peeking out the window. There was no one at the street level worth noting, just the normal folk that flooded the market. He glanced around the storefronts across the street, quickly surveying each face that might be of interest, but when the knock came again—this time louder—he made his move for the front door.

He took care once again to avoid the creakiest of the dusty, old wooden planks that decorated the floor, his bare feet applying only the lightest of pressure with each step. He was still nude, the only article on his person being the gun drawn low and to the floor and tightly gripped in his hands. He closed the bedroom door behind him, looking one last time at the woman in his bed, whose hair was falling in such a way that he was of a mind to make like no one was home and sneak right back into bed with her. There was a beauty in her panic.

There was silence for a moment as he crossed into the living room, and then three more knocks, heavy and purposeful, rattled the sheetrock that formed the walls of the apartment. He pressed his eye to the viewing hole, and there stood the man with the scarred face under a fedora. He inhaled from a pipe that turned the blacks of his eyes a sinister orange. Though it gave the man a devious presence, Sam let out a sigh of relief, let the revolver fall to his side, and undid the deadbolt and chain lock before twisting the knob.

The burned man tilted his head up, and the cool morning light illuminated his face so the scars reflected their deep folds. Sam always forgot how cruel the work that had been done to the man's face looked, though he was reminded each time they came across each other. Smoke crept from the man's lip as he exhaled pipe smoke, and his mouth curled in such a way that he presented Sam with a minor smile.

"You could come up with a code or something, you know?" Sam said. The burned man's eyes fell to the gun in Sam's hand, then to his nudity, and finally back up to Sam's face.

"I suppose that *would* be wise," the burned man replied. He brushed past Sam, allowing himself into the apartment without so much as a request. "Nothing I haven't seen before, though. We both know if you've seen one, you've seen them all." Sam looked down to his exposed lower torso. He was a well-equipped man, and never thought of himself as just another crayon in a box, but the burned man took no interest in Sam's body, and so Sam went on about grabbing the pair of slacks that he'd tossed carelessly on the living room floor and placed them over his legs.

The burned man's eyes fell on a book resting on Sam's kitchen counter, which read *The German Language*. "Brushing up, I see?"

"When I can," Sam replied. He'd taken it upon himself since the episode at The Whispering Oak to revisit the language. Most of it came easily due to his background, but he was making an effort to understand the finer points and subtleties, since that would help if he had to go behind enemy lines, and now that the burned man was in his living room, he was sure that time had arrived.

The burned man picked up a beer bottle that had toppled over among a pile of empties. A roach scurried across the counter with the shifting of glass. "Taking care of yourself?"

"Laying low," Sam replied. He placed the gun on the table in the dining area, and made his way to the faucet. He drank directly from it, forcing water down his throat in large gulps.

"They make tools for that, you know?" the burned

man said. "Glasses, or cups, I think they are called. They come in all sorts of varieties too." The burned man gestured to a seat at the table. "May I?" Sam nodded. Sam's superior grabbed a glass ash tray and tapped his pipe into it, then packed it with yet more tobacco. Sam recognized the smell—it was the same smell that had lingered in the apartment since the first time the old man had shown up unannounced. It took Sam weeks to get it out of the linens.

"I hope you've enjoyed your time off," the burned man said. As he spoke, the door to Sam's bedroom creaked open and the brunette whom he'd left in his bed materialized. "Looks like you have." Once the woman realized that the fear written on Sam's face had been unwarranted, she stepped out of the doorway. The burned man surveyed the woman. She'd donned the dress she'd been wearing the night before—only slightly wrinkled—and fixed her hair just enough that a walk of shame wouldn't likely be recognized as such. She entered the room clutching her purse. Sam thought she looked more beautiful now than in the bed. The burned man locked eyes with him and gave him an approving nod.

"I'll be on my way," the woman said. Her cheeks turned a rosy color as she collected her heels from the floor near Sam. "Work, and all that." She left the room without so much as a goodbye, and Sam wondered for a moment just who had used whom. He *liked* that. A man like him couldn't afford to get caught up in relationships. People in Sam's orbit had a way of getting into trouble, and he didn't like including bystanders in his misdeeds. He'd wished that perhaps she might have left her information so he could get in touch with her once more, though.

The door slammed behind her and the two men were left in silence save for the crackling of the burned man's pipe tobacco. Sam reached into his pocket and retrieved a crumpled pack of cigarettes, lit one, then sat staring at the man.

"I hope you've spent as much time resting as you have doing"—the burned man paused while looking around the disheveled room—"whatever it is you get up to." The burned man reached into his coat, retrieved a folder, and opened it to display yet another dossier not unlike the last one Sam had been provided. Pinned to the top of the document facing him was a black-and-white photo of the dreaded weapon—*Erdschlag*. It had been photographed from a distance that suggested someone had discovered it from the depths of a thick forest, its long barrel inching out of the front of two large warehouse bay doors. Behind it, hoisted on a pole, the soft, defocused emblem of the *swastika* hung from a banner, and there was a team of men in coveralls moving about its base.

"We've found it," the burned man said, snapping Sam out of the hypnotized state he'd been sucked into.

"Where?" Sam asked.

"The Black Forest," the burned man replied. "The plans were smuggled by an office liaison—a defector." The burned man turned the page and displayed the black-and-white image of a woman.

She too had been photographed without her knowledge. Sam took a notable interest in the photo. She was *gorgeous*. Her blonde hair fell in bouncy curls that kissed her chin mid-step, and she had striking, fearful—looking eyes that displayed concern that she was being watched.

Sam ashed his cigarette without removing his eyes from the photo. "So you're not going to blackmail me this time?"

The burned man rose from his seat, placed his hat back on his head, and buttoned his coat closed. "Do I have to?" He retrieved the file from the table and ensured Sam got one more glimpse of the weapon—and the woman—before it left his view. Then he deposited it back into his coat before pinching the top button. "Now that the bombs have started flying, none of us are safe. There'll be a car here at 8 AM tomorrow to take you to D.C.—I assume you'll be in it."

3

The near-infinite expanse of the dense, dark forest remained undisturbed. Its slumbering quiet was kept that way by the sentinel-like figure-eight patterns of the golden eagle soaring above the canopy. Who better to oversee all of its visitors than the majestic creature—favored by many a civilization for its prowess. This one in particular favored the River Enz. Though the small river was only twenty miles from the much greater Rhine, she found her prey frequently, rooting it out of the river's banks and rarely turning up empty-handed. Recently, she'd found an abundance of rodents scurrying up and down the water's edge. Though she was far larger and more powerful than her victims, it was her sly and stealthy attitude that made her so dangerous. She relied not on her brute force, but her patience and attention.

She had force in spades, of course. Thick, sharp talons decorated her toes, and her strong beak was capable of paralyzing her target with ease. It was her craft, though—at least near the River Enz—that separated her from the myriad of other birds and hawks that populated the snaking body of water. Her prey was unaware they were being hunted, unaware that above them, waiting patiently, was a soaring predator that struck only when the moment was right.

She operated alone. This was a necessity if a predator was to destroy its target, for having a partner or companion would only complicate the process; if she was to accomplish her task, distractions and missteps would mean going home disappointed. Some days she was successful, and others she was not, but on some primal level she was aware that it was the nature of the battle. If she failed, she'd become that much more adept for tomorrow. Today, however, was already tomorrow for her, and she was determined to feed.

It didn't take long for her to spot a small mouse. One might think to recognize such a small detail from a great distance would be difficult. It was the movement of the mouse, though, that gave away his position. He was the only thing that moved in an otherwise serene landscape, and that was enough to gain her attention. Mice too were fond of the River Enz where she hunted. Frequent traffic by humans in the last two years had made it a viable place to find scraps of their discarded food. The eagle knew this too. She observed the habits of her targets, and though they didn't learn from their mistakes, *she* did.

She glided gracefully, allowing the wind to carry her. Her wings functioned without much effort, and her hollow bones didn't weigh her down. She made no noise either, and the mouse, with his head buried in the ground, did not pay attention to his stalker above while it remained at great heights. He was unaware of the things that lurked—the things that sought to kill him. She knew this, and she used it to her advantage. The cover of trees aided her hunt, and she was careful not to reveal herself until she was absolutely sure she would accomplish her task. One wrong move, and she would expend valuable energy.

She descended effortlessly and arched her wings to allow gravity to do what it did best while she circled the rodent in broad, wide movements. To dive too early would have been unwise, and though her brain did not reason at the high level of a human's, it functioned on almost an extra-sensory level in regard to the hunt. She fell farther, closer still, and saw that the mouse had found some food of his own. The tiniest of his movements were very visible to her, and that's what made her exceptionally good at her job. After circling around him once, twice, and even three times, she arrived close enough to the tree line that she was prepared to strike. She watched as the mouse became distracted with the food he had discovered.

A cloudy, overcast sky provided extra cover that she'd never requested. It would help her, though, because when she did find the right opportunity, the mouse would not be alerted to her presence. A bright, sunny day had the potential of casting a hard shadow above him when she descended. That was just the nature of the game they play. Each party had their advantage, and the mouse's skill was that he could quickly hide if necessary. There was a maze of pockets and tunnels along the banks that had been created by both him and his community, among other wildlife that called the river home.

When was the right moment for her to strike? Even

she did not know. One could say she *felt* it, and though that may not be a scientific explanation, it was the truth. That moment had arrived, though, and without warning, she fell dramatically and violently, and her wings pointed erect and sharp like blades. However, they were not the weapon she used—she used her claws.

The mouse sensed the danger, his intuition not so dissimilar from hers. Perhaps it was the displacement of air, or the smell that preceded her, but he knew he had been found. His head arched, darting from left to right, but he saw no threat on either side of him. His body twitched nervously, and he searched frantically for his route of escape. He found it almost instantaneously, and sprang forward off his hind legs—too late. The shadow from above encompassed his tiny body.

Just as soon as he found his escape route, he felt the powerful gust of air engulf him, and before he even knew what hit him, the talons tightly gripped his torso. A moment after he felt the pain of the attack, he was risen high into the air, his escape route disappearing quickly from his sight, and next he saw the limbs of the trees—a sight he was unfamiliar with. He squirmed feverishly, attempting to pull himself free of the eagle's grasp, but with every movement he made, she only clutched him tighter. Soon the ground below became barely visible, and then all he could see was the wide expanse of forest fading. The last sight the mouse saw before his demise was glorious—*romantic*, even. He saw the way the attacker had carried out her task, and knew the mistake he'd made before he took his last breath.

She didn't need to travel far to feast. Only two short miles away she'd built a nest near a structure that she'd developed a symbiotic relationship with. The goings on of the men busily constructing a machine of death provided her with the remnants of food that had attracted the rodents she fed on. For the men, the exchange was not of material goods, but of a metaphorical one. She was the emblem of their national flag, and to have her hover above their place of work was a sign—perhaps from God, some even believed—that the work they did was *divine* in nature. One man in particular had taken note of her, and she him. The flashy decorations that adorned his clothing had captured her attention before. That man was Lothar Eichler, and though she didn't know his name, everyone at the place she called home *did*.

———

She landed on the limb of a large tree near the site. Lothar Eichler fixed his eyes upon her admiringly as she spread her wings in large arches and went to work on her breakfast. She was a glorious creature, grand and cunning in the ways that only a predator like her could be. They shared similar air space, she at the top of a long branch that jutted out toward his location, and he at the top floor of a warehouse that could house a game of American football. He too had started his morning, but his enjoyment was found in a cup of black coffee, meditation about the day's work ahead, and the quiet he could only enjoy before the sun made its debut. When the sun did wink over the tree line, the droves of men that frequented the location daily arrived and began work on the massive undertaking housed in the floor below him.

He was a tall and striking man, finely manicured

and kept, suggesting he traveled not in military but bureaucratic circles. Blonde hair swept across his head with a slick sheen—there wasn't a single misplaced strand. He exuded a sense of pride and nobility. Though he wore no party regalia, he dressed in the long black coat typical of his associates.

It was from up there, in his private office, that he monitored the work they did. He didn't watch because he was concerned with thievery or laziness, but to assure that the construction and modifications were being done to specification. He couldn't afford to tell his superiors that the machine that had cost so much of the nation's precious money and resources needed more time—or worse, that it didn't work as promised. Eichler's father had taught him a valuable lesson, a mantra, in his early childhood: do it right the first time, *every* time. Eichler had lived his life by those words, and they'd been haunting him since he'd failed in his mission to America.

He had not failed, not *really*, but he had not succeeded either. His goal of enticing American entrepreneurs to take part in his project had been foiled and stained by the spy that had penetrated the confines of The Whispering Oak. Who he was, Eichler still did not know. Had he been working for the Americans? The British? He hadn't sounded Russian. Regardless, the mysterious man had scared his investors off, and now Eichler was tasked with proving the power of his war machine with action. It wasn't his job to figure out how to fund the machine, not really. That would have been the job of Göring or Krosigk or Speer. Eichler had been reporting to Reich Minister of Armaments Fritz Todt before the man's death. Now he had to answer to Albert

Speer. With the changing of the guard came rewards—specifically loosened purse strings—and Eichler thought that his weapon of destruction, *Erdschlag*, would be his way of proving his own worth. Surely the Führer would know it too when Eichler fully demonstrated the weapon's capability.

The sun rose and bathed the dark office in a warm glow, and Eichler nursed the simmering cup as he approached the viewing window that overlooked the massive tank. Like clockwork, the screeching of the massive doors that granted entry echoed inside the building, and the star closest to the Earth painted the machine in harsh orange light. Eichler smiled, a grand, proud curl that stretched far up the cheeks as he looked on his work. The machine was gargantuan—and there was no other like it. It was so huge that it resembled more of a mobile fortress than a vehicle. It was anything but easily maneuverable, but the incredible, nearly three-hundred-foot-long barrel that stretched longer than the entirety of its body made up for that. Eichler had never seen the machine perform—no one had. It was built purely on speculation, but if it was made to the specifications of the machine's engineer, Emil Sauer, then it would do its job. Sauer had assured Eichler that anything he designed was built to work. He did not fancy himself a tinkerer or fiddler—those were jobs for children. Sauer got results, and that was what had attracted Eichler to him.

When the morning light had fully revealed the interior of the space, it came as no surprise to Eichler that Sauer was already working, perhaps even through the night. The old man didn't sleep much. He'd claimed that one needed less sleep as they aged, and Sauer had a firm belief that the machine was the last project he'd work on in his lifetime—and his *best*. It was his magnum opus, and yet Eichler got the strange feeling that Sauer did not *want* to be there.

Eichler didn't know how the machine worked—not really. He understood the basic functions and controls of a tank, but he didn't dare claim to be familiar with the finer tunings of such an incredible weapon. It was Sauer who knew those details, and he would translate them for Eichler so that he could present them in the many meetings regarding the project.

The machine itself would mystify even the most seasoned of engineers: a moving castle on wheels with enough firepower in its massive barrel to level a small town with a single shell. Its predecessor—another mighty tank dubbed *Schwerer Gustav* and designed by Krupp—had inadequacies. Sauer had simply improved upon it in a slew of ways, the most important of which was a better method of transportation. The *Gustav* was a glorified bunker-buster designed for use at the Maginot Line. Though it was a terror all of its own, the team tasked with firing it found its mode of railway transportation unmanageable. Sauer had seen to it that *Erdschlag* would not suffer the same immobility. Sauer had done away with the rail-reliant bogies, and retro fitted a proper design with more efficient treads.

Of course, that presented other problems, mainly the engine power required to propel the machine. It was a resource guzzler, mainly of gasoline, but it made up for that—or so Sauer and Eichler were hoping—in sheer power. They would know soon enough; the project was just about complete, save for a few minor technical adjustments, and soon it would be leaving its home in Höfen and making the trek to where its cousin Gustav had displayed its own power near the Maginot Line. There, Eichler hoped that it would prove its mettle, and then be pushed along through Paris and to the northern section of France, perhaps Calais or Dunkirk, where it could be aimed directly at London. It was the ability to cover that great distance that made the project all the more enticing, because *Erdschlag* would not just fire a limited-range shell—it would fire a *rocket*. A rocket would do what a shell couldn't: travel nearly 200 km and clear the Strait of Dover.

The idea that London could be nearly leveled in a few short days made Eichler sure he'd be able to find his place among the Führer's party leaders. There was no way he was going to steal Speer's spot. The Minister of Armaments and War Production had too close a relationship with the Führer, but perhaps a new position could be created for Eichler. Eichler liked the idea of becoming *Anführer der Schweren Munition*, or Leader of Heavy Munitions. Eichler would be sure to grab the ear of Martin Bormann when the time came. He needed a direct line—a meeting. Getting to the Führer required punching through a wall in the same way his tank would, and Eichler knew the right people to speak with when the time came. Even managing to grab the ear of Göring would do. *Erdschlag* would be his ticket. After all, it was Eichler who had overseen the project, he who had traveled to America and dealt with the spy. He had earned it—*deserved* it.

Never mind that Eichler had tipped his hand. Sure, the spy had seen the plans, heard the discussion, and seen behind the curtain. Regardless, it had been months since that encounter, and Eichler hoped his enemies had not obtained any information of real value, and that they were unprepared to do anything about it. Still, Eichler had an uneasy feeling because he had not made that information clear to his superiors. He had merely lied and explained that the Americans had turned the support of the project down because of the attack on Pearl Harbor. The timing was impeccable. Had the attack not happened only the morning after the fiasco, he might not have been able to get away with the fabrication. He was lucky the project hadn't been stalled—or worse, canceled entirely.

In addition to the construction team that had been finalizing the tank, Eichler had requested support from the *Wehrmacht* just in case of a siege effort by enemies. Despite the project's high budget and its proximity to France, he had only been provided men to do daily foot patrol around the location the tank was stored. No one was allowed in or out of the facility with any materials regarding the construction of the machine unless cleared prior. If that wasn't enough, the project's management team had been surveilled a great deal. They were being watched—Sauer and Eichler included.

A whistle echoed through the structure, vibrating the very metal of the tank's housing as it reverberated around the room. This signaled the start of the day, and with it, groups of men began to funnel through the large doors. Eichler had his own private entrance to the top deck of the building, and that too was protected by two armed guards that would only allow people in or out with permission granted by Eichler himself.

The construction of *Erdschlag* was a symphony of sorts. With the start of the day came the clanging sounds of metal on metal, the purr of motors hoisting cranes, and the whining and hissing of grinders and welding machines. The production of the armored assault vehicle had employed no less than six hundred men from conception to finalization. It required heavy lifting and elbow grease. A man who had no background in weapons manufacturing could find employment on a project like *Erdschlag* as long as he knew how to work a wrench and follow a schematic.

Soon those jobs would be turned over to the men who would be educated in the tank's finer details, and all of the knowledge the builders had gained up to that point would be passed along to the soldiers who would participate in the movement and firing. The tank would need hundreds of men just to ensure its successful operation. In short time, *Erdschlag* would roll out of the large bay doors that had kept it secret with a *new* team. Eichler himself would be in the tank's cabin to ensure successful arrival at its first destination, Rügenwalde, where it would be tested. And then, he would turn its barrel toward Hitler's enemies.

4

The chariot waited on the corner at 8 AM sharp, just as the burned man had said it would. Exhaust rose from the rear of a black Dunham Adventurer as its hot engine idled in the cool March morning. Sam—always keenly aware of his neighborhood—had never seen it before and was sure it was his ride. He lit a cigarette while stepping off his front steps, and as soon as he approached the car, he heard the transmission switch from its "park" position. There was no time to waste.

Sam peeked into the window, and the man sitting in the driver seat gave him a curt nod. He opened the door, climbed in, and took one last glimpse at his apartment. He did things like that in his profession: simple good-byes—not out of nostalgia or mourning, but because Sam had reconciled any time in a place could be his last. He wasn't one to stand on ceremony, but that apartment had been one of the first places he'd really felt at home.

The driver didn't say a word, but simply stepped on

the gas pedal and took off. As with the morning prior, a patron was arguing with the grocer on the corner, and Sam was happy to be rid of both them and yesterday's hangover. The driver's eyes had been fixed firmly on the road ahead—an unwavering, calculated attention that Sam assumed had no intention of being disturbed. Sam was tired himself, and so he made no attempt to speak to the man.

It was an odd sensation, being picked up by a driver and having little to no communication as to the direction they were headed or the fare, but after the last trip he'd taken with the burned man, the leather seat Sam sat in was a step up from a truck rattling through the woods. Where they were headed, Sam still was unsure, but he'd lain awake for the better part of the night setting his affairs in order in preparation. A massive yawn signaled he'd be asleep soon enough. He'd slipped three months' rent under the land-lord's door, left the faucets running with just a light drip to avoid frozen pipes, ensured the windows were sealed, and secured any leftover food or trash to prevent pests.

The hum of the Adventurer's motor was soothing. The irony that it was a Dunham he had been picked up in before venturing into the dark corners of Germany was not lost on Sam. Earl Dunham had been clear about his anti-war ideology and his feeling toward what he referred to as "financier war-makers." Mr. Dunham had been both supplying the Nazis and also the British, and even recently America, and that wasn't preference, it was just capitalism at its finest.

Once the vehicle had cleared the high cubes of stacked apartments that formed his neighborhood, the sun began to warm his chilled skin through the rear window. They were heading west. Sam found his eyes heavy, and he tilted the fedora he'd thrown above his head, let the brim fall just above his brow, and sank into the comfortable seat. The last things he remembered seeing were the high stone arches of the Brooklyn Bridge, and then he was fast asleep.

When he woke, he felt the drool of a deep slumber creeping down the corner of his mouth. The car had cradled him to sleep, and he lurched forward in a panic, completely at a loss for where he was. He quickly recognized the skyline of Washington, D.C. before relaxing back into his seat. The driver caught Sam's eye in the rearview, then returned his focus back to the road without saying a word.

The tall, pointed tip of the Washington Monument was the first giveaway, but Sam wasn't sure if he was yet in the city or in a nearby state, like Maryland or Virginia. He didn't know the geography of the area well, and the row-house-style neighborhood they were currently passing through didn't look too dissimilar from the Brooklyn architecture he'd just left behind. He'd imagined he'd been teleported like in one of those science fiction magazines. The time displacement he'd felt was easily rectified; he'd reasoned he must have been asleep for at least three or four hours. He felt refreshed and alert, the way one does when they've had a good, solid rest. He didn't remember dreaming, and yet the image of the woman lingered in his mind.

Once again, he'd been given such minuscule amounts of information. Did the burned man know something he wasn't revealing? Sam wouldn't put it past him. The nature of this line of work was often filled with misinformation, lack of information, or dishonest intentions—it came with the territory.

What did it matter to him, though? The burned man had made good on his promise—Sam became an American. He had the paperwork to prove it, and even if he did run into any problems, he had the burned man to straighten it out for him. He'd gotten what he wanted—a life of his own, a place to call home—and now here he was, getting right back to it.

Perhaps it was the tank, *Erdschlag*, or perhaps it was the presence of guilt he felt for knowing what he was capable of and sitting on the sidelines. Maybe it was simply boredom. Whatever it was, Sam didn't care, he was already feeling the rush of lacing up his boots and that sensation of pumping adrenaline, that zone he could only get into from doing what he did best. The life he had thought he wanted had been, for all intents and purposes, empty.

Sam knew that if he was being called in, it wasn't going to be a simple errand. He was going behind enemy lines, into the belly of the beast, and he would have a target on his head the size of a billboard if he didn't attempt to blend in. Still, he could feel his heart throbbing, and not in the way that it had from the hangover, but the way it did whenever the excitement of the unknown coursed through a man's veins. That excitement, though it could make a man feel alive, was the kind that came only with *danger*.

"Where are we?" Sam asked the driver.

The driver peeked through the rearview mirror, locking eyes with Sam. "Virginia, a little west of the Potomac." His voice was gruff and short.

Sam grunted, fiddling in his pocket for a cigarette

and a lighter. "Where we headed?"

"Ahead," the driver replied. Sam hadn't expected him to be specific. Why would he? Sam didn't even know the burned man's real name, let alone where he worked or lived.

They traveled along the great river that snaked through the nation's capital for roughly another twenty minutes. Finally, as its mouth opened wide enough that Sam lost sight of the opposite plot of land, he found himself on its banks, and the car pulled into an empty lot. At the edge of the lot, a lone warehouse stood.

The structure was grand, and fitted with long, tall panes of glass that had been frosted to prevent any type of indication of the activities inside. The siding, which was composed of bricks, had been neglected. Long stretches of moisture had run down its face, and nature had attempted to reclaim the property with mold and algae. Present directly in the center of the building, were two large steel doors that had been covered in a rust of autumnal hues.

"Here we are," the driver said. Sam surveyed the building, sure that the driver had made a mistake. That theory was quickly dismissed. Sam could read the driver's eyes, and they flicked toward the front entrance momentarily as if to direct him toward the building.

Sam exited the vehicle, and gravel crunched beneath his feet. The car growled, then peeled off without another word from the driver. Sam stood for a moment, grasped the collar of his coat, and closed it tightly. It was cold, and he grabbed a cigarette and lit it if only to get his heart pumping faster for warmth. He looked around himself briefly, and there at the edge of the water was a dock with a large boat anchored to it.

It was a freighter, currently loaded with supplies, and his instincts told him that it was not the building he was to be briefed in, because a building did not travel. A boat, however, did. He made his way across the empty lot, traveled across the old, rotted wooden planks of the dock, and then saw a ramp that led to the boat's deck. Sam ascended and found himself on the deck of the massive ship. He was surrounded on all sides by shipping containers of various colors and sizes. Though the boat itself bore no markings Sam could see, the shipping containers did. Each of the containers in front of him had been painted with white letters that read "O and W."

Well ain't that grand? It was the cargo of gun manufacturers Ogden and Walde, both of whom Sam had cornered only months earlier; they'd been pinned inside The Whispering Oak by the spy when he'd leveraged a grenade as his escape plan. It didn't surprise him that their name should pop up again, and it made sense that if he was going to get into Germany and through naval blockades and military outposts he was going to need camouflage only a business trading with the enemy could provide.

"Ahoy," a gravelly voice behind Sam said. A cloud of smoke twirled in the gusty air on the water, and the burned man appeared in between two canisters, there to meet him as expected. He waved Sam toward a watertight door that had been left ajar, and he followed without so much as a "hello." Sam walked through the lingering smoke, the smell he'd begun to associate with the mysterious man more so than old timers with a fondness for traditional tobacco methods. Sam preferred cigarettes—when you were done, you'd toss them for good. That fit a man of his character better. The burned man flung a door open, and soon Sam found himself descending a long, narrow set of steel steps.

"Is this headquarters?" Sam asked.

"Something like that," the burned man replied. "We don't have a headquarters, as you might imagine, since the nature of our work—and its degree of accountability—leaves us with very little in terms of a 'home base.' We're a lot like you, Sam, just sort of going from place to place."

"You always say *we*," Sam said. "But it's only *you* I ever deal with."

"I'm full of surprises." The hard, metal stairs clanged with every step, and soon the old man reached a door at the base of the steps with a wheel attached to its face. It was a watertight seal, like the one before it, and he clenched the pipe between his teeth, gripped the wheel, and loosened it. The door opened with an unholy scream. The burned man allowed Sam to step through, and then closed the large door behind him, resealing it.

The hall was dark and uninviting. A small bulb at low power lit the way, but the ship had only been utilizing its hazard lights, so the red glow permeating the hall made Sam feel as if he was descending into hell itself. "This way," he said, then brushed past Sam once again and continued down the hall. The ship's motors turned, and a deep, guttural vibration from the large craft's innards rattled every bolt and screw inside.

The burned man opened one more door, and a flurry of sound assaulted Sam's ears before he'd even glimpsed the source of the commotion. Once Sam stepped through, the room opened up to a large area that Sam imagined had once been a cargo hold. Now it was a base of operations. There were men at desks on radios, an endless stream of chatter from all angles, and the riffling and shuffling of papers as bodies moved about the room. This, it seemed, was where the burned man had run his missions from—a *mobile* base.

"Shabby, perhaps," the burned man said. "But it gets the job done, and it ensures we're in a location where people never start asking questions."

"What about them?" Sam asked, tilting his head toward the employed. "You've got a lot of people here with the knowledge of this place."

"They don't go anywhere." They traveled along a corridor flanking the grand room. "They live here, or there, or wherever we might be." The men and women inside the room quickly spotted Sam, each pausing briefly from their individual functions and jobs to take note of the newcomer who had entered their top-secret space, though none looked surprised by his arrival. It seemed if you traveled at the burned man's side, no one asked questions. "Come on. This way."

They left the room, traveled through another corridor—this one now well lit and far more inviting than the previous—and the burned man pointed a finger down the hall. "The dormitories are over there. That's where you'll find your quarters if you need them. Do you want some shut-eye? We've got a bit of a journey ahead."

"I'm fine," Sam replied.

"Right," the burned man replied. "Then I suppose we should get on with it." The ship vibrated once more, now a roaring that seemed to suggest it would soon be on its journey. Sam followed the old man once more, deeper into the bowels of the ship.

Down another corridor, the burned man led Sam to a small office that had been retrofitted into the ship. He took a seat in his chair and guided Sam to another that sat opposite his desk. Sam pulled a cigarette from his pack and sparked it. A two-way mirror sat behind the burned man so that he could see the actions of the crew working behind him.

"You're doing a great service by coming back," the burned man said. He flicked a match against the back of a box and pressed it to his pipe. He wrapped his teeth around the stem then sucked the air into his throat to get the tobacco burning. "My employer is well aware of your efforts. They didn't go unnoticed. You uncovered information we had suspected but had been unable to confirm—perhaps might have even stopped it in its tracks. There's legislation now. I thought you might like to know that."

"I'd love to meet him," Sam replied, smoke sinking from his nostrils as he leaned back into the creaky wooden chair. "Your employer, that is."

The burned man let his head fall back casually. "Unlikely. The value of your skillset can't be overstated, but it's necessary to keep a degree of cushion between people like you and him—in case our actions are... questionable."

"We've gone to war," Sam said. "What could possibly be questionable about the next moves?"

"Smuggling a German defector into our own territory, for starters," the burned man said. "I don't know how the press would feel about that—or the people."

Sam said, almost choking on his cigarette, "You want to me get her out?" The burned man nodded casually. "But she already gave you what you needed."

"Not everything," the burned man replied. "She's withholding."

"Smart girl," Sam replied.

"She's been communicating through an intermediary with our friends over in London," the burned man said. "Seems she's attempted to strike up some sort of deal with them in exchange for safe passage. We wouldn't have taken it for anything other than it was—morsels, if anything, and knowing the Krauts, perhaps even disinformation—but it just so happens that our friends across the pond investigated the details. They all hold up. She's been very specific about her demands: America or bust."

"And they want us to do the job," Sam added.

"You've got it." The burned man sucked at his pipe once more, letting the stem hang in between his teeth for a moment. "They've got men on the inside. She provided two Special Operations Executive boys in hiding with even more detailed schematics as proof. They've been doing a bit of their own digging over there pertaining to weapon storage rail lines. I've got to hand it to her, these were good. No idea how in the hell she got them out. Seems they've retrofitted the machine for rocket-fire. It's got the Brits all sorts of worked up."

"Why not bomb the facility from the air?"

"Too dangerous," the scarred man replied with a gust of smoke. "The madman's spread his troops across the whole damned place. They keep the tank hidden in a secure facility with anti-aircraft artillery to boot. By the time our fighters or bombers could get within range, they'd likely succumb to shell fire. We can't just swoop in—not till we can get some troops across the west, that is. That's not going to be any time soon, as I'm sure you've heard, and that's just too damn late. They'll do the job, but we owe her a favor."

"How am I going to get in there?" Sam asked.

The burned man smiled. "Don't worry. We're not going to just turn you loose like we did last time. It's too risky. We've got to be sure you get where you need to go this time. Our friends in London are having a conniption that we might not act on this."

"So why don't they send in *their* embedded?"

"Seems they've got too much stake in the ruse," the burned man replied. "Can't afford to take the two men they've got off their post and bring in more. You would understand that. The sooner we can assure them we've got our best people on it, the sooner we can get them to move their pieces around the board the way we see fit. We do *this*, and they do *that*, so to speak. That weapon's just as much a concern to us as it is to them." The burned man shifted in his seat, tapped his pipe once more in the ash tray, and folded his hands on the table. "I told them they'd get our best."

Sam thought about it for a moment as he pulled a whiff of smoke from his own cigarette. The act of smoking always helped him think. It was if the tobacco injected ideas directly into his bloodstream. He exhaled the smoke, and said matter-of-factly, "So I've got to link up with them."

"That's right," the burned man groaned in agreement. "This is the one, Sam. The one that puts us over the edge. I've already spoken to my boss about your actions in New York, and he's of half a mind to let us set up our own division—though it wouldn't be on paper. I'd be the head of the department and it would consist of the management of these… *unique* types of jobs. You know, the ones that brute force and bullets can't always solve."

"Who would *I* report to?"

"Me, of course." The burned man smirked in such a way that the folds of his scarred skin wrinkled. His battle-damaged eye winked slightly. "You don't *have* to participate. I don't think that's the option you're looking for, though. We're not going to win this war with brute force. With the help of the east, we'll close in eventually, but it's going to be long and bloody. We need someone on the inside. What they do is triage, and what *you* do is surgery."

"So how do I get in?" Sam asked.

The burned man leaned forward in his chair again, rested his elbows on the table in front of him, and loosened the collar of his shirt. "As you can see, this is a freighter, and this freighter has clearance to get through Gibraltar, and subsequently, France."

"You put the pressure on Ogden and Walde, I assume?" Sam said.

"It didn't take much. Knowing what we knew, we could have pressed the boot firmly down on their necks. It was in their best interest to aid us, rather than fight us. There's plenty of guns, and we don't need theirs. So they'll be sending the Germans a delivery. *You're* the delivery, of course," the burned man said matter-of-factly.

"In a container?" Sam's voice rose in disbelief. "You can't be serious."

"How else do you expect us to get in? Surely you've been put in more precarious situations before. You'll have enough supplies to last you the trip. The container's been customized to allow for your survival and, well, comfort, if you could call it that. When it arrives at its destination, you'll need to break free before they go digging around inside. We've recovered a *Wehrmacht* uniform for you to blend in, so you're not a sitting duck when you get out. Meet up with the SOE guys and see to it that this woman gives them everything else they need. Then, get her back here. You'll have forty-eight hours from your arrival."

"What if she's got nothing?" Sam asked warily. "What if she's just leading us on?"

"That's always a possibility," he replied. "But that's for me to worry about. She wouldn't have given up the plans if she wasn't serious—plans, I'll remind you, that *you* failed to retrieve."

"That wasn't part of the deal," Sam argued. "I came out of there with exactly what you wanted, and I almost died doing it."

"Buyer's remorse?" The burned man's nostrils flared, and a hint of disgust followed. "I can still smell the dough on you. Need I remind you that only two months ago you were picking flour from your fingernails?" Sam took his meaning, and didn't push the battle any further. The spy inhaled from his cigarette, deescalating the combative state they'd entered. "We do this for them, and they take care of the weapon. If there is anyone who can get her out of there, it's *you*."

"And where exactly is that, anyway?" Sam asked.

"*Pforzheim*," the burned man replied, and every muscle in Sam's body tensed. The burned man continued to speak, but his voice had become muffled. Sam could *hear* the words, but they weren't registering any longer. The room began to spin, and then, he only saw black.

5

Sigrid's fingers twitched with every snap of the typewriter's keys. She'd been making mistakes, uncharacteristic of her skill level with the machine. On more than one occasion she'd accidentally struck the runic, thunderbolt-like "*SS*" symbol that had been retro-fitted near the "9" key on the typewriter. The key taunted her—a vicious reminder that if she was caught, it was that department that would deliver the punishment.

She'd been the fastest typist in Germany, of that she was sure. That was how she'd been hand-picked by Eichler to oversee all information arriving and leaving at Flussrand. Her dexterity had suffered after her first attempt to contact the Americans. She'd been chan-neling the tremors that had been wracking her body down into her fingers to compensate for the fact that now *she* was the enemy. Noises felt louder, colors brighter, and smells stronger—all a byproduct of the heightened senses she'd been experiencing since she'd gone rogue, since she'd become a *Verräterin*.

No matter how convinced she was that no one knew of the actions she'd taken, the fear she'd been seen lingered all through the day and into the night, creeping into her sleep like monsters plaguing children under their beds. Most evenings she was unable to sleep at all, and after several nights in a row with lack of rest, on the third or fourth night she'd usually collapse. Once she'd even hallucinated that the Führer himself had kicked her door down with a leather boot and dragged her in front of his cohorts for judgment. That final surrender by her brain to her body would serve as a minor rejuvenation until the cycle repeated all over again. She still hadn't gotten a response—from the Americans or the British— and the stress was wearing her down, not just mentally, but visibly.

Dark semi-circles had begun to form under her eyes like sinking crescent moons. When in the company of her coworkers, she placed the blame on the expedited nature of the project and the demands it brought with it. She would often show up at the building unkempt and fix her hair in the office beside Eichler's. That meant she'd have to get in even earlier than him, and he was usually there before sunrise. That type of behavior was the nature of her position, and all she could do was assume her superior didn't think anything strange about it.

Being so close to the man overseeing the project had its privileges—and its downsides. For one, she'd been aware of nearly every development regarding the secret tank and had a better idea of its nature and timeline than most of the men involved in its construction. Not a single shred of information regarding the project didn't pass her desk first before reaching its final destination. On the other hand, being around Eichler so often kept her in a perpetual state of unease.

She'd tried her best to hide her anxiety-ridden state; her stone-cold German demeanor camouflaged the fear from the betrayal she'd committed, but it was eating at her, slowly, and constantly. How much longer would it take? How much longer until she got her answer?

She'd given them enough information to strike fear in even the bravest of men, and she hadn't received any indication that what she was offering was of any value or that the Americans were ready to work with her. She'd wished she had gone straight to them, though she hadn't been able to figure out *how*. One didn't simply come and go as they pleased from the motherland. Getting to the British was blind luck, but speaking to the men across the Atlantic brought with it a range of difficulties she was unaware of how to navigate. She could only pray that her contacts from the northeast had taken what she'd given them seriously and that they would recruit *their* allies across the pond to help see her plan through.

"I *saw* you," an accusatory voice said beside her. Sigrid shivered and fudged the document at hand by striking a "b" key where one didn't belong. There, standing at the corner of her desk and staring down at her with sharp, powerful eyes, was Eichler. His height compared to her sitting position made him look like a tower. His stature covered her in shadow, leaving only the light of the submissive glint in her eyes staring back at him. Her fingers stopped, resting on each key of the typewriter while she froze with dread. Her lips parted slightly, hanging on a word to release from her mouth

—just a word, *any* word. None came. Her voice squeaked, emitting a sound to which no proper word belonged. "Before your trip to Berlin, at the *Schwarzmühle*," Eichler said jubilantly, "I was up on the balcony area."

"Of course," Sigrid replied. She let out a cool release of air, allowing her chest to fall where the stale oxygen had clung during the suspense of his statement. Then she took one more breath inward, her lungs shaking as she did so, and collected a response. "The men invited me. They usually find themselves there on Friday night, not that they really get a weekend off."

"I suppose they'll find the time when the rotation begins," Eichler replied. "Did you have a good trip? It wasn't too long, I hope."

"Always nice to return to the city."

"I'd be lying if I said I wasn't jealous," Eichler said with a smirk. "I've met with the *Oberkommando des Heeres* and they'll be sending over the flak battalions and three hundred men of the *Waffen SS*—some of Wittmann's finest, they tell me."

"How long will the training take?"

"Just several days, I suppose," Eichler replied. "Don't tell me you're ready to leave me just yet. You're the only one I've had with some sense, the only one I can *trust,* that is." A cold chill ran from Sigrid's skull, down her spine, and to the small of her back—Eichler noticed it. "Cold?" Eichler asked compassionately.

"A bit," Sigrid lied.

"The warmer months are coming," Eichler assured her. "And with that, we'll likely be gone from this dark, lifeless place. I was never one for the Black Forest. It's an uninviting cave if you ask me. With any luck we'll be on to Rügenwalde, and then perhaps Berlin. I'll need you there, Sigrid." Eichler glanced at the paper inserted in the typewriter, noticing the unwelcome 'b.' "You made a mistake."

Sigrid blushed, then removed the paper from the mouth of the typewriter and tossed it into a bin before placing another where it had been. She returned her attention to the keys and started a new document. Eichler stepped away and began to shuffle short, soft steps across the room, pressing his knuckles against the bottom of his chin. He frowned. "Let's just hope that von Braun can work out some of the peculiar details on that rocket business. The Führer's not particularly impressed, you know?"

"I didn't know," Sigrid replied timidly.

"He thinks them far too costly—long-range artillery with fins, he says. I found the A-4 quite impressive, if I'm honest, but I'm afraid they're still unreliable. It would be a colossal letdown if they didn't work. We've retrofitted the entire design of this model just to accommodate the things and they don't even have consistent specifications." Eichler paused at the large glass pane that looked out over *Erdschlag*. The men below were still busy at work with its fine-tuning, and the soft, distant clanging of metal beating metal only irked Sigrid further. "Everyone is in search of the next big weapon, and we're all working hard to ensure the Americans don't beat us to it."

Eichler's gaze turned back to Sigrid. "I'll feel much safer once the new team has arrived." Eichler extended a hand out toward the viewing window. "These men are engineers, not soldiers. I've been skeptical about the comings and goings of those involved with the project.

All it takes is one untrustworthy person to reveal the weaknesses of the machine."

Sigrid's teeth chattered, and she clenched her jaw to silence them. She gripped her skirt tightly with the fingers she still hadn't managed to stop from shaking. Eichler stepped toward her, grabbed a large folder from her desk, and opened it. His eyes narrowed when they fell on the schematics Sigrid had held in her own hands not long before. He wiped the paper with the back of his hand. "Sloppy," Eichler said. "The least they could have done was kept the document clean. What are these, pencil shavings?"

"I didn't see," Sigrid replied. The fear flared yet again, burning inside her like someone had poured accelerant on a dying fire that had only recently been extinguished. "I just waited while they took what they needed."

"And fingerprints," Eichler said, examining the documents with a look of consternation on his face. He swiped at the prints; they'd been well preserved with the impressions of lead from the pencils. Sigrid's heart raced so intensely she could feel the thumping in her ears. "I should have had you do it," Eichler said. "Had they been held in the wrong hands the whole thing might have been rendered useless." Eichler groaned from deep within his throat and closed the folder. "At least I know you get things done."

"I can't sketch," Sigrid said. "My skills stop at effi-cient typist.' "

Eichler smiled. "See to it that this goes back in the safe, Sigrid."

"I will," Sigrid replied. She wanted him to leave, to vacate her space so that she could take a normal breath.

She'd almost blown it, and all because the men she'd shared the information with had been sloppy. But she had been careless, not them. She'd been in such a rush to get out of the secret space they'd been squatting in that she hadn't even thought to dispose of the evidence. Another move like that and she'd be shot in front of a rifle squad—or worse, sent to one of the camps.

"And one more thing," Eichler said, hanging in the doorway to his office. "Has Sauer received a copy of this?"

"He hasn't, sir," Sigrid replied. "I haven't seen him since I returned."

"You should speak with him," Eichler replied. "He seems to be suffering from a bout of exhaustion. I can't say I fault him. We could all use a bit of rest, and the work has been particularly demanding in his case. I suppose some unrest is to be expected when one is investigated."

"Investigated?" Sigrid asked.

"You hadn't heard?" Sigrid shook her head from side to side. "Seems old Sauer had some questionable *associations* in his past. I vouched for him, of course. One can only go so far, however, when dealing with the *Gestapo*. They have their own ideas. We'll have to keep an eye on him."

Sigrid's mouth went dry with the mention of the word 'Gestapo.' She licked her lips briefly. "I'll see to it."

Eichler shut the door firmly behind him and sat in the office that flanked Sigrid's. She rose from her desk, massaged the wrists that had gone stiff since her superior had walked into the room, and swiftly stepped to the window that provided the bird's-eye view of the tank. Below, Emil Sauer had been deep in heated discussion with two oil-smeared men in fatigues, a clipboard in hand.

Sigrid walked silently from the office and closed the door behind her with a soft click. Once she was at the rail that overlooked the gargantuan project from the top floor, Sauer took notice of her, and waved abruptly to disperse the men he'd been speaking with. She descended the stairs two at a time, and met him at the base of the tank.

He had a short, sinewy torso. His frame was more like a teenage boy's, rather than an aging man. The tread of the machine at his back was taller even than him, and it was clear engineering and not sport had been his calling. As she approached, his gaze revolved around the room, monitoring the activities of those that saw to his instruction. When she met him, he pointed to the figures on the document in his hand as the two walked alongside the tank. "This is an updated schematic of the barrel assembly," he said. "You'll see to it that this crosses Eichler's desk when you return?"

"Yes, sir," Sigrid replied. "And this one is for you." Sauer, without warning, proceeded toward his office with Sigrid in tow.

"I take it your trip to Berlin went well?" he asked.

"As well as one could hope."

"Excellent," Sauer replied. There was no excitement in his voice—it was cold, and calculated. "If you'll stop in my office, I'll need to make a record of this before it goes up the ladder. Some adjustments should be noted. You've got a moment, yes?"

"Of course," Sigrid said. Sauer hooked left at the center of the room, and the two trekked down a hallway that had been constructed away from the proximity of the tank. He stopped at a door, dug in his pocket for a set of keys, and inserted one into the lock on the door in front of him. "It'll be just a moment." Sigrid stepped in and he closed the door behind him.

Emil Sauer's office looked as if it had been hit by its own heavy artillery shell; a mess of papers littered not only the desk, but even the floor. Coffee mugs—the insides were stale with the crusted black remnants of dried coffee—functioned as makeshift paperweights, each of which was holding some variation of the mechanism being constructed or its finer details and parts. A smoky smell mixed with the offensive odor of mold and mildew, and Sigrid's nostrils nearly met her upper lip at the stench. She'd never seen Sauer like this—overworked and overtired. He drew the shades at the window, the glass of which revealed only a cluster of trees leading almost infinitely into the dark forest beyond. Even in broad daylight, the trees rose so high and so dense that one might mistake the time.

"How are you, sir?" Sigrid asked sheepishly.

He surveyed her face, then understood what she had intimated. "Oh, so you've heard?" He paced behind his desk. "I was sick," Sauer said. "Sick."

"I could imagine," Sigrid replied.

"The *Gestapo* inquired about my loyalties," Sauer spouted. "All because of some relatives I haven't seen or heard from in ages. As if the work I'm doing here isn't enough."

"I'm sure you made clear your loyalty."

"They'd asked why it had taken me so long to join the party," Sauer growled. "Asked me about my childhood, my family, my beliefs. It went on like that for nearly a day—all because of some records that had been dug up, and were probably inaccurate, mind you."

"Herr Eichler might have vouched for you," Sigrid suggested.

Sauer waved his hand dismissively. "Eichler's a fool. The men don't respect him. They only answer to him because he has the title." He leaned in toward her and said softly, "I hear what they say about him. They whisper and laugh. The things they say, I won't repeat, but it's safe to say that if I didn't function as the intermediary between him and the men, this project never would have seen the light of day. He can't do anything right. He's another product of wealth who'll climb the ranks—despite his failures—just like the rest of the party leaders."

He rifled around for a cigarette in his pocket, retrieved one, and offered it to Sigrid. She declined with a wave of her hand, and he struck a match to ignite it. After inhaling, he cocked his head curiously and scanned her face. "You don't look well."

"You're one to talk," Sigrid said. The delivery had been snappy and resentful, and she quickly felt foolish for speaking in a tone unbecoming of a subordinate. Sauer didn't argue the point. Both parties had seen their individual reflections in mirrors enough over the last several days to know that they had developed flawed complexions, but the stress of the project was wearing on every man—and woman—in Flussrand. "You might try less of those." Sigrid motioned to the cigarette.

"Only a day ago they were of half a mind to send me to a work camp. Can you believe that? Me! After that, what does a cigarette worry me?" Sigrid's eyes fell to the ash tray he flicked his cigarette into. The butts were piled so sloppily in it that more had toppled off the sides than remained in the tray itself.

She grabbed the tray, tossed the remnants into the garbage, and deposited the empty tray back onto the desk. "You're liable to start a fire like that."

Sauer's eyes lit up. "Now there is an idea." She smirked. "Burn the whole thing down." He inhaled once more from the cigarette, relaxing his shoulders. Sigrid jokingly pressed her finger to her lips to hush him, and the two shared a moment of respite. "What came of your meeting?"

"Just a project update," Sigrid said.

"Don't be foolish," Sauer replied, directing the burning cigarette at her. "They're watching every little detail. You can be hauled off for the most minor of infractions now, you know? They were probably checking *you* out." Sauer's insistence that the motherland had entered into a full-blown police state did not help put Sigrid at ease. "They'll eat their own if it means purity—no stone left unturned."

"You're the one who's foolish," Sigrid retorted. "They'll keep someone with a brain like yours, not a typist's."

Sauer grumbled. "That's ridiculous. Brains mean nothing in this regime—loyalty above all else." Sigrid shifted with unease. "But loyalty doesn't win wars, Sigrid. Bravery does." He pulled on the cigarette once more, exhaled abruptly, and then flicked it into the ash tray. The cherry exploded with a flurry of sparks.

6

The room was dark, and faceless, blurred masses maneuvered around Sam's obscured view. Blood had dripped into his eyes, painting his sight with a translucent, rosy curtain that was the visual representation of the pain he felt *everywhere*. His body was screaming at him, gasping and pleading with him to just shut down, to give up, and to allow himself to dissolve peacefully into the infinite blackness where there would be pain no more. His fingertips burned where the cuticles were exposed to cool air, and with every light breeze he felt the odd, exposed tingle where the fingernails had once occupied the hands tied behind his back.

His face throbbed with a deep, profound sensation from within his jaw. His head fell forward. After many attempts to hold it up—to glimpse the faces and the features of his assailants and freeze them in his mind for the moment he would have his own hands about their necks—it finally fell. His clothing, a grey-colored canvas, had been drenched with blood. Where the liquid had stained it, the color evolved into a deep charcoal. The amount that had leaked from his brow, snaked down to his mouth, and dripped from his chin had gathered in the seam of his pants between his legs and formed its own small basin where the liquid had pooled.

"*Er wird sterben,*" a voice said from his side.

A hand grabbed a fistful of the hair at the back of Sam's scalp forcefully, tilting his head backwards and revealing a mass silhouetted by the lone light above him. This man, different from the one who'd spoken previously, said, "*Noch nicht wird er nicht. Er sprach nicht.*" The man released Sam's head, and it fell once more at the neck and hung over his chest. He could barely see, let alone hold his head up any longer.

He didn't even remember what had happened before he'd gotten so banged up. His memory leading up to that moment had a been a nightmare, a carousel of pain and torture and flashes of violence and injury that he came in and out of like a sleepless, feverish night. They were keeping him alive. Whenever he collapsed, they let him be, and as soon as he came to, they started on him all over again until he was out cold. There wasn't much more he was going to be able to take—not because he was close to breaking, but because he was at risk of losing too much blood or going into shock. They hadn't planned for that. He hadn't talked, and because of that, he was close to death.

It takes a special type of person to endure the type of torture that Sam had undergone. Most men would have spilled their guts the moment the first fingernail had been pried from its resting place, the first pinky finger broken, or tooth pulled. The blunt trauma was the least agonizing. Any boy who'd gotten into a fight had learned how to take a punch without crying. It was the removal of the two teeth that was particularly painful; it was Sam's least favorite—not because it hurt at the moment of extraction, but because the pain became more and more intense as time went on.

He wouldn't tell them what they wanted to hear, though, and that was the only thing giving him the resolve to keep going. What would they do next? It didn't matter. Nothing they could do to him now would be worse than what they'd already done. They were desperate though, and Sam worried the tactics they'd employed thus far would make them get *creative*. Now he was hoping he'd collapse again, hoping he'd fall into that black void of relief where he could be rid of the constant barrage of assaults, if only for a minute, just *one* more minute.

He was angry—angry with the men who'd been toying with him for nearly eight hours, and angry for allowing his pride to withstand the pain they were dealing him. He'd always suspected this would happen. He'd always suspected his time would come.

The time had come, alright, and now he was looking the devil in the face, only the devil wore a soldier's uniform. He had no hooves, but leather boots, and no horns on his head, but badges on his breast. He came with friends and he carried a dagger and a pistol rather than a pitchfork. The devil spoke once more. "*Schlagen ihm mehr ins Gesicht. Wenn er nicht spricht, bringen wir ihn nach Pforzheim.*" The boots clomped behind him, and the screeching of the door at Sam's rear forced his ear drums to throb. Once the door slammed shut, the sound of each of the steps became more distant. Sam was alone with the devil's minions once more.

The next blow to the face came swiftly, connecting his cheek with all four of his assailant's knuckles and forcing more blood from his mouth. Another impact came from the side his head had been forced to, and his head bobbed back the other way. Another jab came once more, and he was right back where he had started. They were toying with him, mashing his head back and forth as if it was some type of children's toy. The pain was so great in every area of his body that each punch started to meld together, and soon he couldn't differentiate between where they were coming from by the pain. The only indicator left was the motion of his neck alternating between his left and right shoulder, and he hoped that he would fall into that sleep once more.

But he woke—not in the cold, light-deprived room of the men that had been banging him about like a rag doll, but the clean, sterile, white glow of an infirmary. The featureless forms that had been going to town on his face now had clear detail, and the one in front Sam quickly realized belonged to the burned man. He, too, was slapping Sam, desperately attempting to snap him out of whatever funk he was in. Luckily, he was slapping not with the hard, rock-like stumps of fists but with feathery, open palms.

"Don't do that," a man in a white coat said.

Sam leapt from the table, arching his back forward and touching at his face feverishly, and he found that the wounds that he'd remembered being inflicted only moments earlier were just a memory—a *bad* memory, and perhaps his worst. His face was free of blood, and he couldn't detect any pain in his fingertips or jaw. Long, vertical spikes displayed on the screen of the EKG monitor bounced up and down like a roller coaster. In his chest, he felt every throb that corresponded with the alerts of the machine.

"God damnit, Abel," the burned man barked. "What the hell was that?" Sam didn't answer right away. Instead, he collected himself, wiped the wet hair that had fallen on to his forehead out of his face, and sat up straight on the bed. His skin was warm and damp, the way a man feels after the first few minutes of coming down from an intense cardiovascular activity. He took deep breaths, slowing his heart down manually with every inhalation and exhalation. The EKG told him he'd taken it down from a roaring 160 beats per minute to a much more comfortable 110.

His mind raced, darting backwards in time to just what it was the burned man had said that had thrown him out of whack. He didn't need to think very hard—flashes of the images that had just been replayed in his dream-like state drew him to the word with ease. It was one lone, frightful word: *Pforzheim.*

Sam felt the motors of the boat churning from beyond the room, carrying a deep hum from its core and to each individual nook and cranny in its bowels. Then he looked through the porthole and saw the light from the sky pouring through. Beyond it, only the glistening blue waves crashing down on each other like they were stuck in some eternal battle looked back at him.

Sam sat upright on an examination table while a doctor in a white coat tended to a heart monitor nearby. He paused for a moment, surveying Sam's complexion before balling up both fists and placing them on his hips. "You look a little green."

"It's the water," Sam replied. "Sea sickness, is all."

"We've got medication for that," the doctor said. He was a clean-shaven man, with a tightly trimmed hair line and a broad chest. Sam quickly deduced that he hadn't come from some prestigious medical school, but likely was a Navy medic who had been transplanted into the burned man's operation. "It happens to a lot of people—at least, those of us who don't have sea legs. Your vitals are fine."

"Would he not have cleared me otherwise?" Sam asked, then nodded to the burned man, who'd been posted up in the corner of the room with his arms folded against his chest. He gave Sam a look of indignation.

"Well, I'll leave you two to it," the doctor said before he exited the room. He left Sam and the burned man in a silent space save for the low moan of the ship.

"I'm not a doctor," the burned man said. He slouched into the seat in the corner of the room, and, naturally, packed his pipe with a pinch of tobacco. "I'm not a fool either."

"It's the boat—"

"We were still *docked*," he interrupted. He placed the pipe between his teeth. Sam had never seen them, or the man's face, in such unflattering light. The teeth were yellow-stained, and one of the canines had even been broken; it was cracked at the tip, which made it sort of look like a fang. He'd looked uglier than Sam had ever seen him—a vicious, injured animal that was ready to attack. He hesitated to light the pipe, and his eyes hung on Sam's for a moment, untrusting suddenly, and concerned. "*Pforzheim*," he said once more. This time, Sam didn't collapse, but his chin lifted defensively as if he'd been backed into a corner and been left with nowhere to run. "Despite the heft of this ship and the gross waste of resources it would be to turn it around, I have no problem doing so if that's what I need to happen."

"Not necessary," Sam replied. "We've got work to do."

"Then what is it?"

"Bad memory with that place, is all," Sam said.

The burned man rose from his seat, leaving the clean illumination of the window that had been casting sunlight on his face. He exhaled from his pipe, grabbed it by the base, and tapped the burn marks with the stem. "My face wasn't always this pretty, you know." He walked softly, walked toward the far corner of the room with slow steps, and let his eyes wander out toward the window and the infinite expanse of sea outside. "To tell you the truth, most days it still hurts. Nothing a little scotch can't cure, but the nerves never healed right. Sometimes if I sleep on it wrong, the sting comes back. I've often wondered if it's really the pain I feel, or the reminder of it—like my brain has been misfiring and *remembering* the feeling more so than actually feeling it."

"Like a phantom limb," Sam replied.

"That's right," the burned man said, pointing the stem of the pipe at Sam. "I know plenty of men braver'n me who'll tell you that." He continued pacing, now letting his eyes fall to the floor and chewing on the stem of his pipe once more rather than inhaling from it. "Thing is, that limb's gone, and they ain't getting it back. The pain lingers, but it ain't *real*, not in that way. There comes a time with all pain when you just get so used to it that you forget it's even there, you just go on with it and accept it as it is. You're still here, still kicking."

Sam took the burned man's meaning, though he couldn't help but disagree. Sam wondered if perhaps his efforts long ago had turned the old man into a sociopath, an emotionless weapon that only carried out tasks and had little else left inside the tank other than that of the ruthless orders he'd been tasked to carry out. The burned man stopped, laid his eyes on Sam once more—not a hint of sympathy inside of them—and inhaled from the pipe. "You don't learn to shut the rest out and you'll make mistakes, Abel. That's the way it goes. Fear causes men to make mistakes. Mistakes get men injured—they get men *killed*." Smoke curled from the burned man's lips and shrouded him in a haze that blurred his face amidst sun coming from his rear. He sat in a haze of his own making, his eyes cold and unflinching. "But I don't need to tell you that."

"Why me?" Sam asked. "There's plenty of men —*American* men—who can be trained to do what I do. Why did you come for me?"

"You've already said it," the burned replied. "You're just a man—that's it. You've got no allegiance to cloud your judgement, no ties to any single identity, no junk in the attic that makes you swing this way or that. You're just a man with a reputation, and that's the kind of man I need. You just put the knife between your teeth and climb over the top. I need a weapon, a gun I can point that doesn't jam. I still think you're that man. I hope I don't stand corrected."

Sam was that man. He enjoyed the pleasures any other man enjoyed, but not in the same way. He enjoyed a beer, and a cigarette, and a woman—though not in that order. What Sam enjoyed most, though, was the idea that he was different from other men in the sense that he didn't mind jumping into the snake pit. He enjoyed it, if he was honest, even if the snakes were venomous. What bothered Sam, what disturbed him the most, was just how much like the burned man he really was. "You never told me how you found me," Sam said.

The burned man snorted for a moment. "Your name got around during the mess in Europe. Don't think people didn't talk. It was only a matter of time until someone found you. I was just happy I got to you first. There were a lot of people asking questions—*dangerous people*—many of whom were looking for you. I figured, any man who's got that big of a price on his head is a man I want on my team. I want the man that makes his enemies scared to shut their eyes at night. That's you. At first I wondered if I had made a mistake, if I'd put a rogue wolf in my employ, but then after that grenade business in New York, I *knew* I'd found my weapon." Sam felt calmer already, felt reassured in his efficiency as exactly what he was: a spy, an infiltrator, a *killer*.

"And I want more of you, Sam," the burned man said proudly. "I want to replicate you, damnit, to clone you if I could. I want an arsenal of you." The burned man made for the door, grabbed the handle, but then stopped for a moment. "Take the time you need. We've got some debriefing to do. Oh, and if anyone asks, your name when you're around here is '505.' "

505? The door shut, and Sam was left alone again. He'd finally cooled down, but his clothing was wet with the sweat he'd suffered during his episode. He'd never blacked out before, not like *that*. It was different than the collapse he'd suffered during his torture—that was due in part to a mixture of shock and pain. This, on the other hand, was likely a panic attack. He felt buzzing in his head, and with it a sort of light-headed, floaty sensation.

Outside the window the sun had retreated, shrouding the room in a drab, shadowy hue. He stepped from the bed, pressed his face against the window, and looked out to the horizon. The Atlantic blanketed every direction in sight, and there wasn't any deviation in the image except for the grey bulk of clouds where a storm had been gathering. He was happy to be in a large craft, if only because a small boat would likely be tossed around the sea if the storm had any real strength to it.

He looked to the ocean below. The waves were still engaged in battle, slapping against the hull of the ship and spraying white explosions of salt and liquid. There was no land visible from his position any longer. He was on his way, and the mighty ship would cut his path despite Mother Nature's displeasure.

7

———

The universe had conspired against Sam and tested his truthfulness regarding his seasickness. The freighter had gone headfirst into a storm—a violent number that would have caused anyone with a weak stomach to lose their breakfast. Traveling directly through the storm wasn't the safest method of transport, but the burned man warned Sam that time was not on their side; the quicker they could get Sam into the enemy's territory, the quicker they'd find out just what resources their allies could provide. The sky had turned so dark from the rolling clouds that one might have assumed they'd traveled through the night. Four hours later, when they'd come out on the other side of it, the sun had resumed its place in the western hemisphere to bid them a good night.

Sam spent the evening watching the post-storm sunset from the ship's deck. It was quiet, and meditative, and a reprieve from the internal noises of the ship and the busywork of the people working inside of it. Sam understood why they hadn't taken a plane—a plane couldn't transport an operation like the one below his feet and would likely only get as far as London or Spain before needing to refuel. Worse still, even if they made it there on a plane, they still wouldn't have a reliable entry point into Germany.

"It's the perfect cover," the burned man had said to Sam earlier. "The ship can get through any blockade in Gibraltar—friendly or otherwise. If it's an Allied inquiry, then we'll be waved through, and if it's the Axis that's curious, the paperwork will show that we're just merchants transporting goods for the war effort." It *was* a good plan. Ogden and Walde had been shipping weapons with little regard for affiliation or intention since the Führer had set foot in Poland. Any treaties or agreements banning the sale of goods to enemies had been all but swept under the rug within the context of this operation, and Sam was sure the burned man had seen to it that no harm or penalty would come to the old gun manufacturers. It helped that everyone aboard the ship dressed in the garb of shipping merchants, rather than government employees, and the shipment had been expected in an Italian port frequented by Ogden and Walde anyway.

Sam would have liked to see Italy, but it was unlikely he'd even witness the light of day while passing through. He'd be confined to the shipping container until it arrived at its destination—at least a day or two spent quietly and patiently waiting in a pitch-black cube with some rations and his thoughts. He'd be locked in before they arrived in Genoa, hoping no one inspected the crates upon arrival, driven via truck through southern Germany along the border of Switzerland, and then deposited somewhere in a munitions depot at Pforzheim.

Pforzheim, Sam thought. *The heart of the Schwarzwald.* He shuddered again at the thought. The last time he'd seen Germany he'd never thought he'd work up the resolve to return. He'd only made it out by the skin of his teeth and he'd lost everything doing it; his home, his belongings, and even his damn *name*. Yet here was, staring off into the sunset of a Pforzheim-bound shipping vessel.

He'd made himself a promise as the setting sun flared against the horizon: he'd kill himself before he'd ever go through that type of experience again. He'd cut his throat, hold his breath, or perhaps put a bullet between his eyes. When a man became a spy, no one ever came for him. He had no friends—no *real* friends—and if, or when, he was found out, it was up to him to survive on his own.

He understood the inherent risk with what he was about to do, and yet, like a drug addict taking too high a dose, he still felt that urge to push the envelope—just one more hit. No addict ever remembered how bad rock bottom felt. As soon as the effects of the terrible experience wore off, they searched for more, and that was Sam, an addict for the *thrill. I won't overdose this time.* That's what addicts always tell themselves before they *do*.

When the sun had finally vanished, leaving the deck of the ship in a cold, wind-ridden blue shadow, Sam retired to his quarters. There wasn't much else to do but sleep for the night. He had plenty of time to be briefed, and plenty of time to go over his plan in his head, as well as the details of the plan with the burned man. Unlike the events in New York at The Whispering Oak, this plan was likely to become a multi-pronged operation. Sam wondered if he'd see *Erdschlag* with his *own* eyes. He thought it best to steer clear.

Sam's head hit the flimsy pillow that was on his bed. The blanket he'd been provided had been made of a cheap wool that made his skin itch, so he tossed it off the bed, more comfortable with the idea of being chilly than waking up with rashes. He'd slept in sub-freezing temperatures on missions before, so a little cool air was nothing to be bothered about. In fact, it was always far better to deal with a chill than attempting to get shut-eye in sweltering climates.

Now that his eyes were heavy, he found the motors beneath him soothing—a white noise that began to lull him to sleep and silence the racing in his mind about the possibilities that lay ahead. He'd have a full day upon waking, and many sleepless nights after that, so he took the opportunity to get a good sleep. Soon, his mouth hung wide, and his eyelids closed softly. The mighty vessel cruised into the black void of the Atlantic, and Sam traveled into his own black abyss.

The clanking of silverware woke him the next morning. The sun shined through the porthole window and confirmed his suspicion: he'd slept through the night. The heightened state of alert that had been a byproduct of his training and lifestyle rarely allowed him to do so, and Sam Abel would wake from a deep sleep with even the slightest change in the direction of the breeze. On the freighter, though, he was safe. With the burned man he was protected.

He opened his door, and at his feet lay a tray with all the fixings one could want, as well as an envelope tucked into the corner with his name written on the front in neat cursive. The plate on the tray was decorated with two eggs sunny-side-up, two strips of bacon, a mountain of potatoes, and a cup of mixed fruit at its side. There was orange juice in a small glass, and a mug of coffee with a small cup of cream next to it. *Just what the doctor ordered*, Sam thought. Perhaps it *had* been the doctor who'd written the note, but he was too hungry to check.

He ate the fruit first, not because it was his favorite, but if he started with the meats he'd never get to the necessities. Once the fruit was finished, he gobbled the eggs down. The wet yolk ran down his lower lip as if he'd never learned proper table manners. Then, he slurped the black coffee down his throat to wash them back. He attacked the bacon, crunching it rapidly before forcing the potatoes in behind it. Before he'd even finished, he took a crack at the envelope and pulled the paper out of it while sucking yet more coffee down.

He unfolded the paper and read from the top, "After you've finished your breakfast and tea, we'll go through your loadout. Take a left when you leave your dormitory, then head straight toward the starboard side and down the alleyway until you see the sign that reads 'Below-Deck Storage.' Continue down the staircase, and you'll find yourself in the engine room. Take a right before you go any farther and we'll meet in the room labeled 'Storage 1.' "

Tea? Who on Earth would refer to their coffee as tea? He'd also never heard any American refer to a bedroom as a 'dormitory.' He put the same clothes on that he'd worn the day before, lit a cigarette, and closed the door behind him.

The alleyways were quiet except for the low hum of the vessel. It was a welcome distraction from the noisy streets of Brooklyn, and he'd wondered to himself if it might not be so bad to quit spying altogether and learn how to become a merchant. The pay probably wasn't bad, and it likely wouldn't matter who he was or where he came from—a fitting career for a man of no nation. He didn't know the first thing about loading cargo or navigating the sea, but the idea of getting a day's break in an exotic location or being away from home for months at a time was enticing. He hadn't even had a true home until just recently.

He followed the path laid out for him by the person who still had yet to be named, and arrived at a water-tight door with a window that had been blacked out. He looked around, but there was no one in sight. He tapped on the door with his knuckles, and the door responded with tinny clangs. The door opened, and there stood a well-groomed young man with a smile across his face. He wore a sport coat, and though his undershirt bore a collar, the top button had been undone and it was not hugged by a tie. He wore spectacles, and he pushed them up to the bridge of his nose before reaching his hand out to Sam jubilantly.

"You must be him," the young man said. He was British, and Sam wondered just how in the hell an Englishman had joined a secret American outfit like the burned man's. Sam shook his hand, and the man kept shaking it awkwardly. His eyes were bright and eager, and a lone, slim curl of black hair bounced against his forehead as he continued the gesture. Sam did not return the same excited demeanor of the man, who, Sam thought, was starting to resemble more of a boy.

He was lanky and underweight, just under six feet tall, and wore khaki pants against the blue jacket that made him look like he'd been ready to walk into a private school. "Newton," the man said. "At least, that's the name they've given me. I'm told no one really uses their real names around here."

Sam almost let his real name slip from his lips, with the hiss of an 's' like he'd been a snake warning a predator of its strike, and then his namesake clicked. "505," Sam replied.

"Right, then," Newton said. "Let's get on with it." He stepped into the room, and Sam followed behind him. What Sam found was not a storage room, but an armory. The room, like many of the others inside the ship, had been augmented heavily. It had previously been a hollowed-out storage facility, with a long hall that stretched to the opposite end they'd entered. At the back, a set of targets featuring nondescript men hung and had been printed on papers with zones on their bodies—it was a shooting range. Flanking Sam on either side were shelves of weapons, and a workbench where this Newton must have done his tinkering. Newton sealed the door shut once more, and turned to Sam. "For the noise. It can get quite loud in here, though you can't hear much outside of the room. It's been retrofitted so that it's near soundproof. Can't have the sound of gunfire echoing through the ship all day, can you?"

"Where are you from, Newton?" Sam asked curiously.

"London, originally." His cheeks grew red and flushed, and he froze for a moment, his mouth parted slightly in a near-perfect circle. "I suppose I wasn't supposed to tell you that bit."

"Your secret's safe with me," Sam assured him. "And how did you get here?"

"Fair enough," Newton said. "Studied physics and

engineering at university for some time."

"How does a kid wind up with a job like this?"

"Well, you've got to really know what you're talking about, for starters," he said. "I suppose that's why they call me Newton. Apple from the tree, and all that. Bit of a rag, I assume. Of course my mother says that everything there is to know about engineering and physics is already known. Told me it was a waste of degree and that I should study law or finance or some such. She thinks I'm working with Alaskans on an oil rig. Told her that's about the only job I could find. Mommy knows best. Keeps her from calling, though."

Newton's eyes landed on the shelf behind Sam. "Turns out the degree comes in handy when you apply it to guns and explosives and all those nasty bits. Took a few design courses as well and those have come in quite handy. So, ever use an O and W 40?"

"Can't say I have," Sam said. Newton walked to the shelf, and Sam followed behind him. Newton pulled a handgun from the shelf.

"Be happy they're not handing you a Luger," Newton said. "This one's a bit of an upgrade. The Germans should have let that one die in the first war— far too many quid to produce. It's a reliable little weapon." Newton pulled the magazine from the gun. "Heel magazine release, single stack—a good design if you ask me—single-action or double-action trigger. That means you can safely chamber a round, use the safety-decocking lever to lower the hammer without firing the first round, and carry her loaded and ready. First shot's a double-action pull." Newton aimed the gun at the target, and dry-fired it with a dull click. "First round's ejected, hammer cocks again, and a fresh round's chambered for single-action semi-automatic firing." Newton dry-fired the gun again, then pulled the slide, inspected the chamber, then turned the barrel to the floor and handed the weapon to Sam.

Sam gripped the pistol and aimed it at the target over the top of the barrel. It felt light in his hands, as if barely any effort was required to lift it. Sam *liked* that. He examined the grip, which possessed a wooden finish.

"Oak?"

"Walnut," Newton replied. "Just over a pound in weight overall. Has a nice slap to it, too, but very little recoil. Quite easy to service in the field as well. Wish I could send you off with something you were fond of, but if you're going to look the part, you're going to need to carry the right tools as well."

"Why this one?" Sam asked, guiding the gun around the target.

"Used by both sides, compliments of our *friends* at O and W," Newton said. "Too risky if you were to tip someone off. Many of the soldiers out there will be carrying what you are, and that means ammunition will be abundant should you need it. I suppose you like going about your work in a more a quiet manner—only way to get a nail in is with a hammer, though."

Newton went to the cabinet and grabbed a full magazine, then handed it to Sam. Sam gave him the empty, slapped the full one into the grip of the gun, and loaded a round. "Make sure you've fired eight. If you remove the magazine, and you've only fired seven rounds, there'll still be one at the ready in the chamber. Shoot a man in the right place, and one round is liable to do the trick."

Newton handed Sam a pair of earmuffs and safety

glasses. Sam put on both and stepped toward the target. "How does she feel?"

Sam drew the gun, readied it, and fired a single shot at the target. The gun emitted a deafening crack—nothing subtle about it—and then ejected its empty casing to the left-hand side. The shell hit the floor with a *clink* while Sam witnessed his work. The first shot hit the shoulder of the target, and Sam was momentarily displeased. He paused for a moment, readjusted his aim, and fired seven more shots in rapid succession. Each struck the head of the target, with only minor deviations where one hit the eye and one pierced the nose. Sam ejected the magazine, checked the chamber, and placed the gun on the small table in front of him. "I like the sight."

Newton adjusted his glasses before he took a good look at the target, and his eyebrows rose into long inverted "u" shapes. "You're a fine shot, Mr. 505."

"Can't afford to miss," Sam replied. "It'll do."

"Brilliant," Newton replied. "I'm quite fond of it myself. I'd wager when this is all over there'll be other companies chomping at the bit to recreate this bugger. It's ahead of its time, really." Newton stepped over to the shelf once more. "And your rifle." He pulled a long carbine with a wooden finish on its stock from the rack. "Here we are." He cocked the bolt, checked the chamber, and then handed it to Sam.

"A C30a," Sam said as he examined the rifle from top to bottom. "This one I know."

"It's a newer model—Carbine 30c, to be exact. Standard issue over there, at least for a lesser man of the infantry like you'll be playing." He pointed to the center of the barrel. "You'll see this bit here"—he pointed to the 'M/35,' label—"which means it's a commercial production by Meisner—no *swastikas* or eagles anywhere to be found. These were spread about as carbine models to circumvent Versailles, so it's not *technically* a rifle. I thought you might like to know that in case anyone gets smart. It shouldn't be a problem—they've distributed many through the ranks." Sam placed the rifle stock against his shoulder and up to his eye, taking aim at the targets afar. "Good for at least fifteen hundred feet without a stock, and surprisingly accurate. Not likely you'll be using this, I imagine, but it completes the show. That's a noisy tool, though. Something tells me this piece will be more your speed."

Newtown held a dagger outstretched from his hand, and Sam handed him the rifle before taking it. "You'd be correct," Sam replied.

"I figured," Newton said. "I imagine you're more of sneak and slice sort of fellow, if at all."

The pommel of the dagger widened toward the base. A crown of oak leaves had been milled around the circumference. The handle was braided in a butter-scotch finish down to the cross guard, which had been machined in such a way to display an eagle perched on a *swastika* with its wings outstretched. Wrapped around the handle and draped across the hilt was a braided rope that ended in an acorn. Sam unsheathed the blade from the pebble-finished scabbard—which also had been adorned with oak leaves—and twirled the finely sharpened tip close to his face. It was a fine knife, despite its affiliation, and Sam clutched it in his hand then slashed it through the air once. Newton took an awkward step backward. Sam then spun it his hand, aimed the blade below his fingers, and swung it once more, now slicing in a downward motion. Newton smirked. It was obvious that Sam was just as well suited with a blade as he was with a pistol, if not *better*.

"More of a decorative piece, really," Newton said. "But I suppose there is an art to what you do. This one's got a bit of a sting to it." Sam sheathed the blade back into its home.

"Let's move on to some custom bits," Newton said cheerfully. There was a hint of pride in his voice that didn't go unnoticed by Sam. *This* must have been what Newton was really recruited to do. "Potassium cyanide capsule." He pulled a small glass vial no bigger than a thumbnail from the shelf, then displayed it in his hand for Sam to witness. "We'll put it in a protective housing for you, and it'll be stitched into the sleeve of your uniform should you need it."

"Then what?" Sam asked.

"You bite it, of course," Newton replied. "Don't suppose it will feel nice on the teeth, but before that registers, well, I suppose you won't be feeling much pain at all. The Germans are quite fond of these themselves, from what I understand."

Sam examined the small capsule in his hand. Despite the horrid nature of a tool such as a suicide pill, something about the quick death put him at ease. If things got too hot, it would be his ticket out. He'd never had that option before—not *last* time.

8

On the ship's deck, the burned man puffed from his pipe with Newton at his side doing his best to tolerate the smoke. Their long coats flapped like tattered flags with each punishing gust of the wind. Sam stepped foot on the deck, and the icy chill of the morning hit his skin with the ferocity of a welding torch's flame. He'd clutched his shoulders, embracing the last bit of warmth before the chilliest leg of the journey. He'd had a pretty comfortable go of it up until this point, but that would all change very soon.

He'd been wearing nothing but the under garments he'd been given, which, although helpful, were hardly warm enough. He could finally see land, and he caught a glimpse of the Italian coast. Newton was holding a cleanly pressed *Wermacht* uniform draped over his forearm, and beside him two men in coveralls waited with toolboxes in hand.

The burned man handed Sam a small paper bag with a little heft to it. "Rations," he said. "Just make sure you clean up after yourself. Water has been placed in a collapsible bag as well. Don't leave that behind either. It's all been made manageable in case they go digging around the cargo—and we should assume they will."

"One last smoke?" Sam requested. The burned man nodded. Sam looked down at his near-naked body, and then to one of the crew members—he'd had no pockets with which to store any personal belongings. The man dug through his coveralls, retrieved a cigarette, and handed it to Sam. Sam placed it in his mouth, and it was then lit for him. The man removed three loose cigarettes and a book of matches and offered those to Sam too. He then placed those inside the ration bag.

"Don't leave those behind either," the burned man said. "And don't smoke them in any situation that's going to get you caught."

"Who's the one going in here?" Sam asked smartly.

The burned man returned his signature groan over the inhalation of his pipe. "Just because I'm willing to risk you doesn't mean I *want* to lose you."

"Right, then," Newton said, holding out the uniform. "I'd leave the uniform hanging, despite the cold. It's nasty out there, I know, but you don't want to be rattling around in there and dirty it up. It should be clean-pressed, sharp and all that. That'll at least buy you a day or two until you can get it pressed if you need to."

"Can you recommend a tailor?" Sam asked. Newton returned a smile. He then handed Sam the holster for both his handgun and combat knife, and Sam grabbed those too, followed by the rifle he'd been provided. He slung that over his shoulder, and a cool tremor ran through his body.

"Oh and, erm," Newton said, then pointed to the

sleeve of the uniform where the cyanide capsule head been sewn in. "We've arranged that bit in there." Near the cuff of the sleeve, a small impression rose slightly above the uniform fabric.

"Let's get on with it," Sam said. He pulled the cigarette from his mouth and tossed it off the rail of the boat, into the ocean below. "The longer I stand out here the smaller my dick gets." He walked into the container, content to at least be free of the wind chill. Inside the container, there were long rows of wooden crates, and one small alcove for Sam to trek through and get behind the tall stacks. Each box had "Ogden and Walde" printed on its broad side, and serial numbers that differed from box to box below the company's logo.

A mouse scurried out from inside the container, scampering past Sam, and he stomped his foot down to see if there'd been an infestation. Four more skittered out, darting and zig-zagging and taking new refuge on the deck of the ship where'd they surely find a better temporary home than Sam himself was about to have. It was disgusting, but reassuring, because Sam thought that if they could manage in there, he could too. The wind howled against the container, whistling and singing a song to Sam, the nature of which signaled the chilly journey to come. Through the open door, the burned man and Newton stood waving to see Sam off.

"There's sacks in there," Newton said. "They're meant for making sure the cargo doesn't shift and bang around, but they'll be good to keep warm until you get to where you're going." Sam grabbed one, draped it over his shoulders, and closed it around himself like it were some sort of makeshift robe. He'd been through worse, but it certainly wasn't anything to brag about.

The man with the flame-scarred face said, "Alright," then turned to scan the horizon where they'd meet the land they'd been fast approaching. "They'll be out there soon with telescopes and binoculars and such. Let's seal it up." Sam hung the uniform from one of the crates, then secured the rest of his belongings between another two just in case there was any aggressive movement during travel.

Newton saluted Sam. "Good luck, chap."

"Thanks," Sam replied, but he didn't return the salute.

The burned man stepped forward and shook Sam's hand with a firm grip, though he didn't say anything at all—not a good luck, or a godspeed, or a be safe. He didn't need to. It was implied. He simply said, "Forty-eight hours."

Newton grabbed the slide lock on the inside of the door and removed it from its holster, displaying it for Sam. "We've modified it," Newton said. "As soon as you've gone quiet and the coast is clear, you just give this a yank, turn, and throw all your weight into the door. Make sure you relock it before you've gone on your way, just to clean up your tracks."

The burned man took a step back, and the two crew members grabbed the heavy container door and swung it shut. It screamed on the hinges—metal scraping against metal—as the light began to dissipate. The door closed with a reverberating *clang*, and Sam was left in silence and darkness. He bade farewell temporarily to both sunlight and people.

It was only an hour or so before Sam felt the *clank* of the crane secured to the container, and soon the *whir* of the winch that hoisted him up off the boat and into the air. It was a strange sensation—knowing that one was lingering high above solid ground and yet unable to see just how high they currently were. The crane operator had handled the cargo clumsily, and when it had found the ground again, Sam was glad he'd braced himself for the crash.

There were voices at one point: muffled, Italian syllables Sam couldn't make out in detail. He imagined they were discussing the fate of the cargo he'd been in, and that meant he was still at risk—not time to relax just yet. When the voices finally died down, he felt another crane take hold of the package, and then came the guttural rattle of a diesel engine. The driver shifted gears, signaling they were off on their journey, and Sam wrapped himself in a second blanket and braced himself up against one of the crates.

He slept for most of the trip, not because he needed to, but because he forced himself to. The complete darkness he'd been left in made it less difficult. He used one of the matches at one point just to reorient himself, but most of the times he navigated the container he'd just felt his way around like a blind man. He wished a man could sack away the extra sleep for those special reserve occasions in which one was on the job for more than one cycle of the sun.

He'd woken every time the monstrous truck had slammed its brakes or switched to a low gear to traverse a steep grade, but the black interior saw to it that he quickly dozed off again once the commotion had settled. It went on like that for at least another day —uphill, downhill, sweeping around sharp curves, and idling at intersections. Sam wondered if it was the driver's unruly traversal of the European countryside that had woken him so frequently or the fit his body was throwing over the absence of nicotine in its system.

Soon, the vehicle had entered more flat terrain, and Sam slept through that comfortably. He suspected he'd cleared Switzerland. Whenever he woke, he ate one of the rations—they were of the same god-awful brand he had given to the horses the last time he'd entertained a mission for the burned man, but a gurgling stomach had very little preference. He'd finished his water, sparingly sipping it at intervals, and pissing in the corner of the crate when he had to. He'd held his bowel movements, not because he found it manageable, but because he didn't want to be forced to stew in the smell of his own filth. The urine was bad enough. There would be plenty of forest to dump waste in the *Schwarzwald*. His only fear was that he'd be forcing a hockey puck through a small pipe. Just when he'd thought the temptation of a cigarette would best him, he finally heard the truck's motor cease.

He debated putting the skin of his enemy on, but the commotion of voices outside of his makeshift home urged him to do otherwise. It would do no good to get the uniform dirty—or bloody—this early in the game. When the sound of metal thumping against asphalt made its way to Sam's ear, he was sure the cargo had been removed from the truck. Soon the ignition of the diesel motor interrupted the silence, and after a moment of idling, the sound of gears changing grew more distant. Sam took the opportunity to peek through a small crack that had been left in the crate for oxygen, but no light could be found—it was night.

Outside, Sam registered the crunching of dirt

beneath the boots of a man approaching. The steps drew nearer and louder, until finally they were outside the container, which allowed Sam to smell the smoke of a cigarette. He'd kill—quite literally—for a cigarette, but now was not the time. A little patience and he'd have the freedom of a breather and the ability to tend to all those luxuries he'd been holding back from.

"*Wohin get das?*" the man said. Now that the truck's idling wasn't masking the sounds outside, Sam could hear the small intricacies of the words spoken around him with better clarity. He returned to the far end of the container, retreating behind a column of crates that had been stacked in the back.

"*Das sind Waffen aus Amerika,*" another man replied. "*Diese bleiben hier in Pforzheim. Riecht nach Urin.*"

"*Ich werde es mir ansehen,*" the man replied, and Sam heard him fiddling with the lock for the door to the crate. Sam acted hastily, grabbing the uniform he'd worked so hard to keep clean, the rifle, and his pistol holster. He removed the blanket from his body, draped it over one of the crates nearby, and retreated again to the back end of the container. The door opened, and the glimmer from a small spotlight above the container spilled in slightly. Sam shielded his eyes, which had become so accustomed to the darkness that they stung upon contact with the light. Cold air whistled through the crate, but the fresh smell of forest and greenery was a welcome change from mildew and rust. The man entered, and Sam could tell by the heavy *clunk* from the heel of each boot that he was a soldier.

Sam placed his eye against the gap between two of the crates and saw the man lean in closely to one of the crate's faces. He used his rifle to pry at the lid, popping the wooden top off and peeking inside; Sam kept his breath silent—his heart rate remained steady. The soldier, who Sam could see was dressed in a *Wermacht* uniform not so dissimilar from the one he would soon be donning, closed the lid and slung the rifle over his shoulder. Then he turned down the aisle Sam had retreated behind, and continued his search of the container.

Each step closer the soldier took was another advanced in the direction of certain death for Sam —*click, click, click*. Sam grabbed the blade with a feathery grip, unsheathed it from its scabbard, and pressed his back firmly against the crate. The soldier pulled on his cigarette, and the wall opposite Sam glowed with a soft, rusty illumination. The soldier took another delayed step… and another.

Sam held the dagger firmly in his hand, the eagle staring back at him with majestically spread wings, as if he too was screaming, "Strike!" No, it was too soon to take a man's life, too much of a mess, too much of a sloppy start. What would he do with the body? He didn't even know *where* he was yet other than the fact that he'd made it behind enemy lines. The soldier took another step toward Sam, sniffing at the air.

"*Widerlich,*" the soldier said softly to himself. Sam thought it smelled like piss, too. He'd been smelling it for nearly forty-eight hours now. The soldier wandered forward, and now Sam could smell his cigarette. He said he'd *kill* for a cigarette, and now he might have to. Sam clutched the handle of the dagger more tightly now while he held his left hand free and his fingers open and outstretched, ready to grapple. He'd go for the man's throat—silent death. If he punctured the neck, the man might scream, but if Sam cut his trachea, he wouldn't be able to.

Luckily Sam hadn't put the uniform on just yet. If he had to take this man out, he'd be covered in blood. No one ever tells a man how much blood there is to manage when he cuts another man, or shoots an enemy in a haphazard way—he's got to experience that himself to know just how to kill a man as cleanly as possible.

The soldier stepped forward again, shifted one of the boxes, and was now examining one just near Sam's head. Sam retracted his elbow, got the dagger as ready as he could to do the dirty work, and flexed the fingers in his left hand in preparation. He'd grab the man by the collar and slash at the throat. Sam bared his teeth, clenching them together like a violent animal. His only hope was that the man didn't attempt to pull his service weapon. There'd be no getting around that type of noise; Sam wasn't currently in a war zone.

The soldier shifted the box back into its place of origin and turned on his boot. Sam let his breath out with a light hiss between his teeth. The steps wandered back to the front of the container, and then the door closed behind him. Sam was left in darkness once more as he returned the dagger to its scabbard.

The time had come. He placed all his gear on as quickly as possible, and hoped he'd done everything properly to look the part. He had some resources at his disposal now, including all the items that had been packed in the sack that he hadn't yet touched. He felt like he'd hit the lottery, and most importantly, he was finally feeling *warm*. Now in uniform, Sam understood the burned man's insistence that the spy be at ease with his actions—wearing the clothing of the enemy was breaking the rules.

The last thing Sam did after ensuring he'd left no evidence behind was grab the shaving kit from his pack and run the blade across his face. A small mirror inside the kit revealed just how much stubble he'd accumulated over the past several days, and there was no way a soldier in uniform was going to go out into the world looking like a grizzly bear. Once satisfied, he ran some aftershave across the skin, which forced every pore on his face to cry in the bitter air. It felt as if he'd thrown a bucket of ice water across his face, but it increased his alertness. He felt good—well-rested, finely tuned, and energetic. Now he had to get out of this uncomfortable box and on with the mission.

Sam climbed up on top of one of the crates and took a peek outside though the hole in the top corner. The area was all but silent, save for the flute-like song of the wind through the field outside. Upon further inspection, he deduced that he was inside just one container among many. He'd arrived at some type of shipping yard or munitions storage facility, perhaps one which would deliver supplies to front-line troops; all the more reason to get on with it and out of the territory. He waited for a moment, confirmed he heard no enemy soldiers in the vicinity, and hopped off the crate.

Sam grabbed the small rod on the door and slid it upwards until the lock loosened. He held it before it could swing on its hinge, and looked through the crack in the doorway once more. There was no one present. Then he craned his neck around the door in the oppo-site direction—still no one. He exited as quietly as possi-ble. He was *free*.

The night was calm and agreeable. The soft breeze gliding through the landscape was romantic and, combined with the smell of the *Schwarzwald's* rich plant life, Sam dared say it brought a smile to his face. It had been years since he'd experienced that sense, that of thick, dense foliage and rarely disturbed nature. It was a far cry from the pungent stenches and dizzying commotion of Brooklyn. He was reminded that man had a relationship with nature that the advent of the industrial age had driven a wedge between. It was a relationship he missed—deep in enemy territory or otherwise.

Tall trees rose up around him in every direction, providing a sort of canopy to the storage area and only further blacking out the already obscured night sky. He'd need to get his bearings and find his way to Pforzheim. The city's center would be the place he would rendezvous with his allies. Since the container had been bound for a location near the city, he was confident it wouldn't be far.

He traveled down a corridor boxed in by containers, carefully avoiding the tall, revealing lights that had been erected to illuminate the area. There were infantry trucks parked alongside a structure that Sam assumed was the office area for the location, and cheerful voices emanated from inside. The men were partying, and none the wiser to his arrival. He paused at an intersection when two men making their rounds passed through, waiting silently where the shadows had pooled in the area that the light didn't touch. Both men were armed, and dressed similarly to Sam, though they carried custom accessories unlike his. Their boots did not match his own, and they had regimental numbers on their uniforms. They were chortling and smirking, discussing something about their post that Sam paid no mind to. After they'd passed, he continued onward until he met a fence that surrounded the property.

Rather than climb up and risk the commotion, he managed to squeeze through a weak point along the dirt ground where the fence had not securely met it. Sam started on a swift jog as soon as he had disappeared into the tree cover. The man of many names was free and clear to continue on to the next task—on to find his friends from the other side of the pond.

9

Sigrid had waited for a response long enough. The SOE men assured her they'd contact her, and they hadn't. She couldn't bear the anxiety of waiting any longer for a morsel of information regarding her exploits, so she'd taken it upon herself to go see her British friends on Friday night. She'd caught a ride with one of the mechanics recruited on the project, fibbing about visiting one of her friends, and had made it as far as a walking bridge that led into the town center before parting ways with him. Though there was a bite in the night, she'd dressed warmly and had wanted to feel the fresh air after being cooped up in the office for several days.

She headed toward the house of her co-conspirators on the intersection at Leopoldstraße and Zerrennerstraße, and relaxed herself with the smell of the River Enz along the way. She'd been quite fond of the musty odor of the cobblestone walkways and the lingering scents of dinners being cooked at homes. Though the smell brought a warmth of its own, the blacked-out windows that hid the innards of residential activities signaled there was still a war going on. Constant reminders to limit window lights were common, since the government believed that would deter bombing raids. Pforzheim had not yet suffered any akin to other, greater cities of the Reich.

She arrived finally at the market square. There had been a smattering of locals among the fountain in the center of the gathering place, onlookers gawking at a sight Sigrid had not prepared herself for. She could not initially make out the scene. Something had attracted the attention of the people and obscured her view. She continued forward, curious as to just what it was that had captured their interest. After several people had departed the fountain area, clearing a gap for her to see, she made out the bodies of two men hanging from long ropes.

Nooses had been tightened around their necks, and their feet dangled roughly three feet from the ground. Their faces had been heavily distorted, twisted and mangled into unrecognizable features. Sigrid gasped, cupping her numbed fingers to her mouth to silence the audible yelp, because it didn't take much longer than a few seconds to recognize their faces—they were the British spies she had divulged the precious information to.

Their bodies swayed limp in the breeze. They had been stripped of their false *Ordnungspolizei* uniforms. Someone had awarded them the minute decency of their undergarments. Even *evil* men have standards regarding indecency. Sigrid grew closer, and the stressed wood creaked louder above the dangling bodies. Indifferent townsfolk passed by. It nauseated her.

Above both men, a sign that read *"Tod für Spione"* had been written in dark ink and large lettering for all to read—"death for spies." Below that, the British flag had been hung. It waved in the wind, its edges ripped and tattered and flickering with a defeated ripple. Their necks were red from the abrasions, their faces were bloated and swollen, and their eyes bulged lifelessly from their sockets. Both men's tongues hung lazily over their bottom lips. The muscles in the feet had relaxed, their toes pointing to the ground as if they were ready to perform in some twisted ballet. The necks had grown long and unnatural, each bone separating from its original structure. The men looked as if they were ready to be drafted into an amateur basketball league.

Sigrid gripped her neck sympathetically, massaging the throat with both hands as if it would make the sight more bearable. It didn't. She could wind up suffering the same fate as both men, or perhaps, if she was lucky, she might have the quick death of a rifle squad or guillotine. Didn't the brain still function after being removed from the head? Didn't the eyes still see and the mind still feel pain for a brief period after the head had been separated from the body? She'd heard rumors, but even then those ideas paled in comparison to that of struggling painfully as one prayed for the life to leave the body. What was worse was that it was she who was responsible for this unholy display.

She quickly buried the guilt. She hadn't acted alone. The men had willingly taken the information. They had known the risk and, most importantly, had reconciled the dangers of war and espionage.

Sigrid moved swiftly for the alley that occupied the gap between two nearby buildings. The hanging men were out of sight, and now, out of mind. What was done was done. Her rapid breathing and fluttering heart reminded her that right now, she was still *here*. She needed to go to the location they had been using, needed to find out if anything had been left behind that could help her. She *needed* to know.

She traveled purposefully, navigating through the alley and using a shorter route than she had initially planned. The thought that perhaps the men had been discovered in the location had crossed her mind, but she thought it more likely they had been discovered out in the open, perhaps in the streets, precisely as she had warned them they may. If she was caught in their hide-out, she might be questioned too, but the reward of discovering new information far outweighed the risk of being caught. The damage had already been done—she only hoped they hadn't been tortured before they'd been killed and revealed details about her own participation.

The apartment building at *Leopoldstraße* and *Zerren-nerstraße* showed no signs of activity from outside. Each of its many blacked-out, front-facing windows only reflected the dark night sky and the faint, glossy sheen of the waxing moon. This neighborhood was more quiet, and Sigrid idled across the street from her destination as a man pushing a cart with cheeses passed by. She didn't dare use the front door for fear of being seen, and once she'd worked up the nerve to get a look inside, she made her move, hiding her face behind the collar of her coat as she approached.

The rear door showed no signs out of the ordinary—no scuff marks or breakages or scrapes. It had been shut firmly, which convinced her that it was likely the men had been discovered while milling about or looking for supplies. She'd warned them that their disguises had faults, and she suspected it might have been their negligence that had finally done them in.

She searched above, looking around the windows of residents who lived in the building adjacent. A woman was busy beating a rug. Dust lingered in the cool night air. She'd disobeyed the black-out orders, as some did. A stern warning would come her way soon enough via the *Ordnungspolizei.* She took no notice of Sigrid before retreating back through her window.

Sigrid opened the door cautiously, rushed inside, and closed it behind her. The silence within the building alerted her to the sound of her own ragged breathing, and the climbing of her heart rate into the triple digits. Could the *Ordnungspolizei* be waiting for her arrival—or worse, the *Waffen SS* or *Abwehr?* She could be falling into a trap of her own making, and what would her excuse be for being there?

Although she forced those thoughts back into the deep recesses of her mind—which brought about the curious sensation of losing her dinner once more—she resolved to continue forward, if only out of dangerous curiosity. She stepped delicately, and with each foot planted on the wooden planks at her feet, the floor groaned. There wasn't a light source available, only the reflection of the moon bouncing off of various structures surrounding the building and trickling in through the windows at the top of the stairwell ahead.

She climbed the set of stairs, unnerved that the wooden steps there were in a weakened state, and therefore, louder under her feet. When she arrived at the top, she found the door the men had been stationed behind closed and undisturbed. Inside the apartment, she would get her answer, whatever it was. She half expected a gun to be drawn to her temple upon entry, but she continued regardless, her legs functioning as if they had their own brains that would propel her forward. When she arrived, she paused, focusing on the choppy inhalation and exhalation she'd been unable to quell, and slowed it to deep, consistent breaths.

Sigrid grabbed the knob, turned it, and opened the door slowly. She braced herself, biting her lip and closing her eyes while preparing for the hail of bullets that might greet her. Perhaps they wouldn't hurt as much if they came rapidly and abundantly—perhaps her death would be instantaneous and it wouldn't be the worst way to go. It would be better, she reasoned, than the fate that had befallen the British men.

Those bullets didn't come, and Sigrid let a relieved sigh leave her chest. Instead, all that greeted her was a quiet room with the remnants of the operation lying scattered about. After closing the door to the apartment behind her, she stepped forward, inspecting what had been left behind. The moon reflected elegantly through the large glass window ahead. She suspected that may have been why they had chosen that room among the others. The door that had been removed from its hinges and turned into a makeshift table was home to a grouping of half-burned—and still flickering—candles and extinguished cigarette butts. Beside them, a small helping of Irish whiskey remained in a glass jug, and there were two canteens beside it.

Their clothing was lying scattered around the room, but she thought she remembered seeing it that way the first time she'd met them, and it showed no indication that the room had been ransacked. A smattering of documents had been left behind, scattered around the table in no orderly manner. Surely if they'd been discovered, any of their work would have been confiscated—that idea gave her a small bit of relief.

There was a folder on the crate, and its title was labeled at the top in pencil. She grabbed the folder, holding it in the light of the dancing flames in the candles. It read: *Yellowfin.* The amber glow of the candle gave Sigrid pause. How long had the men been hanging? She was not a medical expert, and couldn't deduce the time of death—so why were the candles still burning? Surely they wouldn't have been foolish enough to leave a flame lit after leaving the place.

There was a shift in the air, a displacement of the stale nature of the room, and it tickled her senses in all the wrong ways. There was no open window, and she'd closed the door behind her, so why the change? She was not alone. She placed the folder back on to the table before reaching quietly into her skirt and removing the Luger. Her back was turned to the sole bedroom inside the apartment—the only place someone else could be hiding.

The thumping of footsteps came rapidly, each one increasing in speed in relation to the last. She turned and drew the gun to the source, but the gun was quickly swatted away after an aggressive crack to her forearm. It tumbled out of her hand, rattling against the floor beside her. As soon as the movement registered, she found a knife at her throat. The hilt revealed itself: a *military* knife. Sigrid Lang was no slouch, even if she'd never seen any real action. She proved it quickly, delivering a swift knee to the groin of her attacker, and the man crumpled down to the floor in submission.

It was indeed a *Wermacht* man—*Heer*, in fact. When Sigrid's eyes finally caught the light of the moon against the dark green fatigue, it hadn't surprised her. *Of course.* They'd left a soldier in waiting, sitting in the shadows and ready to strike. He'd do it with his knife to keep silent. He'd subdue her, take her as his captive, and deliver her to be judged.

She lifted her foot, arching her knee high above her waist in preparation to bring it down, but the man, whose face had been indiscernible in the poorly lit room, grabbed her foot and yanked it. This action pulled her weight from the leg she'd been leaning on and sent her collapsing to the floor with a hard *thud* on her back. The impact stole the air from her lungs. Sigrid choked, struggling to catch a breath.

The man rose, towering over her and driving the knife down once again toward her shoulder, but she rolled out of the way of the weapon and the glimmering point hit the wooden plank with a *ping*. He pulled at it, but she disabled his weapon quickly, kicking it with the sole of her foot. The action sent the blade tumbling along the floor and out of her assailant's reach. She finally caught a breath of air and rose to meet him. He leapt to his feet, squaring up with both fists, and sent a jab directly into her face. Sigrid caught it with one hand and delivered her own hook to his jaw. The worst mistake a man could make was to underestimate her.

She'd met her match, however, because he delivered his own strike to her throat with a fist full of curled knuckles. It tapped the trachea in just the right way and sent her stumbling backwards as she clutched at her throat. It was controlled, and efficient—not an attack meant to kill, but disorient or disable. It *worked*. The damn attack had nearly knocked the breath out of her once more.

The man's hands rose, the fingertips curled in a manner that presented an offer to grapple. Sigrid returned the request with the same gesture before they both lurched forward. The clash came like lightning. Sigrid felt the man grab the back of her head, and she clutched his arms. A quick swipe of his leg by her own sent him crashing, and she landed on top of him.

Now she had her thighs wrapped around him, squeezing at his ribs in an effort to subdue him—the glint of the dagger on the floor beside his head caught her eye. She struck him in the nose, then reached for the knife. Now she had him, and she placed the knife at his trachea, the tip of the blade brushing against the soft skin with every breath he took. All it would take was one little poke, just the tiniest amount of force and the man would be gurgling on his own blood and silenced eternally.

He grabbed the blade with his free hand—to Sigrid's surprise—clutching the sharp edge without a hint of fear in his eye. Sigrid thought he was mad. That notion quickly subsided when she noticed his gloves. He struck the backside of her forearm with the other hand, seizing upon her surprise, and her elbow screamed with pain. The sensation of her elbow almost being forced out of its socket caused her to loosen her grip, and she dropped the knife. He threw her off of him, sending her backwards. The base of her skull hit the wood, sending a tremor of dizziness vibrating throughout her body. In front of her eyes was the Luger she'd lost, and she grabbed it clumsily.

She rose and drew the gun to his face. She was too slow—he quickly grabbed her weakened forearm, bent it at the elbow— allowing her to keep the gun in her hand —and redirected it. He lurched forward, and now their faces were almost touching. His eyes darted feverishly back and forth between both of hers. His teeth were gritted, and yet he stopped his assault.

Neither said a word. She felt his warm body against hers, the rise and fall of his chest from the exertion of the tussle. He had her, because soon Sigrid felt the cold barrel of the gun below her own chin. He didn't pull the trigger, but instead stared back at her with anticipation. She felt his hand cradling hers, his index finger wrapped around her own, both lightly resting on the trigger. The inaction told her everything she needed to know—*stop or die*.

"Willst du hier sterben?" the man asked. Sigrid's hand trembled. Why *hadn't* he just killed her?

"Du wirst mich aufnehmen und ich werde sowieso sterben." She'd rather die alone in a cold, dreary apartment than be tortured and ultimately still killed.

The man loosened his grip slightly. "Behave, and I'll let you go." Sigrid was blindsided—he spoke *English*. "Understand?" The realization this man was not her enemy set in quickly, and Sigrid loosened her finger on the trigger to signal her submission. The man removed his hand from the gun, held his hands out, and stepped back from her with several steps. Sigrid let the gun fall to her side.

"You speak English," Sigrid said.

"And so do you," the man replied while retrieving his knife from the floor and sliding it back into its scabbard. "I'm Sam, and I'd like to know what the hell happened to the men that were *supposed* to be here."

10

The clacking of multiple pairs of boots outside the apartment sent Sam to the window. He hid his face, peeking through the glass to ensure that the two of them hadn't been heard. Three *Ordnungspolizei* men had been doing their rounds on the street level, though they seemed unaware of the two enemies hiding above their heads. Sam watched as they marched away and the sound dissipated. His attention returned to the woman across from him. She deposited the Luger in her blouse, patted the top of her head to fix her hair, and ran her hands down the seams of her clothing, smoothing the fight out of it.

There was a mystique about her, a nature of mystery and elegance. Joan Bennett, Sam thought. Her eyes were cold and piercing, and her hyper-gold hair parted neatly at the center. It fell to the sides in large wings where it had been lightly curled. Her lips were thin and stern, and her skin was unblemished, dream-like, even. There was a light glisten of perspiration reflecting in the moonlight—she was more beautiful than in the picture he'd seen. Though her breathing was still rapid, Sam sensed she no longer held any fear for him.

"Sigrid Lang," the woman said. She dragged the back of her black-gloved hand across her glistening cheek. Sam, of course, pulled a smoke from his pocket and struck a match to light it. The cigarette dangled between his teeth, and he offered her one. She accepted the offer, and the cigarette shook between her trembling fingers before she pressed it to her lips. He lit hers, then his, and finally flicked the match to out the flame.

"There's nothing to be scared of any longer," Sam said. "I'm not going to hurt you."

"I'm *not* scared," Sigrid snapped. She inhaled hard on the cigarette, then sucked the smoke in even deeper with a hiss through the thin gap in her teeth.

"You're shaking—" Sam started to reply as his eyes fell to her spasming hand.

"That's adrenaline," Sigrid interrupted. "I didn't expect to find a knife to my throat when I came here."

"But you did," Sam retorted. "You just didn't expect to find *me*." He exhaled the smoke into the cool moonlight. "Which means that you're the one who gave up the information."

"What information?" Sigrid asked.

"Don't be coy," Sam said. "You gave yourself up the second you tried to kill one of your own." Sigrid didn't reply, and her lack of response was the biggest tell she could have given. Sam waved around the room. "So, where are our friends?"

"Dead," Sigrid replied somberly. "In the town square —hanging."

Sam's face contorted into a shock-ridden one.

"What?" Sam inhaled from the cigarette once more, and began to pace. He shook his head back and forth in defeat. "Well that's just swell."

"You're American," Sigrid said.

"I'm *working* for Americans," Sam corrected. "I'm just a man, same as any other."

"But you speak German," Sigrid said.

Sam flicked the ash from his cigarette. "*Ja.*"

"*Dein Deutsch ist gut.*"

"I practice," Sam lied. "So what's your deal?"

"Deal?" Sigrid asked. Her head tilted with confusion.

"Your angle, your job," Sam replied. "I'm assuming you're the one who provided the plans. There can't be *that* many lady defectors."

"I manage all the comings and goings in regard to the project," Sigrid said. There was a pride that rose in her voice, and she stood straight when she said it. "Documents, budgets, reports, schematics—that sort of thing."

"So you're a secretary," Sam offered.

Her eyes narrowed. "Administrative assistant."

"Right," Sam said, a small smirk forming on his lips. "A secretary."

"You can call it whatever you want… " She trailed off for a moment. "I know that in America your women are confined to the kitchen, but over here we're treated with respect when our skills warrant it." She inhaled from the cigarette once more, her face disapproving and dismissive. Sam thought her aggravation only made her more alluring. "And I'll remind you that I'm the secretary who nearly killed you only a moment ago, and if I wanted to, I could have done it."

"You never had a chance," Sam replied. "If *I'd* wanted it, we wouldn't be having this conversation. I just wanted to disable you. If I had intended to kill you, you would have never even seen my face."

"Hah!" Sigrid scoffed. "I suppose you would have been doing me a favor." Sam was taken aback by the comment. He'd been called a prick, a jerk, and asshole, sure—but *ugly*? That wasn't one he'd heard before. "You can mock me all you want, but I'm the one who warned the allies of the nature of the threat at hand—the thing that could very well destroy London if they're not careful."

"*Erdschlag,*" Sam replied.

Sigrid paused her smoking. "You know it?" Sam nodded. "Then you know the danger it presents," Sigrid said. "And you know the risk I'm taking in to ensure that its location was revealed. It is not easy to dance around a man like Lothar Eichler—"

"Eichler," Sam interrupted. His face hardened. "He's here?"

"You know him?" Sigrid replied, not in the nature of a question, but with surprise.

Slow it down, he thought. *You still don't know all there is to know about her, or what her motive is.* He was, after all, a spy, and spies didn't give information at will, they *took* it. "We've met."

"Of course he's here," Sigrid said. "You don't think that he would allow the project to continue without his supervision, do you?" Sigrid tamped the cigarette out in the ash tray nearby. Sam could tell it had calmed her, made her feel more relaxed from the tension of their fight. She leaned against the table behind her, crossed her legs and her arms, and said "So, Mr. American.

What's your plan?"

"Sit tight," Sam replied. "When the coast is clear, you and I are going to see a man on a boat."

"No," Sigrid said defiantly.

"No? That was the deal," Sam replied. "You presented the information in exchange for safe passage for yourself out of the country and into America. Then you're going to trade secrets with my boss."

"That was before those men died," Sigrid barked with a finger pointing toward the blackened window. "Now someone needs to destroy the weapon." Sigrid's face began to show displeasure, even fear, once more. "That was the plan."

Sam snorted. "Sweetie, I'm not here to play saboteur, I'm here to get you out of here."

She grew angry, partially because of Sam's comment, and more so because he seemed to have found it funny. "What does that mean, 'sweetie'?"

"It means hush up and keep your voice down if you ever want to get of here," Sam pointed toward the window. "Or we'll wind up like them."

Sigrid stepped forward, pointed an extended, almost knife-like finger in Sam's face, and said, "That was not the deal!"

Sam didn't flinch. "You didn't make it with *me*." She backed off, pacing around the room, running her fingers through her hair and muttering to herself. "I've got my own orders."

"And what are those?" Sigrid asked.

"Last time I checked, you wanted to trade information for a way out, and now you've got it, so it's on the Brits to blow the damn thing up, not us."

Sigrid laughed, at first a light squeak, and then an

almost maniacal wheeze. He let her go on like that, giggling like a lunatic until tears gathered at the corners of her eyes. She stopped, caught her breath, and regained her composure. "Blow the damn thing up. Spoken like a true American. What's your plan?"

"Leave," Sam said with a brazen confidence.

Sigrid's eyes nearly crossed, her face utterly complexed. "What do you mean 'leave'?"

"I was supposed to meet two men here who are… well… they're tied up, it seems," Sam replied. "They were supposed to hand you over to me, and then we get out."

"Typical," Sigrid said. "Just as I'd expect. You come in with your gear and your guns and your cigarettes and you think you'll just walk into a massively surveilled country and walk right out. Is that right?"

"S'right," Sam said. His expression was cocky, and smug.

"Well you'd be mistaken," Sigrid said with disdain. "Because my reasoning for doing this was not just to flee, it was to destroy that machine."

"Good," Sam said cheerfully. "I admire your tenacity and moral compass. I'm sure whoever they send to do the job will appreciate it too while they take care of the dirty work." His attention turned to the papers scattered about the desk, and he tossed his own cigarette into the ash tray before riffling through the stack. "So, if you'll quiet down, we only need to hold out a bit longer so we can get back home."

"No," Sigrid said. "We need to go to Flussrand."
Sam paused. "Where?"
"The tank. It's in Flussrand."

"I'm not sure what's not registering here," Sam replied. "This isn't a sabotage mission."

"Then I'll excuse myself," Sigrid said defiantly. "And you can tell your American and British friends that the exchange of information was dependent upon the destruction of the machine. If that's not what you've come here to do, then we can forget the deal and they can figure out things on their own. Or, you can help me destroy it and they can get what they want. I'm not going to tell you anything unless you agree to my terms."

"I'm not here to make deals," Sam said. "I'm here to get you away from your people and back to mine."

"They're not my people," Sigrid barked. "They haven't been my people for years."

"Sure fooled me," Sam said, looking her outfit up and down.

"You're the one in the clothing," Sigrid retorted.

Sam nodded. "I'm just blending in. What's your excuse?" Sigrid folder her arms abruptly with a frustrated huff.

Sam rifled curiously through the contents on the table. He was thrilled to find some cigarettes that had been left behind and placed all that would fit into his case. There were many documents, most of which contained the word "Yellowfin" labeled clearly. He saw a stack of papers lying on the table beside him. The top paper displayed a map. It was intel gathered from the SOE men's reconnaissance missions. It laid out the warehouse *Erdschlag* had been stored in, details of the guards' shifts, and the geography of the surrounding area. Sigrid reached for one of the documents, then held it over the flame of the candle at his side.

The paper flared, and the flame began to climb up the document, quickly engulfing it in a fiery flicker. Sam grabbed for the paper. "Hey! What gives?"

Sigrid grabbed more of the papers, lit them on fire, then tossed them into an aluminum garbage can. The papers caught further with a *woosh*, and soon the flames were rising above the lip of the can. Sam pushed Sigrid aside, grabbed the can, dumped it on the floor, and stamped on the documents with his boot an in effort to quell the fire. It was too late; only tattered shreds of charred paper had been left behind. "What the hell did you do that for? Those have *value*!"

"I was cold," Sigrid said.

Sam stepped toward her, backed her against the wall, and pressed his face right against hers. "Your body is going to be mighty cold when they find it up here in a pool of blood."

Sigrid showed no fear. Instead, she returned his intense gaze, and to add insult to injury, a shit-eating smirk. "Then I guess you'll fail your mission," Sigrid said with no hint of remorse. "Or, you could help me."

"You've just interfered with a mission that could decide the fate of millions of lives," Sam scolded.

"Eight and half million, to be exact," Sigrid corrected. "And if I have anything to do with it they'll wind up quite alright. I imagine you're a man of ethics—"

"You assumed wrong," Sam cut her off. He inched forward, backing her further against the wall and reminding her that *he* was in control.

She swallowed a painful gulp. The cold of the concrete stung against her back. There was nowhere left to go, but she showed no signs of backing down now.

She'd come too far—got in *too* deep. She held firm. "Even so, I'm sure you'd respect an arrangement with allied parties, and the conditions of my arrangement haven't yet been met, so if you plan on successfully completing your mission, you're going to need to reconcile working with me, and giving me what I want. It would be a waste of time and resources to find that once I've arrived to safety, I don't speak any English at all."

Sam backed off, turned to face away from her, and grumbled under his breath. He pulled a cigarette from his case in an effort to gather his thoughts. He'd been thrown a curve ball and now he'd need to use his own discretion to decide just whether or not he was going to work with this woman—to trust her—and carry on with the mission. He had little choice.

The cigarette flared with an intensity to match his frustration. His thoughts raced as quickly as the atoms bouncing around the burning tobacco. The woman staring back at him with a smug expression and impatiently folded arms only annoyed him more. He paced diligently throughout the room.

How could he know it wasn't a trap? She might be trying to extort him. Had the burned man done his due diligence? Had the British spies done theirs? She might have known their whereabouts all along and been a step ahead of them herself. If so, what was her angle?

"So, what will it be?" Sigrid asked impatiently. A patrol passed by the apartment yet again. Sam pressed a finger to his lips. Of course they'd heightened security. He'd come in tiptoeing and the whole damn city might have wised up now. Two spies had been caught only a stone's throw away.

Once the succession of boots on stone subsided,

Sam turned to Sigrid again. "Lady, you're the one with the demands. What's *your* plan?"

"It's too dangerous to travel tonight. There's a curfew enforced." She folded her knuckles and pressed them against her chin. "And yet, we have a very small window in which to work."

"Why is that?" Sam asked.

"The project is nearly finished," Sigrid replied. "They'll be rotating out the construction crews any day, then bringing in the operating team and moving the machine to Rügenwalde."

"What's in Rügenwalde?"

"Testing. There is no way we can allow the tank to leave its home. Once it is out in the open, it will never be approachable. It needs to be sabotaged now, here, while it is still a baby in its basket."

Great, Sam thought. *Just what I need, to barge into an enemy stronghold.*

Sigrid grabbed a wool blanket that had been left behind by the British spies and laid it across the floor, then another, and fluffed it to form a makeshift pillow. She said, "We'll stay here tonight, and move by train in the morning. The rail to Karlsruhe from Pforzheim is our only choice."

"Any better options?" Sam asked.

"Did you arrive by auto?"

Sam grimaced. At the bare minimum, he needed someone who could navigate. Sigrid grabbed another pile of papers and tossed it into the garbage can, forming a small fire from what had lingered inside. She clasped her hands and rubbed them forcefully over its mouth in an effort to get warm.

Sam extinguished it without reservation. "No. The fire and smoke are risky."

"We'll freeze to death," Sigrid snapped.

"You'll live," Sam argued.

Her lips puckered with frustration. She stared at him, and Sam knew she was searching for words to insult him, looking for something to use as ammunition. She disliked him, yet they'd only been together for fifteen minutes. He could tell her assessment of him shared what many of the other women in his life had viewed him as: smug, cocky, and arrogant.

"I plan on coming out of here alive," Sam said. "So what I say goes. You want my help? Then we do things *my* way."

"And how do I know I can trust you?"

"You don't," Sam replied. "I need you, and you need me, and right now that's good enough." Sigrid grabbed another of the folded blankets from the crate and threw it at him. It landed against his chest with a soft thud.

He maneuvered to the ground and lay flat on his back against the hard wood floor, pulled the blanket up over his chest and to his chin, and removed the gun from its holster. He laid the weapon flat on his chest and faced the door, clutching it under folded arms and positioning himself to sleep like a vampire. The chilled, flat floor wasn't comfortable, but thankfully it wasn't a shipping container. A hard surface was good for the spine once in a while—it had a way of straightening all the kinks out, and he'd done it plenty of times before. He shut his eyes without another word.

Sigrid climbed in to her makeshift bed in a huff. By the time she'd gotten under the covers, a cold shiver ran through her body. It would be impossible to get warm, even under the wool blanket. She lay awake, her eyes fixed on the window. She'd be unable to sleep well tonight, and yet something about Sam's presence made her feel at ease. She imagined he slept with one eye open, yet he was snoring in only a matter of minutes. Outside, boots stomped against stone.

11

The stein in Lothar Eichler's hand had become warm. The absence of beer—combined with the prolonged grip of the mug—had left only foamy remnants. Despite the commotion and chatter of off-duty troops letting loose at the *Schwarzmühle*, Eichler sat in silence, immune to the rowdy patrons crowding his space at the lone table on the second-floor balcony. His eyes had been fixed firmly at the door, noting all of the comings and goings of the locals and men in his employ. He glanced around the sea of bodies below once more, his attention bouncing from the tops of heads and faces. He didn't dare mingle with those who'd be considered below his social status—not just because it was unwise, but also because he knew few respected him.

"Another beer?" the bar waitress behind him asked. He contemplated another drink for a moment, considering that perhaps, even as late as it was, one more beer might be in order. He'd already felt the numbing sensation in his teeth that was a point of no return. He had a weak tolerance, and one more beer was exactly enough to make his head spin when attempting to sleep, or worse, to cause him to wake with a hangover. Eichler waved her off. Three beers was enough for the night.

Eichler took one last swig from the glass—a disappointing helping of mostly froth. He placed his jacket back on, left the waitress some coins, and stepped down the staircase that led to the exit. He'd been spared the better part of the noise while separated from the rest of the crowd below, many of which he saw daily. Several men saluted him—albeit reluctantly—as he passed by, and he returned the gesture out of necessity.

He'd almost made it to the door, when a rowdy uniformed soldier bumped into him, splattering beer on the shoulder of Eichler's jacket. His compatriots stood at attention, recognizing Eichler's rank and quickly glancing with warning at their clumsy friend to follow suit. The soldier straightened his torso swiftly, pumping his chest and saluting Eichler once his face registered. Eichler swatted at the spilled liquid.

"I'm sorry, Herr Eichler," the man said, his eyes afraid to meet the man's he'd disrespected.

"Maintain some element of respectability," Eichler said sternly. "You are on time off in uniform, not at a bachelor's weekend."

"Yes, sir," the soldier said.

"What's the cause of such jubilation?" Eichler asked.

"Everyone's been a bit rowdy after the town square event."

"What town square event?" Eichler asked.

The soldier eased his stiffened body. Another of the men stepped forward and said, "The capture of the spies, sir." Eichler's attention shifted to the man, a patrol officer that he recognized as one who'd been on vehicle surveillance near the construction site. "Two British men, displayed for all to see in the city center. That will teach them." Eichler stormed off abruptly without another word spoken.

He arrived at the square. The gathering had still been quite large, even in the late hours. Soldiers drank openly in public among the locals, their uniforms disheveled, as if some unholy celebration in which all sense of decency had been forgotten was taking place. *It's hedonistic*, Eichler thought. Someone had lit a makeshift fire of scrap wood that rose up in front of the fountain to illuminate the crowd, and the flames that licked upward like tongues from hell rose higher and higher, until they showed Eichler what he had come here to see.

There, the bloated, rotting corpses of two British men hung stretched and lifeless from nooses secured to a wooden plank above their heads. The crowd giggled and sang, celebrating the fate that had befallen two men who'd dared cross the lines established by the war. It infuriated Eichler, and he clenched a disapproving fist at his side.

He drew a blade from his scabbard, and forced himself through the bodies bouncing against his tall frame. He pushed aggressively, throwing several bystanders in his path away from himself in frustration. He climbed the steps of the fountain, positioned himself behind both bodies, and gripped at the rope the first man hung from. Eichler then pressed the blade against the rope and sawed at it until the first body hit the floor with a sickening *thunk*. Several people who had been near the impact took note, and a dull murmur started to spread through the grouping of people. Eichler then moved to finish the job on the second man's noose.

Now that the crowd had been silenced, all eyes fell on Eichler as he continued to cut at the threading. The pleasure of the group morphed into confusion directed toward the man who'd taken it upon himself to end the charade. He paid no attention.

"What's this?" a voice said. A man stepped forward, his rank indicated by the silver braid around his wrinkled collar and shoulder straps. Eichler paid him no mind, continuing to cut at the noose until that body hit the stonework as well. "Identify yourself and your reason for doing this." Eichler wiped the sweat from his brow, sheathed his blade, and stepped down from the fountain steps to meet the man face to face.

Eichler, a glorified project manager, did not bear any military symbols or insignias, but simply wore a black coat and black boots that gave the impression that he was still a force with the party. In place of a proper rank, his size often gave him the intimidation necessary to get his way. Eichler easily stood over six inches taller than the man, and yet the soldier displayed no indication of fear. "You are an *Unteroffiziere*?" Eichler asked.

The man straightened his back confidently. "I am the *Gruppenführer*." He pointed with his finger around the gathering, indicating the men at his disposal. "This is my squad. Which company are you from?" Eichler looked down to his side, and noted that the soldier carried no sword with his uniform.

Eichler asked, "Do you ever plan on being a *Feldwebel*, perhaps *Oberfeldwebel*?"

"My status is pending," the soldier replied with confidence.

Eichler looked at each of the men under his command, then pointed to the bodies that lay dead at his feet. He returned his attention to the man before him, his face fixed firm like stone. "Do you consider this a good example to your men?"

"They are spies—"

"Be that as it may," Eichler interrupted, "this is not a war zone, this is a community."

"It is a warning."

Eichler felt his eyes bulge with rage, and though he kept his composure, he spoke with the intensity of a parent scolding their child. "I don't see enemy soldiers in these streets. I see women and children. I see businesses and schools, not the front line. This is vulgar. You do this as a warning to your enemy where he stands, not at the feet of your own people. Are they *German* spies?"

"No," the man said softly.

"Then *who* are you warning?" The soldier's face fell, drooping vertically like an infant that had been spanked. He had become embarrassed by the dressing down, and no longer looked Eichler in the face. "Look at me." The soldier, whose foolishness now read in his pout, returned his gaze reluctantly to Eichler. "What is your name?"

"Bruno," the soldier replied timidly.

"Bruno what?" Eichler snapped.

"Bruno Schwarz—"

"Schwarz," Eichler barked with a scoff. "You are doing a disservice to your namesake. "Who is your *Vorgesetzte*?" Eichler asked.

"*Feldwebel* Kreider," the man replied timidly.

"*Feldwebel* Kreider," Eichler repeated. "You tell Feldwebel Kreider that if he has a problem with the actions I've taken here tonight then he can find me at

Flussrand." The soldier's expression changed to that of surprise, as if he knew what the location meant and what had been taking place there. Eichler turned his attention to the gawking soldiers. "You two," Eichler said, addressing two of the men. His voice rose with authority, the words coming fast and commanding as he said, "Take these bodies to a morgue where they belong." He scanned the crowd of locals as well. "The rest of you, clean up this mess, put out this fire, and go back to your homes. Show some decency for your country. We are not savages."

He let the words hang for a moment on the quiet gathering. *Let someone disagree. Let them try to challenge my directions.* No one did. "Good evening," Eichler said to the soldier standing before him. He turned on his heel, and this time the crowd parted for him as if he were Moses separating the Red Sea. They watched sheepishly as he traveled off into the distance, a black silhouette skulking into the night.

"You heard him," the shameful soldier said, as if suddenly he had developed a conscience. The other two subordinates who'd been instructed to handle the disposal of the bodies acted quickly, and the party was broken up without hesitation. The fire was extinguished with a dousing of beer, and all that remained in the square was the haze of smoke.

Eichler did not return to his apartment in Pforzheim. Instead, he got in his military-issued truck and drove straight to Flussrand. He traveled in silence along the wide dirt road, accompanied only by his thoughts and the growl of the motor. The moon had been obscured completely by the tall trees on either side of him, leaving only the two watchful eyes of the headlights to guide him. It was maze-like where the tank had been hidden, but the road that led to the warehouse ensured it was impossible to get lost—it had been cut through the forest to accommodate the massive weapon.

Upon his arrival at the first checkpoint, he was met with several rifle barrels. He brought the vehicle to a halt, left it idling, and revealed his hands briefly to show he was unarmed. Two soldiers had been charged with standing guard at a tiny shack that met the edge of a fence blocking or granting access to the project. Few people worked on the project during the night, and the first checkpoint of guards were surprised—and relieved —to find it was the project's manager.

The guard that met his window lowered his rifle and quickly saluted him. "Herr Eichler."

"Good evening," Eichler said without even moving his eyes to meet the guard's. His eyes remained fixed on the road ahead. "Please open the gate." The guard waved to the other, who'd remained at the shack, and the gate's wheels slid across a small track system built into the road. "I want you to triple the number of men at this checkpoint."

"Right away," the guard replied.

"Wake every man from his sleep and increase perimeter patrol. Have them take shifts if necessary. I want no gaps. Tell every man that he should be close enough to never lose sight of the man on either side of him."

"Is everything alright, Herr Eichler?"

Eichler threw the vehicle into gear. "No." He accelerated past the checkpoint and continued farther down the dirt road, shifting through the gears rapidly and grinding the clutch. He abused the tachometer for the duration of the trip. Eichler arrived finally, slamming the breaks with a tormenting screech and skidding through the dirt.

The warehouse that housed the project was dark. It had been sealed shut for the night, and only reflected its large shape in the moonlight, a massive cave without an entry. He walked toward the personal entrance that had been designed solely for him accompanied by two sentries.

"Sir?" one of the sentries asked.

"Keep your eyes open," Eichler said without stopping. He climbed the back staircase, a series of steel steps that only led in one direction, and arrived at the door where they stopped. He fiddled for the keys in his pocket, found the right one, and just as the tip of its teeth pressed against the lock, he paused.

For the first time since Eichler had arrived at the project's home, he felt *fear*. Had someone slipped past the guards? Had they already gotten inside? He settled himself, inhaling deeply, and inserted the key into the door as quietly as possible. Every tooth of the key kissed the inside of the lock with a soft *ping*. Eichler turned the key with absolute silence, and then, readying himself for whatever came next, pushed the door open with a swift swing.

The door slammed against its hinges. Inside the large second floor office only the smooth bellow of air circulating through and rattling the paperwork with a light flicker met his ears. He stepped slowly, careful not to let the heavy thumps of his boots alert anyone.

He arrived at the glass window at the edge of the office, which functioned as the viewer for his beloved project. The soft rose-colored glow of the warehouses hazard lights were visible. They illuminated the tank in a hellish hue, just a black mass with a large cannon floating in a sea of red. With the tank painted in that light, he grew even more proud of it. Perhaps its enemies might be unlucky enough to see it as he saw it: as an instrument of might that brought with it only fear. Eichler's resolve to protect it only grew stronger.

He hustled to his private office, turned a small lamp on to guide his search, and retrieved his keys once more to unlock his desk drawer. The drawer slid open, and Eichler shifted the contents frantically until he found what he sought: his firearm. Since he was surrounded by a small army, he'd previously felt no need to carry it on the premises. That had changed when he'd seen the men hanging in the market square. If there had been spies in Pforzheim, there could be more.

What had they seen? What did they know? What had been reported back home to their superiors? His heart beat rapidly, a sickening thumping that returned the only sound in the silent office.

Eichler jammed the magazine into the gun and chambered a round. Then, he turned to the coat hanger next to the bookshelf behind his desk and grabbed a belt holster. He hadn't used the gun since he'd been to America, a harrowing episode where he'd been cornered— bested, even—by a spy whose name he had not known, a spy who had learned far too much about Erdschlag.

A spy, that perhaps, had made his way to the motherland.

12

Sigrid woke in a hazy state. At first, she was wholly unaware of where exactly she was, but the man in silhouette smoking at the window quickly reminded her. He seemed unaware she'd awoken, and she watched him for a moment as he stared blankly through the window with steely resolve. With each puff of the cigarette, the smoke curled around his head; his exhalation was in a duel with the draft coming from the window. He'd reduced himself to only his undergarments, likely in an effort to keep his uniform looking presentable, and his form was very visible in the light tracing him through the window.

His figure was admirable. The body was toned and muscular in the way a professional swimmer's might be. There was little—if any—fat on him. His thighs and calves were tight, signs of constant movement, a man who never slowed down. His arms were trim but firm, the arms of a man who is hiding some muscle under the skin but still desires the maneuverability and spry nature close-quarters combat might require. The glimmering black hair fell just to the side of his face, a few pieces hanging sloppily from a restless night of sleep. She'd have to fix that if she was to be seen in public with him.

Seeing such a fine specimen reminded her that it had been quite some time since she'd been with a man. She'd never hurt for attention, especially not in the city of Pforzheim or at the weapon site. Nearly every man working on the project knew who she was, not just because she was one of only several women working there, but because of the way eyes seemed to gravitate toward her when she entered a room. It had been the demand of the project and fetching this and that for Eichler—not to mention her activities in the shadows—that had curtailed her private life.

Despite her gender, Sigrid commanded an air of respect in her circle. Few—if any—women were tasked with carrying sensitive documents. Eichler, in an effort to protect the classified documents, had not relied on the shoddy post system currently at play. He preferred to have people who worked on the project, mainly Emil Sauer and Sigrid, deliver documents as his personal courier. Such was the nature of many high-level transfers of information in the Reich.

She shifted lightly, and the wooden floor beneath her whined. Sam's attention darted to her immediately. He had the reaction time of a lurking cat.

"You're awake," Sam said. He smirked while he pulled from his cigarette. "And staring."

Her face contorted once more into that of disapproval. "I am *not*."

"And now you're blushing."

She threw the covers from her body, turned from

him, and stormed into the bedroom. Any sympathetic notions she'd had for him had quickly vanished; there was a job to do. She felt the blood rush to her face; her cheeks were warm and flushed.

Sigrid composed herself in the glass window that caught the reflection of the morning sun—a rear-facing window that hadn't been blacked out—in just the right way that she could see her own complexion. She *was* blushing. She patted her hair lightly, smoothing it where it had lost its hold. She hoped she wouldn't see anyone on her journey that might recognize her. Once she was satisfied with her presentation, her focus shifted to the horizon outside. The sun was inching above the mountain ridge in the distance and casting a cool hue on the city. She shook any prior thoughts she'd had about Sam from her head, and waltzed back into the common area a new woman.

Sam held the bottle of liquor out toward her. "Breakfast?"

"That's alcohol," Sigrid said dismissively.

"Well, there's no coffee."

Sigrid gathered her belongings from the makeshift bed. "You'll have a proper meal when we arrive." Sam tamped the cigarette out in the tray and began to recompose his uniform. Sigrid watched with loose attention as he did so.

"And where would that be?" Sam asked as he placed his uniform on.

"My home."

Sam frowned. "And why would we be going there?"

"We can't go to Flussrand today," Sigrid replied. "It's a Saturday, and too many employees will still be working. We'll need to go tomorrow, but we can't stay here.

Spies have been caught within walking distance, so they'll surely be going door to door. We'll proceed tomorrow."

"I never agreed to go to Flussrand," Sam snapped.

"Well I'm not staying here," Sigrid said matter-of-factly. "So you're welcome to stay and risk being found, or you can come with me, and since you're required to usher me to safety, I believe that means you'll be joining." Sam rolled his eyes, and Sigrid's attention turned to the buttons he'd been securing on his fatigues. "You're going to make the same mistake they did."

"And which mistake would that be?"

"Your uniform," Sigrid warned. "It's all wrong." Sam ceased the buttoning of his shirt, and held his hands out in submission. She sighed with frustration and made her way toward him. "Is this the best your people could do? If so, I fear for your effort in the war. You look like a new recruit." She undid the collar to his shirt a bit, grabbed a handful of dust from the nearby table, and swatted the knees of his pants. Her eyes fell to the dagger. "Hide that. That's not a field knife, it's a dress knife, so unless you're going to a parade it shouldn't be visible."

She stepped back for a moment, massaged her chin, and surveyed his presentation. "Do you have a *Soldbuch*?" Sam patted his pockets, finally landing on the one on the breast of his tunic, and opened the button to retrieve the cardboard book. She snatched it from his hand and flipped it open. "This won't do."

Sigrid pulled a pen from her pocket, followed the grid where items had previously been written in the prior owner's possession, and scribbled information into one of the rows. She forged a signature in the new column and handed it back to him. "Arlo, you're officially on leave. If anyone asks, you were stationed in the Ardennes."

"Where about?"

Sigrid scoffed. "Do I have to tell you everything? I don't know—*Foy* or *Sedan*. Don't they prepare you for anything?"

"The SOE guys were supposed to help with that part," Sam said. The burned man had only provided him with the bare minimum. Sam's cover name was Arlo Krause, and he had the credentials to prove it. He was a frontline infantry soldier. The rest was up to Sam to figure out. His own experience would inform the rest of his journey.

Sigrid buried her hands in her face. She massaged at her temples in frustration. This was hopeless. They were both going to wind up dead. "Your *Soldbuch* hasn't had any records for nearly six months—that will raise eyebrows, so do yourself a favor and don't make any trouble. Any superior would easily see through it. This booklet was pulled from a dead man." She gestured to his uniform. "Which means your clothing was too, and if anyone becomes wise to that, we're in trouble. *Sprechen Sie gut Deutsch?*"

"*Gut genug,*" Sam replied.

Sigrid wasn't convinced. "Just let me do the talking."

"So what's our story?"

Sigrid paced about the room. "We are dating—"

"I knew you felt it too."

"Very funny," Sigrid said with a scowl. "I wouldn't date you if you sprouted wings and flew me away right now." She plunged herself back into thought. "We are due to be married. You were granted leave, and we are visiting family members in Karlsruhe."

"Why was I granted leave?"

"You were injured," Sigrid said. "Develop a limp, if need be, or *I* can give you one."

He frowned. "I'll manage." Sam began to place the boots over each of his feet.

"*Anyone* can be stopped," Sigrid said. Her eyes grew large, even fearful. "And you, well, let's just say you look suspicious as it is. The train ride is short, perhaps twenty or thirty minutes. They pull people's identification frequently to search for undesirables. *No one* is safe. They'll be on high alert now that those two men were found. They were sneaking around in uniform the same as you, and since you are alone and not on the front line, you stick out."

"You've got pretty hefty clearance," Sam said. "Why would anyone even bother to question you? Can't you just flash your credentials or something?"

"I don't have *immunity*," Sigrid replied.

"Right, a secretary."

"Having good credentials is precisely *why* one might be questioned," Sigrid replied, paying the jibe no mind. She retrieved a small jar of hair gel from her purse and pulled some out with two fingers. She rubbed the cream between her hands, and swiped at Sam's hair, smoothing it and giving a wet, healthy shine. After swatting at it briefly, Sigrid ran her fingers through the strands, giving it a convincing look of credibility. "That will do."

She scrutinized his appearance, satisfied that she'd at least made an attempt to make him appear worthy of deceit, and rested a hand on her hip while chewing a fingernail. "Leave the rifle. It's too much."

Great, Sam thought. *Already down one weapon.*

Sigrid searched through the dead spies' belongings once more. She collected the pencils out of a small case on the desk and deposited some of their articles into her bag. Sam thought it strange, especially her unease and suspicious behavior, but suspected she may be attempting to cover her own tracks. He couldn't argue with that.

Sigrid stuck her head through the door at street level. The lone tweet of a winter bird came with the rising sun. The back alley was quiet, and Sigrid nodded to Sam before pushing the door open. They walked purposefully, and Sigrid led.

"Keep your head down and don't make eye contact," Sigrid said in a low mumble. "If anyone engages in conversation with you, a shelling has damaged your hearing and you have me to act as your intermediary."

"A limp *and* a shelling?" Sam asked.

"Don't mock me," Sigrid snapped. "They were one in the same."

The smell of baked goods hit Sam's senses so hard it tempted him to drop the mission where he stood. It was the smell of home, or whatever he approximated as home, but there was something special about the smell. *Lye,* he thought. It was a trick of the Germans, especially in their pretzels, that was often considered a dangerous and toxic method of cooking. For a moment he considered trying to convince Sigrid to make a stop for breakfast, but any deviations in the plan could be dangerous. Perhaps he'd send for some when he safely arrived at his destination. *A guy's got to eat.*

They continued steadily along the cobblestone streets. There were no soldiers or police in sight. Sigrid said, "It's not far. We continue along this path for a few blocks and we'll arrive at the Pforzheim Hauptbahnhof. The Karlsruhe stop is one of the last, and we'll be in plain sight on the rail, so keep to yourself."

"I wasn't planning on making friends."

A car on the street stalled in front of them. Steam seeped from the seams in the hood, and the driver exited to check its condition. He saluted Sam, and Sigrid gave him a nudge with the point of her elbow. "*Salute* him," she said through gritted teeth.

Sam did. There was an irony that did not escape him, a man dressed in enemy clothing walking through the belly of the beast and returning the gesture common to the men who hated him. Sam had reconciled with the concept before he'd even left the freighter. It was not the first time he had worn enemy clothing, and if all went well, it was unlikely to be the last.

"We're never going to make it," Sigrid moaned. "We're never even going to get to Karlsruhe. We'll be stopped on the train and brought in for questioning."

"Relax," Sam replied. "We're going to be fine."

"Perhaps I'll go to Flussrand on my own," Sigrid replied. "Then you can tell your men you jeopardized the mission by being so flippant."

"I was getting on fine until I met you," Sam replied. Sigrid's lips parted. She was going to say something she regretted, but instead silenced her thoughts and bit down on her lip in protest. "I don't like this any more than you," Sam said in a hushed tone. "We should be heading away from Germany, not farther in." Sigrid chose not to reply.

They walked in silence, accompanied only by the brisk tapping of feet against stone. They had unintentionally increased in speed since they'd left the hideout, a subconscious longing to get out of public view and to some modicum of safety—and probably a response to the prolonged bickering the two had been deep in. They were never *truly* safe, not anymore, but four walls and a roof would be better than nothing.

"There it is," Sigrid said. Ahead was the single-level, rectangular structure of the Pforzheim Hauptbahnhof. As predicted, there were soldiers and police standing guard at both the street level and entrance. A locomotive howled as it arrived at the station, and with it came a cloud of smoke that wafted through the air. The sun had made a full appearance, bathing the building in the warm, welcoming light of morning. Many Germans, unbothered and uninvolved with the mechanics of the war, shuffled to and fro both inside and outside of the station. Men with briefcases and winter hats and travelers with luggage went about their business, unaware that two enemy passengers would soon join them.

"I'll get the tickets," Sigrid said.

"I've got money."

"I don't need your money. Make sure you salute each of the soldiers as we pass them. It's customary, especially if they're your superiors." She inhaled deeply, depositing as much of the cool oxygen into her chest as it would allow. She felt perspiration gathering rapidly at the back of her neck, and her hands had become clammy and moist.

Through the flurry of bodies passing through her view, two soldiers stepped forward from the entrance, engaged in conversation. They were heading right toward her. Sigrid recognized both immediately, and froze mid-step. She turned abruptly to face Sam, and her pupils doubled in size.

"What are you doing?" Sam asked.

A debate raged inside Sigrid. Sam saw the two approaching soldiers at her back walking toward them. Panic won the battle, and she grabbed Sam's head, then pressed her lips to his without warning. He grabbed her by the waist, brought her in tightly, and took her cue. There was no exchange of tongue. The synced succession of boots passed by as the soldiers navigated the busy entrance, and Sigrid released Sam the moment they were out of view.

Sigrid stared at him—disdain was the emotion that came to Sam's mind. She backed up a short distance from him, her eyes darting between each of his. For a moment, they just lingered on each other's faces.

"I'd usually offer you dinner first," Sam said casually.

Her eyes flattened to thin lines. "They were security patrol from Flussrand, men who have been tasked with watching the perimeter fence. They might have recognized me. I thought they'd been rotated out. I remember removing their names from the list—" Sam's attention had diverted from hers, sharply focused on something else. "Hello?"

Sam grabbed her tightly without warning, embracing her in his arms, and then kissed her once more. This time, it had been deep and meaningful. Sigrid felt weak in the knees, as if the support of his arms was the only foundation keeping her upright. The surrounding atmosphere seemed to slip away, her senses overwhelmed by the nature of his touch. He kissed her not with the ferocity of suitor, but that of a protector. At that moment, it was only her, and the rest of the activity of the station melted away.

A voice inside, one of reason and doubt, told her to speak up. This was unwise, but desire carried her away like a wave breaking at sea. She hadn't been kissed like that before. Her heart fluttered, flickering inside her like the beating of a hummingbird's wings in an attempt to escape its cage. He pulled her in tighter, and now she felt his hand behind her head, his fingers interlocked between strands of her hair. For the first time in days, she'd felt safe—no matter what fate befell her, she'd have this man at her side, spy or otherwise.

He released her gracefully. Their lips clung softly for a moment, his holding the bottom of hers. She found her hand wrapped around his cheek. She hadn't remembered putting it there—it had happened without provocation. When a space finally opened between their faces, her eyes opened to meet his, yet he wasn't looking at *her*. She was thrown back into the real world as if waking from a dream she hadn't wanted to end, and found it odd that his face did not seem to share in the same blissful emotion as hers.

Her ears heard it first—the sounds of not two pairs of boots, but a large regiment. Then she looked past his shoulder and realized her ears had not deceived her. A sea of uniformed *Heer* men had departed from the station, and were now funneling into the streets of Pforzheim. Her eyes darted frantically at her sides. They were *surrounded*.

Now she locked eyes with him once more, and without saying a word, his were telling hers, "Don't move, don't do anything stupid." The men were armed to the teeth. All it would take was just *one* of them to recognize her, or him, and their cover would be blown. The clomping sounds trailed off and away, and only the station's patrons remained.

There was that look again. This time she looked as if she'd just come out of hypnosis. Her skin became pale, as if Sam had sucked the life out of her. She breathed rapidly, her chest shivering as it rose and fell.

"Calm down," Sam said. Her heart had gone from a gentle flutter to the rumble of thunder, and she'd been pressed so closely against his chest she was sure he'd felt it too. His was at a subtle thump. They remained there for a moment, interlocked and pressed firmly against each other, and his eyes stayed with hers. "We're alright." Sam released her, and Sigrid inhaled a ragged breath.

She fixed her hair where he'd grabbed hold of it, and composed herself, then stepped backward regretfully. "I would feel fine if I wasn't parading around with *you*."

"Likewise," Sam responded. The kiss they'd shared had apparently meant *nothing*.

"This isn't good," Sigrid said. "News of the spies must have spread. They're tightening security at Flussrand."

"And you still want to go?" Sam replied.

"Yes," Sigrid said.

He sighed with frustration. "Well, we're sitting ducks here, so let's move on."

They set off up the series of steps that led to the station's main entrance. Sigrid said, "I'll go get the tickets," then stepped away and left Sam behind to fend for himself.

Sigrid wasn't sure what had caused her more distress, the fact that she'd just been surrounded by a swath of her old coworkers or that she'd been blindsided by the man she was aiding. Her skin was warm and flushed, and she felt an incredible injection of energy, a pep in her step, as she made her way to the ticketing counter. Above it, a series of names listed destinations, and below them the corresponding departure and arrival times. The Karlsruhe-bound train was scheduled to arrive in just five short minutes. They wouldn't have to wait much longer.

The teller welcomed Sigrid with a smile. *"Womit kann ich Ihnen behilflich sein?"*

"Bitte zwei Fahrkarten nach Karlsruhe," Sigrid requested.

The woman at the ticketing counter smiled deviously. *"Wer ist er?"*

Sigrid blushed. *"Pardon?"* The woman motioned to her own lips, making a wiping movement. Sigrid sourced her reflection in the nearby glass; her lipstick had been smudged around her face, and she looked like a clown who'd done a rush job on their makeup. Sigrid grabbed a tissue from her purse and wiped feverishly at the mess.

The woman stamped the tickets and slid both on the counter toward Sigrid. *"Zwei Fahrkarten nach Karlsruhe."* A smirk further crept up her cheeks. Sigrid dug into her purse, retrieved the proper coinage, and placed it on the counter. Then, she grabbed both tickets and strode off without another word.

Sigrid met Sam at a bench across from the track. A sign on the column supporting the structure directed patrons to the underground shelter below the station in the event of an air raid. It made Sam uneasy. The thought that he could be scorched in a bombing raid by his own allies without warning was just the nature of the job. Sam had hoped the burned man had done his due diligence before putting him in danger.

After a too-long period of waiting on one of the benches near the ticketing counter, the train to Karlsruhe finally arrived in the station with a deafening whistle and the squeal of blow-off steam. Sigrid and Sam wasted no time rising to their feet, and they were the first to arrive at the train's doors. Their tickets were collected upon entry, and they quickly found seats in one of the middle cars. They sat silently, neither speaking a word, and the train signaled once more that it would start its journey. The train chugged out of the station, and they were greeted with the rolling hills of the German countryside—and a brief respite. Sigrid's attention remained fixed on the window—neither Sam nor she had gathered the courage to speak about what had happened just yet.

13

"*Soldbuch,*" a gruff voice requested. Sam had been lulled to sleep by the vibration of the train, caught in a void between relaxation and dreams. Instinctively, he sat up in his seat and at half-attention. Staring back at him was a bulky, well-groomed man with "SS" thunderbolts patched on the right collar of his uniform. On the left collar, two groups of two diagonal lines had been stitched across the black patch. His shoulder bore a triangle, also with diagonal lines embedded in it that converged at the bottom point.

The officer was a sturdy man, broad in the chest and hard-jawed. His features were sleek and sharp with strong angles that looked as if they'd been chiseled from stone by a craftsman. Sleek blonde hair had been combed from the left side in a neat part that fell to the right. His uniform had not a crease in it, which suggested he had not seen any action as of late.

Sam's lips parted, hunting for the words for a proper

response. The officer repeated himself, and this time it was a *demand.* *"Soldbuch."*

Sam tapped both of his index fingers to his ears, feigned pain when he did so, and tapped Sigrid. She'd been one step ahead of him, and reached into his breast pocket to retrieve the small booklet. She said loudly to Sam, *"Er will deinen Soldbuch!"* She handed it to the officer, and sat back casually in her seat.

"Was stimmt nicht mit ihm?" the officer asked. His gaze skeptically returned to Sam's. He asked Sigrid the question, but he watched Sam for the answer.

"Er überlebte eine Explosion," Sigrid said with a deep sigh. She made grand gestures with her arms and hands, and mimed the explosion of a shelling—overselling it a bit, Sam thought, but he took her point. *"Ich fürchte, er hatte Schäden an beiden Ohren."* She pointed to both ears with a sympathetic expression of concern on her face, and shook her head back and forth after her demonstration. *"Ich fürchte, er kann nichts hören."*

The officer's attention shifted to the small booklet in his hands. He flipped it through it briefly and landed on the page that Sigrid had scribbled in earlier in the morning. His eyes glided slowly down the page, hung on the center, then darted back to Sam. Sam flashed a charming smile, but the man wasn't fazed. He returned to the book, scrutinized the page his finger had rested on, then his gaze lingered on Sam's uniform briefly.

"Es gibt ein Problem?" Sam yelled. Both Sigrid and the officer shifted backwards in response. Sam's question was abrasive, and if Sam hadn't been trying to sell the injury so hard, it might have been an act of comedy.

Sigrid gripped his shoulder firmly. Her nails dug into his bicep, forcefully and sharply enough that even through the canvas-like material of the uniform they felt like five small razors. He turned to meet her eyes before she said, *"Schrei nicht, Liebling."* It was the emotional plea of an embarrassed—if sympathetic—lover.

Sam made like he was reading her lips. *"Es tut mir leid."*

The officer's attention turned to Sam once more, then back to Sigrid. He addressed both of them as he kept the *Soldbuch* clutched in his hand. *"Hast du nicht gehört? In Pforzheim wurden Spione gefunden. Sie waren als Polizisten verkleidet—Briten."* The officer spoke fast in his native tongue, but Sam heard the word *spione*—spies—perfectly well.

Sigrid gasped with surprise and cupped her hand to her mouth. *"Und ich hoffe bestraft."* She sold it well. The punishment angle had been a nice touch.

The officer nodded in agreement to her. *"Auf dem Markplatz gehängt."* He titled his chin proudly with a thin, grim smile. It made Sam queasy. War was war, but a public hanging was barbaric and unnecessary. Sam was of half a mind to pull his dagger and hammer it into the officer's trachea, but thoughts like those were quickly quelled when considering the high stakes of the mission.

"Wann wirst du zurück sein?" the officer asked Sam.

Sam didn't want to keep the act up much longer, and since he'd watched the man's lips move with clear enunciation, he answered quickly. *"Eine Woche—"*

"Nach der Hochzeit," Sigrid said, and she clutched Sam's arm and rested her head bashfully on his shoulder like a gleeful bride. She batted her eyes with an innocent, girlish charm, then planted a soft, wet kiss on his cheek. If it kept up like this—feigning romance in the

company of enlisted men—they might actually be getting married soon enough.

"*Eine Hochzeit?*" the officer asked gleefully. "*Und der Hochzeitsring?*"

Sigrid flashed her hands, demonstrating the black gloves that covered them. "*Zu Hause. Ich kann es nicht unter meinen Handschuhen tragen. Es ist ein kalter Tag.*" She shivered briefly, acting as if she'd still been plagued by the cold weather.

"*In Karlsruhe?*" the officer asked.

"*Ja, in Karlsruhe.*"

Sam turned to Sigrid, smiled, and looked back to the officer. Satisfied, the officer returned the *Soldbuch* to Sam. Sam pocketed it in the breast pocket of his tunic, then stood to salute the officer.

He returned the gesture before saying, "*Es tut mir leid, aber wir müssen vorsichtig sein. Es gibt Grund zu der Annahme, dass es da draußen noch mehr Spione geben könnte.*"

"*Es ist kein Problem,*" Sam said, then returned to his seat. Sigrid let out a long sigh of relief. Sam whispered to her, "Good work."

"Not every situation requires a dagger," Sigrid replied.

"True," Sam agreed. "But not every situation can be solved *without* one."

Sigrid rolled her eyes. "We're almost there."

Despite the tense inquiry of the *SS* officer, the journey to *Karlsruhe* had been quick—roughly thirty minutes. When the train finally came to a halt, Sigrid and Sam made it a priority to be the first patrons out for fear of risking another unwanted encounter. They were in need of some shelter away from prying eyes.

"We'll have to get there on foot," Sigrid said. "I don't have an auto, but it's just a few streets down."

Karlsruhe was a charming city, and far less occupied than Pforzheim. Sam gauged that the latter had been on heightened alert due to both his allies—and subsequently, his—presence. One might not think there was a war at all, but it always looked that way from the side that hadn't been penetrated by enemy combatants. Berlin, Sam understood, had been pummeled relentlessly. Here in Karlsruhe there was a warm, cheery feeling brought by the full arrival of the sun. There was a series of poplars that had nestled many of the nearby buildings, hugging them at the corners where the main streets intersected.

An obnoxious ding alerted Sam as he lit a cigarette at the edge of the Karlsruhe Hauptbahnhof property. It came from the rear, and by the time he caught a glimpse, it had whizzed by him without warning. A disheveled man pedaled furiously on a bicycle, shooting Sam a glower as he rode off and down the street.

"Watch yourself," Sigrid said. "They're very fond of *wheels* in Karlsruhe."

"Why's that?" Sam asked.

"Both Karl Drais and Karl Benz were born here," Sigrid answered. "Though they don't live here any longer. Both reside in Mannheim, but the people won't let you forget." Sigrid searched to both her left and right, and then nodded forward. Ahead of the station, a pocket in between buildings was still bathed in shadow where the light had not yet touched. "Come on," Sigrid said. "This route will take a bit longer, but I'd like to get out of the open. Too many people here know me."

The road they had taken had been decorated with

red flags bearing *swastikas*. Each side of the street featured them hanging from every other lamp post, as if one might need a constant reminder every time they walked a few steps. They hadn't seen any soldiers or police, which set Sam at ease, at least for the moment. He was eager to get into a warm home; he hadn't had a true bit of warmth since the freighter, and the trip on the rail had been so short that it had barely given his body a chance to heat up.

His stomach gurgled with every small restaurant they passed. He thought he'd heard Sigrid's do the same along a very quiet stretch of path that hadn't been interrupted by the frequent rumble of motors passing by. He'd asked Sigrid to stop once, but she'd vetoed the idea quickly for fear of staying in plain sight any longer than they had to. Every time Sam's eyes found themselves longingly fixed on an eatery, Sigrid quickly quelled his desire by reminding him "it won't be much longer."

They traveled along the road with minimal conversation. Sigrid had explained that while Sam's German was acceptable, Germans nearby tended to speak Swabian, a more region-specific dialect, and that his speech patterns would only raise questions. She'd done most—if not all —of the talking thus far, and Sam thought it better that way. If she could handle the dialogue, he could handle the mission.

"Why do you speak such good English?" Sam had whispered along the route.

"My father was fluent," Sigrid replied. "Why do you speak good German?"

"We have history," Sam said.

"After the first war, during the American occupation on the Rhine, many people began to speak English—

especially in the southwest. Some schools even teach it." Sigrid went on about how it was valuable in her line of work, and that her father had expressed the value of knowing many languages, and how English was one of the most important for the future. Much of the world would eventually learn English, he'd said, and that just had a lot to do with trade and economies. Anyone who could speak English would be of high value. Sam couldn't argue with that. He spoke it himself.

"I suppose it made you all the more viable a candidate to Eichler," Sam prodded.

"You never told me how you know him," Sigrid reminded him.

How much did Sam want to tell her? He still hadn't been sure exactly *what* information he was willing to part with, but she'd kept him safe thus far, and if she really hadn't wanted to help him, she'd missed her opportunity when they'd been cornered on the train. Sam tossed the cigarette he'd been nursing into the street, and tucked both of his hands into his pockets. He said, "Eichler came to America the night before the attack on Pearl Harbor."

Sigrid frowned for a moment as if retrieving a fleeting memory. "I remember. I organized his itinerary for the trip. He never discussed what it was about, just that it was an important trip that would aid in the project's future."

"He was trying to recruit some of our industry leaders," Sam replied. "I snuck into the meeting place, cornered him and his friends, and that's when I discovered what he was working on. Our first meeting was anything but friendly."

"How did you escape?"

"I pulled the pin on a grenade while in their company," Sam replied. Sigrid looked dumbfounded—he was out of his mind. "Sometimes you've got to be willing to risk your ass to get out of a pinch."

"So he would recognize you?" Sigrid asked. Worry set about her face, the corners of her lips dropping into a pout.

"I'm afraid so," Sam replied. "I don't think he was very fond of my presence. Seems I ruined his little dinner."

"This would explain why he was so furious when he returned. He was short with me for nearly a week, confined to his office with drink and sleepless nights. I remember it vividly, because one would be unable to forget the morning of the attack by the Japanese."

"That's right," Sam said. "They got spooked once it was clear they might be funneling resources to the enemy, especially with the fear of the government finding out. Once the bombs hit Hawaii, well, it was just a conflict of interest. When we'd figured out what it was he came to pitch them things got a whole lot more interesting."

Sigrid paused for a moment, and stopped dead in the middle of the sidewalk. Sam turned to face her. She'd become confused by the story Sam had just told.

"What gives?" Sam asked.

"So," Sigrid said softly. "The Americans already *knew* about *Erdschlag*?"

"'Course," Sam said. "They're Americans."

Her eyes fell quickly to her feet, and she clasped both of her hands together. She rubbed them nervously. Her face became long—the face of regret. "I have made a grave mistake."

"Don't get down on yourself," Sam said. He grabbed both of her hands and cupped them in his. That calmed her slightly. "We knew, but you got us the *goods*. We didn't know where it was, or where it was going. We didn't even know what it looked like, other than the picture frozen in my mind's eye. You got us something to go on, and well, now I'm here."

Sigrid's gaze held firmly on Sam's. The world around them casually slipped away, and for a moment, it was just the two of them—an enemy spy and a defector hiding in plain sight, comforted by the warmth each provided on the brisk winter's morning. One thing was true: neither was alone any longer.

Sam mostly worked alone, but he would've been lying to himself if he said he couldn't use the help on this one. The plan had gone awry. What would the burned man say if he knew Sam had been traipsing around with the defector? Had an action like that been authorized? Sam imagined the burned man would say, "Whatever it takes." *She* was the reason he was standing here now, anyway.

The rattle of a diesel engine interrupted the fantastical void they'd both been caught in. Sam turned and quickly recognized the form of a military truck turn the corner of the street. It was heading toward them. Sigrid grabbed Sam's hand, pulled sharply, and darted down a small side alley.

Sigrid navigated out toward the opposite end, and they stopped at the broad side of a large series of homes wedged up against each other as if columns in a puzzle. It was a quiet, quaint neighborhood, and maintained with a liveliness evidenced in the potted plants that hung from each homeowner's balcony. The house directly ahead—an off-white structure with dark brown wooden beams decorating its facade—was the one Sigrid had taken particular interest in.

"It's that one," Sigrid said quietly. Sam stopped her stride by stretching his hand in front of her. He edged toward the mouth of the street, took a good survey of both its left and right sections, and saw nothing that he deemed out of the ordinary. He wouldn't necessarily know what "out of the ordinary" was in a town like Karlsruhe, but there were no soldiers or police nearby, and that was a good start. Sam knew what a true enemy looked like, though. It was the man peeking over the top of a newspaper that was three days old, or a child informant kicking a ball down the street. Perhaps it could be the gentleman waiting for *no one* by the side of his automobile—the type that stuck out and said, "I don't belong here." *These* were the people one needed to be careful of—people like Sam.

The thought that Sigrid could have been compromised was not out of the question. Sam, whose eyes had returned to the face of the building, watched intently. He released the clasp that held his firearm in its holster, though he didn't remove it. Just the action of making it more simple to grasp was enough—he was quick to spot a threat, and even quicker to draw.

"What are you doing?" Sigrid asked softly.

"Your English friends were caught and killed, yeah?" Sigrid nodded in agreement. "You can't be sure they didn't talk." A new fear rose in Sigrid's chest via a wave of nausea. "If they're anything like me, then they didn't. They were SOE, so I'm going to assume they kept it together. Still, we don't know that for sure." Sam lit a cigarette. "Did you ever give them your name?"

"Yes," Sigrid answered.

Sam exhaled and flicked the cigarette ash into the gusty tunnel formed by the buildings flanking them. "Wait here."

"Be careful," she called out in a breathy, desperate whisper. Sam paid the comment no mind and stepped into the street, alternating his attention between his surroundings and the home. The house was three stories; the ground level was obscured by a fenced-in portion that had been invaded by an army of vines. The second floor rose up above that, and yet one more floor with a gabled peak formed the third. He first gathered intel on each of the four windows that faced him. Their curtains were drawn, and a small sliver at the sill where they didn't meet yielded only darkness inside the building. Sam walked casually, not with purpose, but with the gait of a wandering civilian taking in the sights. He fixed one hand firmly in his pocket as he nursed the cigarette with the other.

A plump man nearby puffed jovially on a pipe as he lounged in a chair in front of a home. A small record player at his side playing a calming violin made Sam's steps non-existent. On Sam's other side, an elderly woman tended to her garden, and snipped at flowers with her scissors absentmindedly. Neither paid any attention to Sam's arrival.

Sam grabbed the gate that separated Sigrid's property from the sidewalk, then entered a boxed-in and well-groomed garden at the base level of the property. He closed the gate quietly behind him, and was comforted to find that the vines that crawled up each bar forming the gate provided a welcome wall to his activity. He peeked once more into a window at the ground floor, but only blackness stared back at him. Sam rapped three firm strikes with his knuckles on the door.

He placed his ear to the wooden door, listening intently for any commotion. None came. He removed his ear from the door and tossed the cigarette, maneuvered over to the gate, and opened it before waving Sigrid over. As long as Sigrid hadn't been compromised, they were safe—*for now.*

14

S leep had not been Lothar Eichler's ally since the night he'd returned to *Flussrand*. He'd remained fixated on the window that faced the front gate of the warehouse property, steam rising from the coffee in his hand. He hadn't let himself see the bottom of the cup for several hours. He'd even rekindled the cigarette habit that he'd kicked years before, and the smoking tobacco clutched between his index and middle finger trembled with a nervous twitch only further exaggerated by the abundance of coffee. He considered taking a drink, a *real* drink, but resolved to remained focused.

He'd taken note of the comings and goings of every single person present—no matter their significance or lack of—with a hawk-like focus. He'd made it a priority to secure the perimeter fencing and funnel any exit and entry through the entrance's man gate. If someone wanted to get in or out, they'd need the credentials to warrant it. He couldn't pause production for fear of not meeting his deadline, which made him feel open to any manner of sabotage or attack. Any high-value members of the project needed access, and so instead of worrying that there was a threat among his ranks, he beefed up the resistance a threat would meet.

At the front gate, Eichler watched with great anticipation as the soldier he'd chastised the night before, Bruno Schwarz, arrived. His vehicle was held while his credentials were checked. Eichler had prepared his team for the too-enthusiastic soldier's arrival, and he'd planned to put the eager recruit to good use. The truck was waved on and the perimeter gate opened.

No longer two, but *four* armed guards stood at attention at the main gate, each bearing high-caliber rifles with long-range scopes. The men had also hastily constructed another inner fence designed to form a cube before the entrance, a sort of holding area where any threats could be imprisoned if necessary. Beyond the main entrance, the outpost at the head of the road had also been given additional men—sixteen in total.

The perimeter had armed recruits walking in continual lines that followed the property's geography closely, staggered so that each man could see the man behind or in front of him at any time. Each of those men had been instructed to keep one eye on the woods that obscured the property and another focused on the ground at his feet to look for anything out of the ordinary. The men walked strict paths at a distance of twenty feet—no more and no less—from the perimeter fence. They retraced their footsteps precisely to avoid any disruption of the path they had created, and the movement of each man had already run the forest floor ragged from constant abuse.

If all the precautions Eichler had taken weren't enough, he'd also placed a highly proficient sniper at the roof of the structure, whose barrel remained directly at the front gate at the face of the property. Any man who left the property was searched upon exit before being cleared to leave.

Still, none of the heightened security measures taken had made Eichler feel any safer. He wouldn't feel safe —*truly* safe—until the engineering team was out the door and the battalion tasked with operating the tank had been brought in to oversee its testing.

He'd requested air patrol, heavy artillery weapons, and even his own smaller battalion of Panzer tanks to patrol the property, yet his requests had fallen on deaf ears. It had aggravated him to no end. It seemed Reich Minister of Armaments and War Production Albert Speer had other priorities. Eichler's pet project, he believed, was of the utmost importance. A machine that could deliver a rocket at such great distance warranted a special kind of protection. He'd half considered just rolling the damn machine out into the open and utilizing its anti-aircraft artillery as a defensive technique, but he would be showing his hand purposefully, and the more hidden the project was kept, the better chance he had at ensuring its safety.

Eichler knew better than to expect a large assault. That wasn't the way spies worked, not the SOE men who'd hung in the town square, or any other for that matter. *Sabotage* was the name of the game. Tension had been welling up inside him, and it felt like a volcano ready to spew its guts from the mouth. The confirmation of a compromise in local proximity had Eichler out of sorts. His instinct was telling him something was wrong. Who among the men outside could he trust, and who needed to be lined up in front of a rifle squad? He was of half a mind to start lining them up right away and forcing a confession. Put a gun to a weak man's temple and he'll talk soon enough.

And what about Sauer? The old man had undergone questioning by the *Gestapo* recently. The thought that the head engineer of the project could be a saboteur wasn't out of the question. What kind of man would oversee a project of this size only to see its capture or destruction? One who'd incur a sizable reward upon successful sabotage. Sauer had been questioned only several days earlier, and perhaps the SS had been right in their suspicion. Any of the low-level grunts pacing the property could be an informant, a defector, yet how would he know? The men outside had never respected him, and that made him trust them even less.

Eichler breathed deeply in an attempt to calm the rapidness of his thoughts. He'd been tapping the firearm feverishly at his side—it hadn't left his grip since the night before. Sadly, it did him no good. Anxiety was not the key to thinking clearly, and after all, he had men out in Pforzheim to discover any information they could. What might they find?

Someone must have seen something, recognized the two men who'd been unceremoniously displayed for all to see at the fountain. Where had they stayed? Who had they talked to? A few coins might see to it that some information made its way to Eichler—he'd already been waiting most of the morning, now early afternoon, for even the tiniest morsel. If Eichler had any resource at his disposal, it was money, and he'd drain his own bank account if it meant protecting *Erdschlag.*

A tinny knock sounded on the door at Eichler's back. "Send him in," Eichler said to the soldier standing guard, and the door opened.

Bruno Schwarz stood at attention before saluting his superior, and Eichler motioned for him to enter. The guard behind the young soldier closed the door and left the two in silence. Eichler's attention shifted to a small canvas sack gripped in Schwarz's hand.

"I'm sorry, Herr Eichler," Schwarz said shamefully. "About last night, that is. Had I known—"

Eichler raised his palm flatly to stop him from continuing. "All is forgiven. You're an eager recruit and loyal to the cause. That's all that can be asked of a man. Consider this our first meeting. Have you had any success?"

"I have," Schwarz replied, and he placed the canvas sack on Eichler's desk. He undid the buckle and dug in with his free hand, shuffled around inside until retrieving an envelope, and handed it to Eichler. Eichler focused on the top of the envelope. It read "Yellowfin."

"They were hiding in an apartment building at the corner of Leopoldstraße and Zerrennerstraße, sir," Schwarz said. "It didn't take much to figure them out. A beggar required a few coins to give up his information, but it checked out. It's an abandoned building—seems they set up shop there for some time."

Eichler flipped through the envelope. Inside, documents detailing the city of Pforzheim had been sketched with pencil. The streets and rails had been well documented and were particularly accurate. Measurements and geography had been accounted for, as well as nearby areas of interest for bombing raids. There had also been exact copies of the geographical points of interest in relation to the south-western portions of Germany, particularly the Black Forest, as well as its topography.

There was a building on the outskirts of the city where some of the parts for the A-4 rockets had been engineered. This was a facility with a primary goal of manufacturing vital "o" rings. Eichler was familiar with it because he himself had visited it not long ago to procure details and schematics of the prototype rocket for use with *Erdschlag*. This gave Eichler further pause, and his fingers froze momentarily with fear. What he saw next was inevitable, but predictable. After flipping through some of the remaining documents, he found an item that troubled him greatly: a detailed map of Flussrand.

Eichler's teeth clenched tightly. Not only had Flussrand been well-mapped, but a rough sketch of the tank had been drawn in a three-dimensional rendering of its storage facility. He flung the paperwork across the desk with a furious sweep of his hand. Schwarz gulped nervously.

"Come, Schwarz," Eichler said, and the young recruit followed without question. Eichler descended the metal staircase with a series of rapid clangs, then searched the warehouse feverishly. The man he sought was nowhere in sight. He stepped purposefully alongside the mighty weapon, then hooked left down the corridor that led to Sauer's office.

He didn't even attempt a courteous knock, and instead walked into the room without warning. Sauer, more haggard than he'd been even the day before, was currently nose deep in the plans for the tank, a cigarette with overdue ash hanging from his lip. When Sauer saw the look on Eichler's face, and the gun at his hip, the ash fell on to the plans. He wiped at it sloppily, fumbling with the cigarette in his mouth and then rising from his seat.

His brow furrowed quickly into that of annoyance. "What's this about?" Sauer demanded to know. "And who's this?" Schwarz, attentive to his superior but unaware of what came next, didn't speak.

"This is the man who apprehended the SOE spies in *Pforzheim*," Eichler said as he gestured to Schwarz. "And he happened to come across a wealth of information regarding this project." Eichler waited for Sauer to speak.

Sauer scoffed. "Again, Lothar?" His head fell, and swayed from side to side in defeat. "Considering the fact that you're its sole caretaker, you've done more to jeopardize this project than anyone could have imagined."

"I have *protected* this project—"

"You've done nothing of the sort," Sauer interrupted. He pointed the cigarette toward Eichler, darting it back and forth with an accusative point from its cherry. "You compromised the plans in America. You've overworked the crew to the point of exhaustion. Four men were *killed*, I might remind you, as a result of your failure to follow the safety protocols that I laid out clearly for you. You failed to acquire a single *Reichsmark* when we needed it most."

"And yet the machine is complete," Eichler said. His index finger moved from its resting place above the trigger guard and down to the trigger itself. "*You* were the one with access to those plans," Eichler said with a snide growl. "Your signature is on each of them. And might I remind you, *you* were the one under investigation as to your familial connections and your recent whereabouts."

"You accuse me?" Sauer asked. "The only reason that weapon stands erect outside this door is because I am a part of this project." Sauer pointed the cigarette toward the warehouse beyond where the tank sat idly. "*I* constructed that machine, not you! I saw to it that it would work to specification. I retrofitted it with the proper equipment when the plans changed. You don't know how to work a wrench!"

"And who else better to give away all of its secrets?" Eichler asked. "Who better to reveal its weakness and location than the designer himself? What are they paying you, Emil?"

Sauer's attention darted to the gun Eichler held at his side. His lips curled, and he sucked at them before nodding at Eichler disdainfully. "That's why they don't respect you, *Lothar*," Sauer said. "Because you're a weak man. You've never served. You don't know the first thing about construction—or the military, for that matter. Worst of all, you *whine*. You're paranoid, and you're unstable, and you only see what rewards you can reap from your endeavors. You don't want to win the war, you want to rub elbows with the rest of the Führer's loyals."

"Watch what you say, old man," Eichler warned.

Sauer nodded to Schwarz. "In front of him?" He scoffed once more, this time with a chuckled added to the end of it. "He's probably got more charisma in his left toe than you have in your entire body." Sauer pointed to him. "Well, let's hear it, *Gruppenführer*.

What information have you gleaned from the captives?"

Schwarz gulped, a dry, apprehensive swallow. He looked to Eichler for his next move. Eichler guided a hand outward as if to suggest he give over the information. Schwarz's lips parted slightly, then he spoke. "One man said nothing. The other spoke of an informant inside Flussrand—someone close to the project, though he wouldn't say. He mentioned that they were one of few who had access to sensitive files."

"And there, *Herr Eichler*," Sauer said with the most mocking tone he could muster, "is your answer. There are only two couriers entrusted with the management of documents to and from Flussrand and Berlin—myself, and your *pet*. Isn't it fitting that a woman would be the one to leak documents and turn? There's a reason the ministry doesn't entrust them with these types of tasks, and that is because they *can't* be trusted. As you know, I was detained for several days—and if you'd like me to go retrieve the officials who held me during that period, I'd be all too happy to fetch them for you. Your girl, on the other hand," Sauer started again. "Didn't she have a trip to Berlin last week?" Sauer watched the gears grinding in Eichler's head. Then, with a patronizing smile, said, "Ah."

Eichler lingered on the accusation. Despite the evidence Sauer presented, it was difficult for him to believe that it would have been Sigrid. He felt foolish. If it was her, he'd entrusted her with every valuable shred of information regarding the project. She knew *everything*. Now that he considered her for the first time, his mind connected the dots further; the plans in question had been the exact ones she'd been tasked with bringing to the capital. And yet, he *still* didn't believe Sauer.

Eichler stepped from beside the doorway. "Emil, you're being removed from the project until further notice."

Sauer grew red in the cheeks, then slammed his fist with a crack of his knuckles against the wooden desk. "You can't do that."

"I can, and I am," Eichler replied. "Until this business is sorted, Flussrand is closed. We will discover who has been compromised, and if it isn't you—and I pray it's not—then construction will resume. I can't confirm that you were where you say you were. No officials inquired about your past to me, and that gives me cause for concern."

"Of course they didn't. They didn't want to tip me off!" Sauer cried out. "That's what they do. They show up unannounced, to scare you, so you have no time to prepare—just like you're doing right now. And here I am, with nothing to hide. Search my office. Tear the room apart. Go to my home, my wife would be happy to support my story." Sauer's rage had subsided. His eyes had become sorrowful. Though the project had been Eichler's to boast of, it had been Sauer who had nurtured it.

"I will proceed in whatever way necessary to ensure the project's future," Eichler said. "You're to leave Flussrand immediately. If you return, you'll be shot on sight."

Sauer stood, aghast. He hesitated to move, to follow the order and leave. Schwarz's hand moved to his holster, undid the button which secured the strap holding his firearm in place, and rested his hand on its butt. Sauer took the cue and then stormed off. When he passed by Eichler, his superior thought he might have even seen a tear forming in the corner of the elderly man's eye.

Lothar Eichler was still having a difficult time believing his most trusted employee had been a conspirator. He didn't think she had it in her. She always presented herself as timid and attentive. Never would he have suspected her as someone who'd been seeking to bring the project down from the inside. He'd always thought of her as a meek girl who'd just happened to have a particular skill, and furthermore, one who could be trusted. Perhaps, Eichler thought, it was that trait—her apparent trustworthiness—that meant she was anything but. Weren't the silent, contemplative ones always the conniving types?

At his desk, Eichler ran his fingers down the paper schematic, and pencil shavings rolled down toward his chest. The debris he wiped from his tunic had dirtied his fingers, and the dark, pewter-like residue left on the tips settled into the fine grooves of his particular fingerprint. *Fingerprints*, he thought. Panic inside him cascaded in waves like a hurricane at sea.

He pressed his face close to the document. There, faint but visible, were a series of prints on the top-left corner of the document. Eichler looked up at Schwarz, who had been waiting quietly at attention. "Schwarz, what did you do with the bodies I requested you dispose of last night?"

"Instructed my men to hand them over to the morgue, Herr Eichler," Schwarz replied.

"You have a vehicle, yes?" Eichler asked.

"I do," Schwarz replied.

"Good," Eichler said with a sinister purr. "I have one

more errand for you." There was a fire in Eichler's eyes that no liquid could extinguish. He gave Schwarz a very specific set of instructions, then sent the soldier on his way. Eichler returned to his unhealthy fixation with the main gate—not put at ease by the information his runner had procured, but *enraged*.

15

Sam sat at the window and babysat a cigarette. He could sense Sigrid wasn't thrilled with the smell of the smoke, but considering he'd got her home safely after a nerve-wracking journey, he assumed she wouldn't speak up. Sigrid lit a fire while Sam monitored the activity at street level. If anyone was going to try to get the jump on them, he was going to be ready.

The second floor of the apartment was immaculate. It had a sparse but cozy feeling that put Sam at ease if only temporarily. A floor-to-ceiling bookcase at the far wall signaled that Sigrid, or her family, was well-read, and many of the titles were not solely in German, but English, with a select few in Latin. There were old texts peppered in with the new, ranging from all matters of thought from science to philosophy. Opposite that, a staircase led to the third floor Sam hadn't yet seen.

His attention was to remain on the street until he was convinced they weren't being watched. With every minute that passed, he relaxed further. The warmth of the apartment was a welcome change. The fire crackled inside the room, and Sigrid placed two more logs on it. After she was satisfied with the fire, Sigrid stared back at Sam, arms folded.

Sam grunted. "Now what?"

Sigrid sighed. "A warm bath and a meal. The good news is the weapon will still be there tomorrow—I can promise you that. I'll tell you everything I can, but a man needs food in his stomach and a clean shave to think straight, don't you agree?"

Sam rubbed his thumb and index finger against the stubble that had already invaded his face. He couldn't argue with the hospitality, and his stomach whined with anticipation at the thought of a hot meal. The cigarettes had held him over thus far. A cigarette was always a good appetite suppressor, but after too many all Sam was left with was a rebelling stomach and a migraine. Sam's stomach gurgled once more, as if speaking to Sigrid itself.

Sigrid chuckled. "I'll take that as a yes."

Sigrid heated up beef rouladen, a sort of meat wrap stuffed with bacon, onions, mustard, and pickles. The food had been left over from a previous meal, but Sigrid had promised Sam they were even better that way. She cautioned him about the rogue toothpicks inside each roll of meat. Sam enjoyed the tangy burst of interior ingredients with every bite. At the side, mashed potatoes and red cabbage accompanied the beef, and Sam went overboard with the brown gravy, soaking everything so greatly that the remnants of the solids had turned into a soupy mixture he scooped up with a spoon.

Sigrid pushed the food on her plate around with a fork. Sam sensed her nerves had been tested over the course of the week, and he didn't prod. He pulled a cigarette from his pack before saying, "You mind?" Sigrid gestured, albeit reluctantly, that he was welcome to smoke, and Sam chased his meal down with the cigarette.

"It's a terrible habit," Sigrid warned. "Not that it's any of my business."

Sam leaned back into his chair, allowing the food that was pushing against his pants to sort itself out. "It's the *last* thing that'll kill me."

"I could see that," Sigrid reasoned. "I suppose being here is far more dangerous."

Sam exhaled with a long sigh. He waved the cigarette toward the third floor. "What's up there?"

"Bedrooms and such," Sigrid replied casually.

"And such?"

He followed Sigrid up to the third floor of the home. There were three more rooms upstairs, as well as a wash closet. They passed one of the bedrooms, then Sam saw another well-kept room with very little other than a bed and a small wooden nightstand. Finally, they arrived at a room facing the street, and Sigrid opened the door to a space shrouded in darkness. A chair sat near the cool light penetrating the window. The sky had become overcast, and the sun had all but vanished behind a grey sheet above.

"There," she said while gesturing to the chair adjacent to the window. Sigrid turned on a series of lights, and the room reflected twinkles in a myriad of directions. At first, Sam found it offensive. The room was littered with all manner of gears, cogs, rods, and metals of every nature. The room also contained a bookcase, but this one was dedicated mostly to titles regarding engineering and mechanics. Sigrid flicked another switch, and a small lamp dedicated to the workbench she sat at glowed with life. Sam took his seat.

Sigrid said, "Start from the beginning, Sam," as she got to work tinkering with a small watch on the table.

Sam told Sigrid most of the story of his arrival. He went over the mission, the goal, and his instruction from the burned man. Sigrid listened intently for the duration, not saying a word. She was in seemingly deep concentration in regard to the work in her hands.

Sigrid prodded at a blemished brass watch. It did not tick, nor did either of its slim golden hands move. The exterior had begun to rust, and a linked band lay draped over her hands. Though Sigrid's hands were still shaking, Sam noticed a mastery within her fingers. She wore a jeweler's loop over one eye, and the other watched Sam as if it operated independently. After some nudging, the watch popped open with a click. "There we are."

She needled at the gears inside with a thin screwdriver, tinkering with precise movements and a light, graceful hand. "The older, the better, I say," Sigrid said to Sam. "Most men would discard an old piece like this, but it is the elder craftsmanship that was designed to last. Now things are made quickly and cheaply, with little regard to longevity." Her accent began to become more prominent—slight deviations in the consonants— a lisp here and there concerning "s" and "c" sounds— suggested her tinkering had relaxed her.

After one small prod, the watch began ticking with life once more—the soft, subtle heartbeat of a machine. "They all die eventually," Sigrid warned. "Even the most well-made constructions do. Castles fall, bridges collapse, mountains crumble. With time, anything dies. Even a rock, with its near-infinite nature, will become dust over a long period of time after it's beaten down by the wind. It is the nature of things. We, however, can do our best to preserve them." Sigrid replaced the watch's back cover and displayed it for Sam. "Do you know the history of Pforzheim?"

Sam had history with Germany, alright, but he didn't know the intricacies of Pforzheim. His relationship with the country had brought him nothing but pain and torment. It was a place he'd resolved to never come back to, and yet here he was. Regardless of his own personal associations with the country, he humored her as she retrieved another watch from a bench nearby and proceeded to tinker with it.

"We are a people of precision," Sigrid said. "We specialize in it. We like gears and rods, cogs and wheels. We like jewelry and watches. That particular skill, the skill of tinkering and refining precision instruments, has awarded us a unique identity. It makes us particularly suited to engineering." Sigrid displayed the watch face toward Sam. "Tinker this way and you get a reliable tool." The watch's hands ticked in their usual manner. "Tinker that way, and you've got a dangerous weapon." Sigrid extended the watch toward Sam. "Here, you take this one."

"I couldn't," Sam replied.

"You can, and you will," Sigrid said. She motioned it forward once more, and Sam retrieved the watch. He massaged the piece between his thumb and forefinger, admiring the care that had been taken to make such a small machine. The second hand ticked along with a mathematical precision. It was heavy, and well-made.

Sam had never had one like it, and with some polishing, the exterior might not look half-bad.

"Do you understand the nature of my request?" Sigrid asked.

"I don't," Sam replied. "I'm not so sure why you've had a change of heart."

Sigrid nodded. She knew more than she was letting on, but didn't entertain the inquiry further, and instead remained focused on the micro machine in her hand. She displayed another watch, this one more intricate that the last, and leaned in closer to see the fine parts more clearly. "This one is particularly difficult."

"That so?" Sam asked, sounding disinterested. He hadn't come to Germany to fiddle with watches. He'd come to accomplish a task, and the only woman who he'd needed to secure had her eye fixed on a mechanism that wouldn't get them any closer to accomplishing it.

"This one gear in particular must touch a larger one in just the right way," Sigrid began. She dropped the minuscule screwdriver she'd been utilizing and exchanged it for another, yet smaller one. "It sits right next to another that is crucial, and yet it may not touch both. If it does, it risks throwing everything out of whack. There is a very, very small window of error, a thin gap in which to work. It is a delicate balance, and once sitting in just the perfect spot..." Sigrid trailed off as she continued to rotate the tool. The watch began to tick, and she leaned away from it, then released the tool from her hand and placed it on the table delicately. A smile formed on her face. She was satisfied with her work. She leaned back in her chair proudly. "One achieves the desired outcome."

"Is this how you spend your free time?" Sam asked.

"Sometimes," Sigrid replied. "A hobby, one might say, but a way of distraction from the responsibility that goes along with my work. My father taught me this. This type of craftsmanship—I find it calming, and so did he. *Especially* after I made the decision to do what I did."

"About that," Sam said impatiently. He pulled a cigarette from his tin and lit it. The smoke exiting Sam's mouth swirled like a snake toward Sigrid and shone in the exposure of the desk lamp. "If we were going to do it—and that's a big *if*—what would we do?"

Sigrid smiled brightly, then shifted the watch she'd finished working on out of view. She removed the loop from her eye, cracked the knuckles in her hands with a series of pops, and leaned forward. She rested both hands in an interlocked position on the desk. "Just like any other intricately designed mechanism, we'll need to get inside to expose its weakness—and for that, you'll need me."

"You're really serious about this, aren't you?" Sam asked.

Sigrid grabbed a pencil from the desk and placed a sheet of paper in front of her before adjusting herself to sit upright. She sketched *Erdschlag* roughly, leaving out its aesthetic details and focusing only on its form. She tapped the top portion of the tank with the tip of the pencil. "The turret," she said. "This is where the machine's cannon has been mounted. The only access points to the interior—as far as we're concerned—are housed on its third tier."

She traced the pencil along each of the tank's sections, separating them with broadly sketched horizontal lines. "The first tier is dedicated entirely to propulsion and maneuvering. The caterpillar treads take up the bulk of it, and there are three ladders that are deployable when stationary. They're currently accessible. You've got one here," Sigrid pointed with the pencil near the tank's front-left corner, "here, on the reverse rear side," she pointed on the back right corner. "And finally, the rear entry point." She circled the tank's rear section. "You'll need to get in. The exterior hull is nearly impenetrable, but the interior is completely accessible while it remains housed at Flussrand."

Sigrid directed the pencil to the center of the tank. "The machine has multiple drive sprockets to accommodate its demand for power, with the engine located in its rear. Specifications required that the machine possess the ability to maneuver over potentially dangerous terrain—landmines, bombs, that sort of thing—because of that, and its need to accommodate that risk, the gasoline reservoir is located centrally on the second tier and encased in multiples plates of steel. From the exterior, no weapon in existence other than another copy of the tank itself is likely to puncture it from the outside. The inside, however…"

Sigrid lifted the pencil and traced it back to the second tier. "Once you've managed to get on to the second tier, there are only two access points to the tank's third tier, where the main functions are controlled. On the second tier, the machine is surrounded by walkways that encircle it completely. There are hatches for individual gunners that control the anti-aircraft artillery and general cover fire. Don't waste your time with these, they are dead ends."

Sigrid traced the walkway around to a ladder that extended up to the tank's third tier from its broad side.

"This is one of the ladders to the first entry point. There's always the chance one of the crew have locked the door. If that's the case, there's another point on the rear end if you follow this walkway—also a ladder." Sigrid shifted the point of the pencil back and forth between both of the ladders, circling each before tilting her head toward Sam. "Find your way up either of these ladders, then follow the small walkway that runs between both."

"And if both are locked?" Sam asked.

Sigrid lifted her head and cocked one eyebrow into a high arch. "Then you'll be on your way home." Sam let out a hiss of smoke through his teeth, then wrapped his lips around the cigarette once more. He inhaled, moved closer to the sketch, and scrutinized the drawing further.

"If both doors are sealed, you've got far bigger problems," Sigrid said. "That means there is personnel inside the machine, and if so, they've already seen you coming. There shouldn't be anyone there. I have the crew's schedule—in fact, I'm the one who created it." Sam nodded.

Sigrid tapped the third tier once more with the pencil, specifically where the base of the cannon was located. "I suggest this door. That's where the machine is piloted, smaller shells are loaded for its exterior artillery, and any personnel are housed for operations. The interior cabin can accommodate roughly forty people." Above the tank's turret was a traditional hatch that personnel could climb down. "This point is sealed, and requires a ladder. It's an emergency exit, in case of fire or damage to the main access point on the exterior. You won't be able to get in this way, so don't go climbing up to the top and thinking you can dive in."

"And once I'm inside?" Sam said with an exhalation of thick smoke.

"You'll arrive in the quartermaster's room," Sigrid said. "It was placed on top in case a small infantry unit needed to be housed and armed quickly. If an enemy unit attempted to board the machine, infantry would be deployed from here. Exit that room and follow the hallway forward. To your left is a wash closet, and to your right a galley."

"Where's the bar?" Sam asked with a smirk.

Sigrid grinned. "You laugh, but a lot of thought was placed into how this machine would function as a mobile fortress, rather than simply a piece of heavy artillery. The exterior is completely sealed. If attacked with a chemical weapon, a crew of forty could survive inside for roughly one week before exhausting the supplies." Sigrid returned her attention to the schematic, sketching a line on a diagonal angle from the hall. "Descend the stairs directly ahead, and you'll arrive at the primary control room. This is a wide room, roughly twenty yards in length, and ten wide. It's home to all the navigational and telemetric functions. There's even a periscope of sorts for view-finding should the driver have to enter the secure area."

"So this is the target?" Sam asked.

"Not quite yet," Sigrid corrected. "You see, the party leaders required the designer, Sauer, to create a situation room of sorts *below* the main control room, and so the only way to accommodate it was to construct it directly above the tank's gasoline reservoir. The control room itself is protected from assault but this room specifically is a bit of a weak point. It's accessible via another set of stairs. Should the tank succumb to a fatal attack externally—though unlikely—the crew would escape from the top hatch or quartermaster's barracks and descend, but there were no precautions taken should the tank suffer internal damage."

"What's it going to take?" Sam asked.

"Nothing fancy," Sigrid assured him. "A nice little bundle of dynamite ought to the do the trick. The machine is currently filled with gasoline. We made sure it was prepared and ready to make its maiden voyage to Rügenwalde for testing. One good *bang*, and the explosion reaches the gasoline reservoir—all one hundred thousand gallons of it. The plating under the floor of *that* section isn't nearly as sturdy as its exterior cousin. From there, well, the machine implodes from the inside out. There's no way to extinguish it either. Most of its shell will remain, but that will be a useless husk. All of its primary controls will have suffered damage that would render it inoperable."

"Dynamite I can do," Sam said.

"I didn't expect anything less," Sigrid replied warmly. "Better yet, you can find the dynamite *at* Flussrand. Back when they were leveling the property, clearing the bedrock and trees and such, they needed quite a bit. There's plenty left in storage, though you'll need this." Sigrid turned to the shelf on the other side of the room and opened a small lockbox. She displayed a small pen-like cylinder with a brass finish. "This is a detonator—a time pencil, so to speak."

"You made that?" Sam asked.

"No," Sigrid replied. "They were among the belongings of the ones I aided." Now Sam understood that she hadn't taken pencils from the spies' hideout—that had been why she'd been behaving strangely. The items she'd taken were *detonators*.

"The vial contains a spring-loaded striker." Sigrid pointed to the tube's tip. "Inside, a glass vial of cupric chloride rests waiting. The striker is held by a thin metal wire, and after crushing the copper section, the tube will break, eventually eroding the wire holding the striker. The striker hits the percussion cap, then *boom*."

"How do you know this? Sam asked.

"If you can understand a watch's mechanics, you can understand a detonator," Sigrid explained. "You'll need something to crush it, of course. The heel of your boot, the butt of your gun. Just be sure you've inserted it into the end of the explosive, and don't lose it. Without it, you'd only be able to detonate the explosives while inside, and that just won't do, will it?"

"*If* we're going to do this, I'd like to see the fire-works," Sam replied.

"And quite a show it would be," Sigrid said. "You'll want to make sure you're quite clear of the area. You'll only have ten minutes, give or take one or two. Much of the explosion will be contained to the interior, but the pressure of the impact will likely blow out any weak points and, with the right conditions, probably engulf the whole building it's housed in."

Sam shook his head in disbelief. "If you know all of this, why haven't you done it yourself?"

"I'm not a fool," Sigrid said. "It's bad enough I'll have to go in with you. At least with me there, I can aid you—distract patrols, get you inside, and such. I can get you in, but you'll be the one doing the damage. I'm not a saboteur, Sam. I'm a woman with a *plan*."

"You've got your ticket out right here, right now," Sam growled.

"I didn't hand that information over so I could run away, Sam," Sigrid retorted. "I did it so the machine would be destroyed."

"I still haven't decided whether or not that's even an option," Sam replied. "Our chance for escape ends tomorrow night, and that's not much time. If it's going to happen, you'll need my help." Sigrid dropped the conversation and walked out abruptly in a huff. Sam thought it better to let her stew rather than keep pressing the issue.

He spent the rest of the day monitoring the window. His job, as he was still concerned, was to *protect* this woman, but she did have a point. If anyone could get him in and out, it was Sigrid.

And what would the burned man say? Did he know the SOE men were dead? It had likely happened while Sam was in transit, and impossible that London or his superiors would know of their fates. Dead men don't speak. As far as everyone knew, they were still alive and prepping their mission. Would the burned man have redirected the mission if he knew?

Sam had explicit instructions: get her out safely. He still hadn't decided whether or not he was going to help her, but to show up empty-handed back at the freighter would result in two defeats, the first of which was a failure to retrieve an asset, and the second a failure to destroy an enemy threat. Bringing the girl back *and* destroying the weapon would be succeeding at more than they bargained for. Perhaps, Sam thought, the burned man could parlay with London or Churchill or whoever was moving the levers to the north if he was successful in his mission. The Americans could get the British to move their pieces wherever they were required on the chess board of war. Sam did what he always did when he needed to run things over in his head, and chain-smoked while weighing the plan.

16

By the time Schwarz had finished the round trip, night had already fallen at Flussrand. He'd made the best time he could, but a snafu with credentials in Pforzheim had prevented him from getting what he sought until he'd held a proverbial gun to the staff doctor's head. He tore through the dirt road with little regard for either his or his accompanying group's safety during his return. The trek to Flussrand was a treacherous serpent of semi-finished roads switching back along the mountainside. When he arrived, he was granted access once more, yet this time he arrived not with the canvas bag, but a dark, plastic one carried cautiously away from his body. The contents of the bag made him visibly squeamish.

Eichler greeted Schwarz this time and flung the door open hastily. The project manager's paranoia had grown exponentially since his encounter with Sauer. He moved rapidly through the room and waved Schwarz in with rushed, sweeping motions. Schwarz looked nauseous; a queasy, grey color had painted the skin on his face. He pinched the bag between two reluctant fingers, and Eichler snatched it from him forcefully without so much as a "good work," or "thank you." Eichler's nostrils flared in response to the foul odor seeping out of the bag. He placed the bag on a chair, and then retrieved two gloves from his desk drawer. Schwarz looked glad to be rid of the bag, and almost immediately regained color in his face in the absence of its contents. Schwarz lit a cigarette to mask the odor lingering in his nose.

"Did you retrieve both?" Eichler asked while stretching the pair of gloves quickly over his hands.

"I did," Schwarz replied. "The left of each. Good timing too," he added. "They were due to be burned."

Eichler maneuvered to a long, tall, wooden case that rested beside his desk. He floated a finger down each of the drawers, then stopped at the third before jamming a key into a simple lock securing the slim drawer. He slid it open, reached carefully inside, and delicately pulled a long sheet of paper from the drawer before shutting it. Eichler carelessly cleared items from his desk to make space, then placed the paper schematic—the precise rendering of *Erdschlag* that Sigrid had handled during the week—flat on the desk.

"There," Eichler said to himself. He dug in the bag, uncaring of the grotesque nature of its contents, and pulled a bloated, severed hand from inside. The skin had lost all its color, and was now a mixture of cool blue and teal where once it had been a warm pink. Most of the blood had coagulated, forming a rust-colored stump at the wrist only interrupted by the small protrusion of broken bone. Rigor mortis had forced the fingers to stiffen into what was surely a final grasp, and Eichler pried them open with five sickening crunches—each caused Schwarz to wince.

Eichler dumped a jar of black ink haphazardly on to a small mat that had been resting on the desk. The ink pooled in a large glob, and he pressed the tips of each of the dead man's fingers to the spill. Schwarz looked on, alternating between intrigue and confusion. Next, Eichler, now busy at work like some sort of mad scientist, wiped the fingers of the severed hand with a small handkerchief, leaving just enough residue that he could manage a print. He pressed the small tips next to the ones that had been left behind in lead and waited for them to settle. He blew a thin whisper of air on to the drying ink, and once he'd formed a decent print, scrutinized the results. His face darted manically back and forth between the lead and ink copy, and after trying to match both, became dissatisfied with the results.

"No, no, no," he said in frustration. He tossed the cadaverous limb into the garbage at his feet. It landed with an unceremonious thump, and the waft of air that hit Schwarz' face tickled his nose with that familiar grotesque stench. Eichler reached in the bag for the other. He uncurled the stiffened fingers of other man's hand, and those took more prying than the last. Schwarz wasn't sure how much more he could suffer, and still wasn't sure just what the mad scientist in front of him was hoping to deduce with his irreverent actions. He'd scolded Schwarz—embarrassed him in front of his group—for seeing to it that the spies hung, yet here Eichler was playing Dr. Frankenstein.

Once Eichler was satisfied the fingers were straightened enough, he placed the next limb into the ink, and repeated the process. This hand, when he removed it from the paper and surveyed its prints, yielded far more promising results. He recognized the patterns quickly, but did his due diligence anyway. He needed to be sure of the crime—the results of which might lead him down a path he still wasn't prepared to follow. He bent down, contrasting the dry print with the wet, his eyes bouncing back and forth rapidly between each. Finally, he released the hand into the trash with a sickening thud.

This time, he rose slowly from the desk with a forlorn expression forming on his face. As he removed the gloves from his hands, that emotion quickly evolved into that of disappointment, and following right behind it was seething anger. The prints on the paper matched those of the dead SOE spy, and only one person had had possession of those documents.

"Bad girl," Eichler hissed to himself. He questioned the soldier standing by, "How large is your squad, Schwarz?"

"I have nine men with my group," Schwarz replied. "Four of which are currently on patrol, and the others waiting outside."

"Very good," Eichler replied menacingly. "That will do just fine. Are they all armed?"

"Some with pistols, sir," he said. "Only two have rifles."

Eichler turned to Schwarz, then retrieved a small slip of paper from his desk and wrote hastily on it with a pen. "There is an armory on the premises. Hand this to the quartermaster. He won't question it. See to it that you gather ample supplies—whatever you need." Eichler tore the paper from the pad and handed it to Schwarz.

"You've got one more errand to run for me, and you'll need to be quick—and quiet—about it."

"Herr Eichler," Schwarz replied uneasily. "We're supposed to be on patrol. My officer—"

"As I told you last time," Eichler interrupted, "any issues your supervising officers have with my requests can be addressed to me. Leave four of your men on patrol in the city, and take the four you have with you." That time, Schwarz didn't question the instruction. Though Eichler bore no regalia that suggested he was an officer, Schwarz understood the nature of the issue at hand; he didn't question the request any further. Eichler held the head office at Flussrand, and that meant he surely had more pull than even Schwarz's commanding officers.

Eichler spoke again. "There's a defector among us—a woman. I want her alive. Of course, if you meet resistance, then do what you must, but I prefer that she's brought in for questioning."

Schwarz saluted him, turned on his heel, and exited with haste. Eichler lit a cigarette and inhaled forcefully. He flicked the cigarette with a manic, repeated motion. There was no ash left to fall from the cherry of the smoldering end. It was the act of a man whose nerves were becoming frayed. *Damnit. Not now. Not so soon.*

All this time, all the precautions he'd taken, and it had been right under his nose the whole time. He'd been fooled once more, and this time by one of his own. There'd be no way of explaining this scenario away as he had with the events that had taken place in America. He needed to put an end to this fiasco here and now, while there was still time to protect his asset.

If the British SOE men had already been caught,

then what was she up to now? It wasn't over—Eichler was sure of it. He'd force it out of her if he had to, no matter what it took. She was no soldier—no spy prepared for a torturous inquisition. If that was what had to be done, so be it. No one was going to compromise *Erdschlag.* The question was, was she still alone? And if not, would she be returning to Flussrand? Eichler considered that he could just let her return and act as if nothing had happened, but the project was too close to completion to allow that. Every moment wasted was another of risk. He needed to protect Flussrand at all costs.

The thought that Sigrid had conspired with Sauer wasn't out of the question. He'd taken care of one threat, and now he had to see to it the other one was neutralized as well. All the security he'd allocated to the project wasn't enough. He needed *more.*

Lothar Eichler crossed the field in front of the warehouse at Flussrand with long, purposeful strides. The moon on that night was bold and mighty, and lit the path in front of him with a sharp glow. He surveyed all of the men in his employ, now limited to only soldiers patrolling the property. The engineers and construction workers had all gone home for their single day off, Sunday. Now Eichler cursed himself for allowing it. The morale had been low, and he'd been warned of that, and he rewarded his men with a day off—though ill-advised —since the project had been so close to completion.

How stupid he'd been. He'd been worried about something like this happening, and now here it was, just as he'd feared. They'd mocked him for his slave-driving resolve, and they'd chortled and guffawed whenever he left the room. They'd shown little, if any, respect for the man in charge. They'd called him paranoid and incompetent and weak and little—despite his height. Who was foolish now? The project in question was officially jeopardized, and all because of a woman he'd placed in charge.

What would the ministry say if they found out it had been he who'd suggested her employ? He'd be reprimanded for being so foolish. Perhaps he'd even be shot —or worse, removed from any project of its kind. For Lothar Eichler, a failure to secure his place with the other men of high value was worse than death. Never mind that he'd seen it through to its completion. What would it matter if the enemy destroyed it before it could perform its task?

Eichler's blood boiled as he arrived at the small structure near the entrance of Flussrand. There, a concrete post for the patrol had been erected, the first checkpoint to enter the greater property. Whether he was a little man or not, he had a large weapon ready and waiting.

Inside, a few of the soldiers smoked cigarettes and sipped coffee. When he entered, they stood at attention and saluted him, but they were slow to move, and their lack of urgency only enraged him further.

"Where is the one you call Bär?" Eichler asked the group. Each of the men turned to face the figure in the corner of the room in unison. The man had been keeping to himself, facing out through the window. Upon hearing his name, he slid his chair back, and then rose from it with heavy, cement-like steps. He turned toward Eichler, and finally approached. The concrete floor, even with its sturdy nature, seemed to cry under his boots. He stood in front of Eichler, stopped, and hovered above his superior.

He was massive, and had a chest that jutted out with pectoral muscles that resembled the armor plating worn by a soldier of the Roman legion. His head, which bent down slightly just to look Eichler in the eye, was attached to a neck more like a tree stump than a body part. His arms were so thick that when he stood upright, his hands did not meet his sides as a normal man's would. If his stature wasn't intimidating enough, a grim, stone-like expression decorated his face.

"Come with me," Eichler said, and Bär followed.

17

Sam's figure formed a mass of shadow shaped by the silvery outline of moonlight. Around him, a cloud of smoked swirled, only further adding to his mysterious persona. Sigrid paused at the top of the staircase, hypnotized by the silhouette beyond and lingering on the contours of his muscle groups. She worked her way around from the top down, starting at the trapezius, moving to the deltoid, and further to the biceps and forearms before realizing she'd been staring. He sat shirtless, and every so often the glow of the cigarette would illuminate the room with a soft orange ambience that outlined the arches of his muscles.

He sat staring out the window, the cigarette sitting only inches from his lips and his fingers moving only ever so slightly to take another pull. She didn't care for the habit, though she indulged in stressful times; she thought it rather like a newborn wanting for a bottle and judged men accordingly. With each pull at the cigarette by Sam, a soft crackling found her ears.

His attention was focused and unwavering—she likened his behavior more to that of a watchful predator than a man. His body, canted slightly in a way that allowed her to just see one of the eyes, remained attentive and calm. The eye that she could see had something callous about it—she'd noted that earlier the night before when she'd first met him.

What was it in the eyes? It wasn't that something was there—it was that something was *missing*. His eyes were magnificent, and yet they were devoid of humanity in a way that she'd only seen on soldiers who'd seen things no man should see. She'd witnessed the same absence of life within recruits who'd come back from the war, not those of the men with shellshock, but the violent, unhinged type of men that had done unspeakable things, witnessed unspeakable things, and had lived to tell tales.

Her hand found her chest, and she realized her heart was racing. She remained fixated on his figure, and when the cigarette flared once again, she noticed the abrasions present on his back. There were lines, burns, and scrapes embedded in the skin, though they'd aged poorly. A small, circular scar present in the shoulder blade evidenced the exit wound of a bullet, and flanking it on all sides from the opposite shoulder to the back, keloid scars had been left as mementos. Some were large, and some small, and each told no rhyme or reason of the other's involvement geographically. The floor beneath Sigrid's feet cracked under the shifting of her weight, and she held her breath shamefully.

"You're going to need to be sneakier than that if you're going to go on like you have been," Sam called out without looking. His face turned slightly, though it still didn't meet hers.

Sigrid stepped forward slowly, and stopped at the doorway to his room. The moonlight kissed her face with the softest touch, shrouding her in a glistening blue glow. He inhaled from the cigarette once more, then turned to her, and this time, the glorious, cool eyes lit with a fiery glow from the cigarette's cherry. Sigrid wondered if somewhere inside the man opposite her, the devil himself had taken hold.

"You're still awake," Sigrid replied. The comment hadn't been phrased as either a question or a statement. Sigrid pushed the door open and continued forward until sitting on the edge of the bed. Now she was close to the scars, and she glimpsed them more thoughtfully, first analyzing the smaller, jagged ones present on the back, and then stopping on the circular one that had undoubtedly been formed by a bullet's exit. She reached softly for the wound at his shoulder and let her fingers glide with a soft touch over the raised skin. Her breath shuddered, ragged and uneven. Her face fell, and she let her fingers do the work.

"Did it hurt?" Sigrid asked.

"Only after the fact," Sam replied somberly. "You don't know you've been hit until you see the wound. When they clean it out though—that's a different story."

"And these?" Sigrid asked, redirecting her touch to the other wounds present along the spine. She inhaled once more, rough and stilted.

"For a while," Sam replied. Now he turned fully toward her, and his eyes found hers.

Sigrid removed her hand from his body and pulled it forcefully back to herself. Her eyes were sorrowful and wide. She stared directly into his eyes intensely. They sat like that for a moment, neither saying a word, before Sigrid asked, "Won't you sleep?"

"Not till we're finished," Sam replied with a grim purr. She pulled her hand from his skin, and he saw that her blouse fell down her chest in such a way that it revealed the soft flesh of her breast in the cool light. Her face became flushed. He tamped the cigarette down into the tray and turned back to the window, resuming the stoic attentiveness to the outside world.

Sigrid touched his face, her fingers resting on the hard edge of his jaw, and turned it toward her. She stared into his eyes again. His returned an intensity unmatched by any she'd ever experienced—but also one of supreme concern. Her lips parted slightly and revealed just the edges of her teeth. Without warning, she grabbed a fistful of his hair from the back of his head and pressed her lips against his. Then, he lifted her from the bed, prompting her to straddle him with both legs, and his hands found her thighs and made her feel airy and light. Now their faces were locked together, and their lips sloppy with passion, and soon she was against the wall and digging her nails into his back.

For the next ten minutes, no one spoke, but only shared in the auditory exchange of heavy breathing as they made love. Sigrid thought there was something dangerous—rather than romantic—in his eyes when doing so. With it came a vulnerability that she allowed to consume her. She imagined he killed with the same attentiveness. He'd kissed her body in such a way that made her feel like the most beautiful woman in the world, and she let him handle her with all the strength he had. In return she made no attempts at tempering her own ferocity, and soon the two performed as if drunk with love. She didn't know what had gotten into her, why she had taken him like that, but she suspected the danger had done something to her, changed her in some way. Sigrid was buzzing when she finally let him go, a warm, electric-like sensation that radiated from the back of her neck and down to each extremity. She felt every aching muscle that had stiffened from her dangerous travels relax in unison. Sam moved on to the only thing he ever did when his hands were free—reach for a cigarette.

Sigrid pulled the covers above most of her body, which had grown cool in the open air. The sweat both had generated lingered like the remnants of a light rain. She basked in the euphoric sensation for just a moment longer before turning toward him. He lit the cigarette and offered it to her, then let his eyes wander toward her lips as she pressed the cigarette to them.

She inhaled lightly, and then a smile crept at each side of her mouth. "I think I'm beginning to see how one might develop a habit," she said as she exhaled softly. Sam took the cigarette back from her, felt a chill as their hands brushed once more, and allowed himself to stare into her face for a brief moment. Something had *changed* about her. The woman who had held the dagger to his throat the night before and ushered him through enemy territory had become faintly melancholic.

Their eyes held firmly on each other's—neither spoke, and yet each felt the other might interrupt the silence at any moment. It was the most calm Sigrid had felt since she'd carried the plans into Pforzheim and solidified her place as an enemy. She was no different than the man staring back at her. The eyes of the animal opposite her had softened a bit too, now almost unrecognizable from those of the man she'd almost killed only a night before.

"Why did you do it?" Sam asked. The dark spheres in her eyes grew large and worrisome.

She retrieved the cigarette once more from him, took a puff, and held it in if only to prolong the answer. The smoke lingered in her mouth. She averted her eyes away from his as if in deep thought. "You will think I am foolish."

"Foolish is crossing enemy lines and sleeping with them," Sam said as he took the cigarette back from her. He noticed her hand began to tremble this time when he brushed against the soft skin.

"I've seen things," Sigrid said. Her voice crackled before she said, "Things of pain, and horror."

"It's *war*, Sigrid," Sam said.

Her gaze returned to his. "Berlin," she replied. Her eyes flittered nervously, shifting from left to right when they returned to meet his, physically manifesting all of the excitement welling up from deep inside of her. "When I travel to Berlin, all I see is torment. It won't stop there. I can see the future, *my* future, and it is fire, and twisted metal, and smoke, and blood."

Sam gave her his full attention. The state she'd slipped into—he knew from experience—was one of true fear.

"I can see the future of my home…" She trailed off briefly. "And it is worse. The structures tremble with the screams of a hundred assailants from above. The city shakes at its core, one last unearthly scream before its prolonged silence. A thousand bolts of lightning strike it at once, each bringing with it the roar of thunder. It sounds like the beating of hell's drums."

A tear gathered in Sigrid's eye, and the whites became red. The twitching of her eyelid forced the tear to fall, and it rolled slowly down the cheek, leaving only a trail of glistening moisture until it fell to the bed below. "When the storm has stopped there are only screams and panic. The sky burns with light, but not from the storm, from the fires that rage up toward it in protest. Mothers search for children in rubble, and they in turn cry out for their mothers."

Another tear fell, and Sigrid's gaze became distant. She wasn't looking at Sam any longer, but looking *through* him. Her gaze had transferred from the physical to the mind's eye. She was watching this scene play out like a projector displaying a personal movie in her brain. She wasn't here with him, but *there*.

"There is a tower of bodies—all of which are unidentifiable—and it reaches into the heavens. It parts the sky, penetrating the clouds, but blocks out the sun. The city is cast in darkness, and all that is left is the tower of dead. They are faceless, and charred, and blackened. No one knows who they are… but *I* do. They are my friends, and my family, and the people of this city. The bodies on the tower cry tears in such abundance that they overflow into the city. It's *tainted* by the storm that took everything. They are men and women and children alike. Very few make it out alive, and those that do shuffle like specters in the smoke and debris, lost and aimless and confused. They wade through the high waters from the tears that have flooded their city."

Her eyes refocused on his. She was back here with Sam. She wiped the tear from her eye, and took a ragged breath. She said stoically, "That is why I have done what I've done."

She had been rattled. Sam didn't deny that what she had seen she had *felt*. "No one can see the future," Sam said. There was compassion in his statement, but authority. "The Allies will close in soon enough."

"And how long will the world be punished until then?" Sigrid asked. She was *serious*. "Do you know who occupies Berlin? Citizens—not soldiers. They can't fight back. They can't attack. Men are fighting, and people like myself are just caught in between."

"That's the nature of battle."

"No," she said abruptly. "When boys want to fight, they take the battle to the schoolyard. *Your* people are not innocent in this either. How many must die until there is surrender? The Führer has no intention of that, nor do his compatriots. They will take all of us with them, and what will be left?"

Sam sighed with defeat. She wasn't wrong.

She said, "You can deny it all you want. You may think that I am a foolish girl—that I am 'out of my league,' as you say, but I have seen the future of *Erdschlag* and it is *nothing* like what I have seen before. If what befalls Berlin happens in London, I will never forgive myself for my inaction. No man or woman or child should see what I have seen. And I believe that what I am doing is right, and perhaps, if I'm correct, because you are here."

Sam asked, "Why give up the plans and put yourself in danger? What's to stop the people you handed over the information to from taking it and kicking you out the door. Don't think I can guarantee your freedom."

"If I can prevent what I have seen from happening

elsewhere," Sigrid replied, "then that will have been enough. My request to go to America was just an added bonus. I'm not stupid." She had a strong resolve now. Her shoulders were more set, not slouched, and she spoke sharply. "If that machine is mobilized then that will be the fate that befalls many cities—each with its own tower of death and sadness. The Earth will become a shrine to a lack of humanity, hellish tentacles reaching toward heaven, mocking it. Men fight, but what has been created is in defiance of all that is fair. What will be our punishment for this defiance? That I don't know, but I can tell you it is only more pain. I know what I have seen, Sam, and I *can* stop it from happening to others."

Sam scoffed. "But you need *me*."

"Laugh all you like," Sigrid said with dismay. "But if you won't help me then I will find someone who will, and the people you work for will get *nothing. Erdschlag* is not the only information I am privy to. There are *many* copies of documents I have hidden." Her face became frustrated and pouty. "I have done a good thing. You are here, and if you want to help me, to do what I set out to do, then *you* will do what needs to be done."

"And you'll get a free ticket back into the arms of safety," Sam snapped. Her actions might have started selflessly, but she *had* ensured her own self-preservation in the process. Sigrid turned from him. She bit her lip, frustrated by his lack of understanding. She ran her hands through her hair, sat up at the edge of the bed, and gathered the comforter around her.

"I am sure you have done things you are not proud of, Sam," Sigrid replied. "I have seen the way you handle your knife. How many lives have you taken? How many deserved it? What makes you so *just*, because you are American?"

"I told you," Sam corrected. "I'm not American."

"No, you're just their *tool*. There is blood on your hands, Sam. You just think yours is warranted."

Sam didn't continue to prod her. She was right. He'd only been running errands for the burned man because he in turn had guaranteed Sam his own cradle of comfort. The problem was inactivity led to restlessness. Sam had been running for far too long before then, and now he'd become accustomed once again to the thrill of the work. Sam had a taste for the wicked, the rush of adrenaline, and the challenge of the stealthy behavior he was so accustomed to.

"Do you want to know what happens, Sam? Do you want to know what happens if we don't act now?" Sigrid asked in a subdued tone. She didn't even turn to look at him. Instead, her face remained fixed on the window peeking out into the dark street beyond. He pulled on the cigarette once more, intrigued. "I escape with your aid, I find myself in comfort on the other side of the ocean, and the machine steamrolls across Europe. When the troops, your troops, descend upon Europe, they aren't met with the rifles of their enemies, but with the barrel of the weapon. It will make short work of them, I assure you." The cigarette lingered in Sam's mouth as he listened in fascination. "I already know you are going to ensure that I reach my destination, because you are a man of integrity. But before you tell me that I have not committed a selfless act, ask yourself whether the same can be said for you? If so"—she turned to him, and her eyes filled with an accusatory disdain—"you will prove it."

18

———

Sigrid was choking, gasping for air in a desperate struggle. At first, she questioned if what she was experiencing was a dream—a visualization of the suffocation she'd felt since she'd turned—but when she saw the face of the man hovering above her, she knew it was anything but. Sam's hand was cupped over her mouth, and for a moment she suspected he was attempting to *kill* her. She quickly realized the grip on her mouth was not forceful. He pressed his finger lightly to his lips to keep her quiet. She nodded in understanding, and he removed his hand from her mouth. Sam waved Sigrid forward, and she leapt from the bed she'd been fast asleep in only moments earlier then followed him to the window.

A figure hustled down the street, shrouded by the cool dawn light and providing no details other than that of a torso—then another followed. The barrels of two automatic weapons peeked through the vine-covered gates at the front of the property. Two men climbed the fence, then vaulted into the walled-off garden area before taking cover against the building.

Sam pulled her away from the window, directed her into his bedroom, and put his pants on. He drew out the pistol from his small bedside table, checked the chamber, and made sure the gun was ready to fire. He tucked it loosely behind his belt.

"Get dressed," Sam said hastily. He peered out the bedroom window, and two more soldiers had penetrated the rear of the property—they were surrounded. Sigrid sprinted to her room and gathered a pair of slacks and a blouse. Low rumblings of the communicating men outside could be heard on all sides. They were cornered.

"*Wermacht?*" Sam asked.

"Yes," Sigrid replied. "Perhaps part of the reinforcements." Sigrid's demeanor grew wary.

"Do you recognize any of them?"

"No," Sigrid replied.

Sam's attention remained fixated on the doorway. "Where are the exits?"

"One at the front, and one in the rear," Sigrid replied.

Sam contemplated the answer, and before he had another moment to think, a knock came pounding on the front door. It was not the knock of a solicitor, but the demand of enforcers. Several seconds passed before the pounding came again, and this time it was stronger. Sigrid stood a few feet back from the window and waited with anticipation. No one had seen them yet.

"Answer the door," Sam commanded. Sigrid nodded timidly. He followed closely behind her. "Play it normal. If they know, *they know.*"

A tremor provoked by the comment shook Sigrid's

torso. She answered the door, and waiting there was a soldier she did not recognize. On his breast was a tag bearing the name Schwarz.

"Sigrid Lang?" the soldier asked, half-question, half-statement.

"*Hallo,*" Sigrid replied, wiping the sleep from the corners of her eyes. Her cheeks were still puffy and swollen, and the sell wasn't half-bad. Sam lingered in shadow at the top of the staircase listening intently. His hand rested on the grip of the pistol tucked against his back.

"*Gruppenführer Schwarz,*" the soldier stated with a tilt of his head. "*Es hat sich eine sehr gefährliche Situation entwickelt.*"

Sigrid feigned ignorance, her brow frowning in concern. "*Situation?*"

"*Darf ich reinkommen?*"

"*Ja,*" Sigrid replied, taking note of the glowering soldiers lingering behind him. Each man's face was stoic, and Sigrid didn't need any more evidence that this meeting had *nothing* to do with her protection. He gave them a wave, signaling they should stand guard, and entered beside her. Sigrid began up the stairs. "*Bitte komm rein.*"

Schwarz rested his hand loosely on his pistol holster. "*Ist noch jemand zu Hause?*" The question made Sigrid uneasy. She fumbled for the words, unsure of whether or not to reveal her company. Sam swooped in without hesitation, entering the room and addressing Schwarz while wiping what was now wet, unruly hair with a cloth towel. "*Guten Morgen, Offizier. Es gibt ein Problem?*"

Schwarz sized Sam up immediately. He was particularly interested in Sam's military fatigue bottoms. His hand remained fixed to his firearm. *"Dein Ehemann?"*

"Demnächst," Sam replied with a smile. He continued to wipe his body with the towel, wrapping it under his armpits and then running it along the back of his neck.

"Seltsam," Schwarz replied with an inquisitive look on his face. *"Herr Eichler hat deutlich gemacht, dass Sie Single sind."* Sam ceased his drying. His eyes remained locked with Schwarz's. No one moved a muscle, until Schwarz drew his sidearm and pointed it at Sam. *"Sitzen."* Sam took the order and slumped into the armchair behind him. Schwarz redirected the pistol to Sigrid, waving it and her over to the armchair flanking Sam's. She obeyed, and now he had the upper hand.

He let out an ear-piercing whistle, and the other two men who'd been stationed in front funneled into the house and up the stairs. Without removing his eyes from either Sam or Sigrid, he said to the men, *"Alles durchsuchen."* Both of the soldiers moved hastily throughout the home, one ransacking the kitchen with a hurricane of clatter and bangs and the other flinging books from the shelf indiscriminately.

"Now," Schwarz said, guiding the gun back and forth between the two as he addressed them with clunky English, "My English is not so good, ya? You and your friend here speak good, I think, because now that we know you were speaking to the British, that means he is either one of them, or maybe, he is American?" Sigrid swallowed a dry, painful gulp, but Sam showed no sign of fear. "Whatever it may be, I will speak in his tongue since I want you both to understand me clearly."

One of the soldiers, dissatisfied with the absence of

any results in the kitchen, moved for the staircase leading to the third floor. Schwarz said, "We will turn the house upside down, as Herr Eichler instructed, but we already know that you are the one who has compromised information, so I think it is a waste of time. I don't expect to find anything of value except the stolen items that your friend here is parading. Regardless, you will both be coming with us to see him."

Sigrid trembled. *"Es ist alles ein Missverständnis."*

"It is *not* a misunderstanding," Schwarz replied. He smiled, confident in his understanding of the situation. "Do you know that I am the one who captured your friends, the SOE men in Pforzheim? Yes, I was the one who gave the order that they should *hang*. Of course, Herr Eichler thought this was a grotesque demonstration, but I disagreed. Hanging was a fitting punishment for the crime. Both of *you* should be so lucky to know that it is he who will deliver your sentence, because if it was up to me, I would recommend far worse than he likely plans to." Schwarz turned to Sam. "I suspected they were not the only enemies lurking about, and it seems I was correct."

Above, the dislodging of furniture and clunking sounds of Sigrid's belongings scattering about the floor grew louder. The frequent crashes suggested there was no respect in their search. All of the work she had done repairing the watches and intricate jewelry had been dismantled and destroyed without reservation.

"Or," Sam said, and Schwarz directed the pistol's barrel to his chest. "You could turn around, say you found nothing of value, and leave with your life." Schwarz smiled in satisfaction. Sigrid was appalled by

Sam's gall. She'd suspected he was crazy, but what hope did they have of escaping here?

Schwarz chuckled. "I expected nothing less than bravery from *you*. You have successfully penetrated the country—creeping around like your British allies in plain sight—how, I don't know, and I don't really care. Eichler may, these types of details are more concerning to a man like him, as well as those he reports to. I've only been charged with bringing both of you in, so that is what I will do."

"Five men total?" Sam asked. Before Schwarz could answer, he responded to his own question. "Two above, two I saw in the rear, and *you*."

"That is four more men I have than you do, and I think we would agree that is four *too many*."

"I've dealt with worse," Sam replied coyly. More crashes emanated from the third floor, and Sigrid grew more frustrated by the act than with the man pointing the gun in her face. "Do me a favor and instruct your men upstairs to leave the lady's belongings alone. There's nothing here for you to see."

"For a man with a gun in his face, you sure do have particular requests," Schwarz said. "I might make one suggestion, and that is that you maintain silence until it is time to leave. I have a very light trigger finger, and I've been known to accidentally fire when nervous—a bad habit, I admit."

Sam smirked. "Funny. I have the same problem."

A loud crack interrupted the silence. Sigrid thought Schwarz had fired, but Sam remained still and unwavering as he sat calmly in the seat. A small rose-colored stain began to grow in Schwarz's chest, butterflying at first, and then leaking to the front of his chest. Schwarz, unaware of *what* exactly had just happened, looked down at his uniform. When it registered, and his panicked face locked on to Sam's, two more shots followed, and he slumped backwards and collapsed on to a small coffee table that shattered under his weight.

Sigrid eyed Sam once more and realized a small wisp of smoke was rising up from the towel that had been resting on his lap. He removed his hand from under it, flung the towel from his waist, and leapt from the chair with the gun he'd used to silence Schwarz gripped in his hand. The other two soldiers bounded down the steps from the second floor, each brandishing rifles.

"Move!" Sam barked, and Sigrid dove from the chair and under the staircase below the two men. A shattering of glass followed from the floor below, and then a barrage of bullets peppered the living room. The first soldier hustled sloppily in, and Sam fired three shots while tracking him. The first two missed, spraying sheetrock and dust into the room. He still hadn't gotten used to the mechanics of the O and W 40. A quick adjustment fixed Sam's inaccuracy. The third shot connected with the soldier and sent him tumbling face first into the carpet.

Sam let two more bullets loose when the second soldier showed, but *he* was wise enough to hold steady on the staircase and use the wall to his advantage. He returned a barrage, and Sam fired the gun once more—but all he got was a dry, disappointing click.

The man drew the gun at Sigrid, and Sam stood abruptly and threw the firearm directly at the aiming soldier's face. The weapon made direct contact. The hard edge of the barrel hit the soldier's nose, instantly cracking the bridge with a stomach-churning crunch.

Disoriented, the gun fell from his hands, and Sigrid took the opportunity to dash out of her cover and rush him.

She sprinted forward, delivered a punishing fist to the nose—the kind that would make a man see nothing but his own tears—and kicked his lower leg to add one more cracked bone to the mix. He fell to his knees with the wail of an injured toddler, and she scooped his gun up from the floor. He raised his hands in submission when the barrel met his face, but she flipped it around and thrust the butt of the rifle directly into his brow to subdue him.

Sam nodded to Sigrid with approval. He'd seen her in action himself before, but he was reminded of her resourcefulness, and he was impressed all over again. Bullets sprayed between the two, and Sam dove toward the staircase leading above. Sigrid returned fire, but the wild pattern of the bullets suggested she was not as skilled with a gun as she was with her body. None of the rounds struck either of the men, both of whom had retreated behind the wall.

"Come on!" Sigrid snarled, and forced Sam up to the third floor. Another attack followed, narrowly missing both of them. The boots of their enemies moved chaotically across the second floor amidst muffled yells. Sam darted for the guest bedroom, and Sigrid followed. A bullet tore across the room, ripping through Sam's arm and taking a nice thick chunk of skin with it before it struck the wall in front of him. She bolted the door while Sam checked his clothing for extra ammunition.

There was no time—bullets flickered through the door, opening up exit holes through the shattered wood and nearly striking Sam once more. He assessed the wound briefly, and was satisfied that it wouldn't need attention just yet. Sigrid backed against the wall as Sam hit the ground. In front of his nose was the dagger he'd arrived with. He gripped it in his hand, crawled across the floor back toward the door, and the firing stopped briefly. The soft clicks of reloading sounded from behind the door, and Sam braced himself next to the hinges. He pressed his fingers to his lips once more to signal silence and tucked himself against the wall. The door burst open.

"Zeige mir deine Hände!" the soldier yelled. Sigrid did so, raising both arms to display her lack of weapon, and the first man hustled in with his gun drawn in one hand and the other hand outstretched to apprehend her.

Sam's knife penetrated the apprehending soldier's temple with a wet *thunk*. The man stopped, his eyes wide and bulging with confusion, and he gurgled for a moment as Sam held firm. Sam's forearm bulged, the muscles taught. Blood leaked down his arm and glistened against the tight skin.

No one ever explains how much force it really requires to drive a knife through the sturdy parts of a human body—especially to the hilt. Most men jab loosely and strike bone before doing any real damage. Sam's cold, callous eyes met Sigrid's, and she knew Sam was as dangerous as she'd suspected. There was not a moment of hesitation or unsureness in his thrust. Sam pulled the knife swiftly with a *squish*, and blood spewed from the hole he'd created. It shot out in spurts, soaking the wood floor beneath his feet. The soldier's limp body collapsed clumsily into a puddle of his own blood.

The house was quiet. The gunfire had ceased, as had any movement, so now it was just her and Sam, and one of *them*. Sigrid surveyed the stairs, holding her breath momentarily to listen for a reveal. All that returned was the soft ticking of the myriad of clocks from the room nearby. *Tick, tick, tick.*

The sound was nerve wracking, like a time-bomb counting down to an explosive eruption when either he found them, or they found him. Though there were two of them, their enemy still had an automatic weapon. Sam had managed just fine with the blade; the first had been easy. Stopping the other man would take more skill. Sam weighed the window option—they were two floors up. *He* could probably manage the fall, but could she? Sam pointed to a small clock on the bedside table. Sigrid nodded with understanding, clutched the clock, and tossed it into the silent hall.

The clock was struck with a series of bullets, exploding into a shower of tin and gears before it even hit the ground. No good—they were trapped. They had to make a move. If the soldier rushed the room, they might not be able to fight back. Sigrid grabbed a vase from the table where she'd found the clock, then threw that as well. The man had the same itchy trigger finger Schwarz had mentioned, and another flurry of bullets pattered against the wall beside the vase.

"*Scheisse,*" Sam heard the man hiss with a low whisper. The clacking of a change of magazine gave Sam all the signal he needed to make his move, and he snaked around the corner with his dagger drawn. The soldier jammed his ammunition in and raised the gun to take aim, but Sam grabbed the barrel with his free hand, guiding it away from his own body, and sent it forcefully into the man's head. The shot rang out from the pulled trigger, sending a bullet penetrating the ceiling above their heads.

Sam plunged the knife into the man's chest, and found himself lucky the tip had cleared the rib bones and penetrated the muscular tissue. The man choked for a moment, panic filling his eyes as his death approached, and Sam pulled the knife forcefully from his ribs. He flicked the knife fancifully and redirected it to stand straight up from his grip. The next attack came like an uppercut, and the blade went directly under the man's chin and through the bottom of his mouth. Sam removed the blade, grabbed the gun as the soldier's grip loosened, and watched as his prey cupped his jaw. Blood squeezed through the gaps between his fingers.

Sam wiped the blade against the man's pants, then turned to find Sigrid watching in horror. She'd been watching someone *different*, someone barbaric and vicious. She hadn't spent the night with a man, but a *weapon*—a living killing machine of organs, blood, and tissue, something that found it easy to steal the life of a man with no remorse. Her knees buckled, a tremor of queasiness starting from her stomach and snaking through all of her limbs, and then she vomited.

19

———

Sam held Sigrid's hair in a bunched bun at the back of her head while she dry-heaved. Once she'd expelled her stomach's contents, she waved Sam off with a shaky hand and lifted her head from the toilet. The tears streaming down her cheeks carried with them smudged black trails where her eye makeup had hitched a ride. Her face was pale and gaunt. Sam presented her with a glass of water to prevent further retching.

Sam placed a hand softly on her back. "I'm fine," she said abruptly, and swatted at his hand.

"Fooled me," Sam said, unconvinced.

He reached a hand forward, and she took it as she climbed from her knees and fixed her disheveled blouse. She wiped the corners of her mouth with the back her hand, then balled her fists and rubbed her eyes. She took a flimsy, ragged breath in through her nostrils, then exhaled as she looked at her complexion in the mirror. She looked like death, but standing behind her in the reflection was the living embodiment of it.

"I suppose you think less of me now," Sigrid said with a whimper.

"Far from it," Sam replied. "Was that the first time you've seen the life leave a man's face?"

Sigrid nodded shamefully.

"Everyone loses it," Sam said, gesturing to the toilet. "Present company included." She turned from the mirror, her puffed and swollen eyes flittering at his. "It was them or us, alright?" Sigrid agreed with the shake of her chin. Sam clutched her shoulders and said once more with conviction. "Them, or *us*."

Sam released her, then lit a cigarette. "Now listen," he said before a smooth inhalation of the smoke, "We've got a limited amount of time. We made a lot of noise. Seeing as we've just ruined their plans, we've got to make something out of this. It's no use killing a man if there's nothing to gain from it—that's just *murder*. As it is, you're going to leave this place behind, and it's unlikely you'll ever see it again, so I want you to put it out of your mind and concentrate. When you see the other side of all this, you'll forget it soon enough." Sam opened the door, then said, "Keep your eyes up."

Sam walked into the hallway, side-stepping the body that had fallen beside the door. Sigrid actively avoided looking at the corpse, but there was a light patter under her steps where blood had gathered. She followed Sam, who'd now stepped down the stairs, and a morbid curiosity got the best of her. The first man Sam had sunk his knife into had fallen at the doorway to the bedroom. He lay on the floor, his lifeless eyes large and pained, and Sigrid locked in on his face. She shuddered, overwhelmed by the complexion and its lack of color, and worse was that he seemed to be looking right *at* her.

She quickly averted her eyes, then continued down the stairs.

The lone soldier Sigrid had hit in the face with the butt of his own rifle sat unconscious on the living room chair. He was still breathing, and Sigrid felt relieved that she hadn't killed him. The deceased in the room had died by Sam's hand, not her own. Sam pointed to the man, then said to Sigrid, "Translate."

Sam slapped him in the face with the back of his hand, but the man didn't respond. With a sigh of frustration, he cranked his arm back, then swept it across the man's face with more follow-through, and the man snapped back into consciousness. He went through a range of emotions with lightning-like speed; first he was disoriented and groggy, then confused, and finally, when he saw Sigrid and Sam hovering over him, terrified.

"Nein, nein, nein," the soldier whimpered, flailing in the chair with panic. His voice cracked with a pre-pubescent squeal. He was just a *boy*. Sigrid frowned. She hoped Sam had better plans in store for this child than cutting his throat. Everything about his demeanor signified that he was in over his head—a kid sent to do a man's job and unprepared to deal with the heavy lifting it required.

Sam asked the soldier, "English?"

He replied, *"Ein kleines bisschen."*

"Tell him he's alright," Sam said to Sigrid.

Sigrid's face twisted with confusion. She said to Sam, "You speak German."

He turned to her, looking impatient. "That's right, I do, but I want to keep him on his toes, and he'll be more apt to start talking if he doesn't understand *every-*

thing you and I are discussing. That'll keep him in suspense." Sigrid understood.

"Es wird in Ordnung sein," she said to the man. She reached for a small drawer beside her and pulled a handkerchief from it. She unfolded it, handed it to him, and he pressed it to his bloodied nose. His shoulders fell and relaxed slightly with the gesture, but tears had gathered at the corners of his eyes. *"Dieser Mann wird dir Fragen stellen. Wenn du überleben willst, gib ihm wahrheitsgemäße Antworten."* The kid nodded sheepishly. Sigrid turned to Sam. "He will be truthful."

"Good," Sam replied as he grabbed one of the handkerchiefs and tended to his own wound. "Who sent him?"

"Wer hat dich geschickt?" Sigrid asked him.

"Herr Eichler," the kid replied. His eyes fluctuated nervously between Sam and Sigrid. He removed the cloth from his nose to speak more clearly. *"Von Flussrand."* His delivery was feeble and soft, and each word hummed nasally from his mashed face.

Sigrid opened her mouth to translate, but Sam stopped her by holding a hand out. "I got it. Ask him why."

"Warum?" Sigrid asked.

The kid displayed confusion with the question. *"Dich zu finden."* The hairs rose straight in unison wherever they were present on Sigrid's skin. She'd known all along. She'd known the second she'd heard the knock at the door, but the confirmation of her suspicion made her all the more fearful. *"Der Verräter."*

Sam noticed Sigrid's trepidation. "We already knew that," Sam replied. "Ask him if Eichler mentioned me."

"Und er?" Sigrid said, jutting her chin toward Sam

beside her. The kid shook his head from side to side before pressing the bloodied rag to his nose once more.

"Good," Sam replied. "Then all isn't lost." He fixed his callous, piercing eyes on the soldier, then his brow furrowed. Sam inhaled from the cigarette, then said, "Now I want to know about the security where the tank is. What's it like? How many men? Where are they stationed? Is there a permitter fence? What's the best way in—"

"Hold on," Sigrid warned. "One thing at a time." She recognized the boy's increasing edginess with every question asked, and Sigrid decided to slip into the "good cop" role before Sam could inundate him any further. She turned to him and spoke softly, *"Erzählen Sie uns von Flussrand."*

The boy gulped, contemplated the question for a moment, then removed the reddened cloth from his nose and licked his lips. *"Es gibt viele Soldaten. Die Sicherheit hat sich seit der Gefangennahme der Spione in Pforzheim deutlich erhöht."*

He spoke rapidly, plowing through details without hesitation, and Sigrid translated in between sentences for Sam. "He says there are many soldiers." The soldier slowed up a bit while she reiterated the information. "Security has been increased significantly since the spies were captured in Pforzheim. His team was stationed in the town until Eichler asked for Schwarz, his group leader." Sigrid motioned to the dead man on the floor that Sam had shot first. The kid starting speaking again, this time with warning in his tone, and Sigrid followed along. "Many guard the perimeter, mostly on foot, and they're heavily armed. There are checkpoints after the long road the vehicles travel on, and each has men standing guard."

Sam sat on the details for a moment while nursing his smoke. He addressed the kid directly this time. "How do we get in?"

The boy, who'd been speaking with Sigrid exclusively, understood Sam's question loud and clear, and responded with a sloppily pronounced, "Impossible."

"That's not good enough," Sam said, pointing the cigarette's cherry at his face.

"Es muss einen Weg geben," Sigrid pleaded with the kid.

He scoffed, *"Zu Fuß kommt man dort nie rein."*

Sigrid sighed with frustration and looked to Sam. "He says you will never get in on foot."

"That's alright," Sam replied to her. "He didn't come here on foot, correct?"

Sigrid asked the soldier if he'd arrived in a vehicle, and then he pointed out to the street before saying, *"Zwei."*

"Good," Sam said. "Then we'll get in on wheels." The young man's attention shifted nervously between Sigrid and Sam while awaiting the next question. "Ask him what his name is."

Sigrid questioned him, and he replied with, *"Köhler. Rolf Köhler."*

Next, she asked, *"Woher kommst du, Rolf?"*

He pressed his hand to his nose, massaging the bony bridge before wincing. *"München."*

"Tell him *you're* from Munich," Sam said.

Sigrid eyes him curiously. "But I'm not."

Sam pointed toward him with the smoldering cigarette. "He doesn't know that."

"*Ich komme aus München,*" Sigrid said with a warm smile.

"Now ask him where his family lives," Sam demanded. Sigrid showed reservation.

"*Wo in München?*" Sigrid continued.

"*Schwabing,*" he replied nervously.

"*Schwabing,*" Sam repeated with a sneer. The soldier shifted in his seat, almost as if distancing himself slightly from Sam. "*Rolf Kohler aus Schwabing,*" Sam said with a declarative growl. He maintained the intense glower with Rolf, then said to Sigrid, "Tell him that you now know both his origin and his family name, and that if he doesn't help me, you will go there and make sure they suffer because of his lack of help."

"Sam," Sigrid pleaded.

"Tell him," Sam said, and now the ire was focused on Sigrid.

Sigrid addressed Rolf, recomposing herself with a stiffening of her spine. "*Dieser Mann möchte, dass Ihre Hilfe nach Flussrand kommt. Wenn du ihm nicht hilfst...*" Sigrid paused briefly before finishing. She looked to Sam, and he encouraged her to continue with a wave of his cigarette. She turned once more to Rolfe. "*Ich werde deine Familie finden.*" A shiver rippled through Rolf's torso.

Sam exhaled the smoke toward him and maintained the warning-like stare. He mimed the slicing of his own throat with an imaginary knife, then asked, "Understand?" Rolf nodded squeamishly. "Good. *Willst du eine Zigarette?*" Rolf nodded yet again. Sam dug into his tin —he had only one cigarette left. More concerned with the mission at hand, he parted with it, and placed it in

Rolf's mouth. The cigarette trembled between his lips while Sam lit it for him.

"He's very scared," Sigrid said to Sam.

"Good," Sam replied. "A little fear will be good for him. Now he'll do what we need him to."

"I'm not comfortable enforcing that type of threat," Sigrid replied.

Sam grabbed her by the arm, said "Sit" sternly to Rolf, then redirected her toward the kitchen. "You're not," Sam assured her. "Who do you think I am? I'm not a monster. We just want him to *think* that. You're going to the pickup point, and *I'm* going to Flussrand."

"I'm going with you," Sigrid yelled, then reduced her tone to a whisper before saying, "You've lost your mind. You'll never get in without me."

"And you've been compromised," Sam replied. "Better without you than with you. I'll get in there."

"That's your plan?" Sigrid asked.

"No," Sam argued. "That was *your* plan. My plan was always to come here to get you out. You'll get your wish, *and* I'll make sure you get out safe."

"You'll never make it out alive."

"Don't have to," Sam said.

"Don't go."

"Then we both leave," Sam challenged. "But then the weapon stands. If we both go, I risk losing you. If I go, you still get where you need to go. Whether or not I make it out, I accomplish the mission."

"No!" Sigrid hissed.

Sam sighed with consternation. "Listen, you made a deal. You want to do the right thing, and you did it. Now you've got to reap what you've sewn. What will they do with the plans if the weapon gets a chance to take aim? Make wallpaper? Sigrid, you've got what you wanted. Now I need you to get out of my way so I can finish this."

"This wasn't the plan," she said somberly.

"Plans change, Sigrid," Sam said. "You're right, but I can't risk failing on both fronts." He directed an extended, stiff finger toward the window and pointed indiscriminately toward the world outside. "That thing rolls out of Flussrand and your nightmare comes true—there, here, *everywhere*. You've still got value if you get to America. Give them everything you can—details, maps, names. They'll reward you with safety. I know."

"And how do you plan to get out?" Sigrid cried. "Even if you do get out, where will you go?"

"That's what I'm good at," Sam replied with a reassuring smirk.

Sigrid deflated. She'd caught feelings—strong ones—for the ferocious spy who'd put her life back on some sort of semblance of rails, yet now he was marching into certain death with only a dagger. She wished she'd never stolen the plans in the first place. Let *Erdschlag* point its barrel at London—that was their problem; *C'est la vie*, or whatever the French said.

Her newfound lack of empathy sent chills through Sigrid's body. Where were the French now? Trampled by the Führer and filling Nazi steins, that's where. How did Sam do it? How did he turn off that part of himself that only left the dangerous pragmatist active? The minimal amount of time she'd spent with him had been a whirlwind of intense emotion—fear, lust, pain, death—all of which only amplified the other.

Sigrid grabbed his cheeks with firm hands and kissed him once more. The first kiss they'd shared was out of fear, the second, necessity, the third, intimacy, and this one—the final they might share—was goodbye. The kiss was like a dose of a powerful drug. She pulled him in tightly, pressing her body against his, and for one final moment she felt safe in his grip.

She released her lips from his, her eyes fixed intensely on the callous blue spheres glaring back at her. She held firm there for a moment, taking one last glance at the stoic face, and kept her hands still clasped to the firm jaw bones. Her heart pounded against her chest with the vigor of a base drum. Sam looked to the soft hands at his cheeks. He kissed her once more on the forehead with a soft touch of his lips.

"Hallo?" a weak voice called out for the other room. "Hallo?" The moaning of the battle-damaged Rolf broke the tension, and both parties chuckled in response.

They entered into the room and surveyed Rolf. Then, Sam said, "Up," while raising a hand. Rolf rose from the chair and waited for his next instruction. Sam grabbed Rolf by the collar forcefully, threw him forward, and then said, "Gehen."

Sam ushered him up the stairs, past the bedroom containing his dead comrades, and instructed him to sit and wait in the guest room.

"What if he tries to escape?" Sigrid asked.

"He won't," Sam said. "Because he knows we'll find his family." Sam looked to Rolf, then said, "Family—München, *richtig?*" Rolf nodded nervously. "See?" Sam asked Sigrid. "He's not going anywhere. But just in case..." Sam trailed off, grabbed a chair from the room, slammed the door behind him, and propped the chair against the handle. "That's better. Now, go get yourself ready. We're running out of time. Whatever you need to take with you, get it now. You're never coming back." Sigrid let the words sink in. Her eyes wandered around the house for a brief moment, memories of her life flooded in like a levee of history had broken, then strode off to her room.

Sam pulled every item of use he could from the two dead soldiers upstairs. Both of the soldiers had been carrying pistols, though the models differed from the O and W 40 he had been supplied. These weapons were new, and they had Nazi insignias emblazoned on each. Sam took the spare ammunition, leaving behind the rifles for fear they would be too cumbersome to carry on his mission, then searched each of their pockets.

Sam harbored no uneasy feelings about rifling through the property of dead men. Their goods were of no use to them any longer, though Sam had developed a habit of never looking into their lifeless eyes as he did so. The eyes of a dead man can haunt his killer, and Sam's first kill, which had happened a lifetime ago, did plague him for quite some time. Sam never took personal items, though. If the man's body bore jewelry that had been personalized, or valuables other than those that were military-issued, Sam left them where he found them. The uniform he'd entered into Germany with was not the intimate property of the man it had belonged to —it was a replaceable skin any man could don.

Cigarettes, on the other hand, were fair game, so when he felt the tin in the other soldier's breast pocket, Sam's mouth salivated. He opened the tin, and took a deep, long smell of the fresh tobacco. He pulled one from the group, ignited it with the lighter he found beside the tin, and then examined the lighter itself. The initials J.S. had been etched into the side below the *swastika* that rose slightly from the brass. Sam eyed the patch on the soldier's tunic. Sewn into the patch was the name 'Schmidt.' Sam removed the cigarettes from the tin, placed the lighter back in the man's pocket, and patted the pocket with his palm twice before saying, "Danke."

He inhaled on the cigarette for a moment, let the smoke linger in his mouth, and thought about just how the hell he was going to get Sigrid back to safety. Sneaking in wouldn't be easy for her. He stared down at the soldier's uniform as he smoked, and then the idea came to him.

20

Sam stripped the boots from Schwarz's body. Without warning, he tossed a boot to Sigrid. She caught it, surprise stretched across her face in the form of raised eyebrows. He pulled the other from Schwarz's body, then tossed that one to her as well.

"What am I supposed to do with these?" she asked, turning the boot over in her hands.

"You put them on, *Gruppenführer*," Sam replied. Sigrid's eyes nearly crossed in confusion.

He looked at her head while stripping Schwarz of his uniform. "You're going to need to do something about that hair, though. Can you put in a bun or something?"

"I can," Sigrid replied.

Sam grabbed one of the caps he'd procured from the dead soldier off the small table. He handed it to Sigrid. "Get it all under this. Hopefully you won't run into any trouble, but it's unlikely they'd question you if you can talk your way around it."

"I have credentials from Flussrand," Sigrid said.

"Good. Let's hope those haven't been compromised just yet. Tell them you're checking on the shipment from Ogden and Walde."

"The gun manufacturers?" Sigrid asked. "The Americans?"

"It's a long story," Sam replied. "You'll just have to trust me. Do you have a map?" Sigrid nodded, and then rummaged through the piles of books the soldiers had scattered around the floor. She found what she was looking for: a large atlas of the greater *Schwarzwald* area —and spread it across the dining room table. She flipped through the large pages until finally stopping on a geographical layout of Pforzheim, which included the area Flussrand occupied.

Sam leaned into the map, his eyes almost pressed against it as he traced the details with his forefinger, then stopped and pointed. "Here." He tapped it for a moment before looking up at Sigrid. "This is a depot—a launch point for weapons shipments."

"Because it's close to the rail line," Sigrid added. "And France."

"I suppose so," Sam replied. "Once you're in, you're going to want to find a shipping container—a very *specific* container. It's going to have the letters "O and W" printed on the side. It's headed back to America without any issues—I *promise*. You'll know when you've found it, because you're not going to have any problems getting it open. It's scheduled to go back out tonight. I was operating in a window of roughly forty-eight hours. *Be there.*"

"And then what?" Sigrid asked.

"They'll truck it across Switzerland, then Italy," Sam said. "Then you're going to wind up on a freighter. Do not, and I can't stress this enough, make anyone aware of your presence in that crate until you hear the blow of a horn and the waves under your feet."

"Well, you'll be there, Sam, *won't you?*" Sigrid said reassuringly. Though she exuded a false confidence, it was anything but—an unconvincing statement more so than a question. "So all of these details won't really matter because you'll see that everything works out just fine."

"That a girl," Sam said. "But just in case, you'll know you're in good company when you run into the burned man."

"The who?"

"You'll know him when you see him," Sam assured her. "He's…" Sam trailed off for a moment. "Well he's got a real unique look. You tell him everything. You tell him about Flussrand and the plans, about the Brits, and what I'm going to do. Give him as many details as you can. You can trust him. If anything does happen to me, well, he's my only hope. He already knows about you. He knows you made contact with the SOE guys and what you gave them. You'll be in good standing, as far as he's concerned. They may put you through the ringer, you know, considering you're with *them*. But I know you'll do okay. The more you give them, the better off you'll be. Thankfully you speak English. That'll help."

Sam stepped over to the window that faced the street. The military trucks the group had arrived in were parked opposite Sigrid's home. "There's two trucks out there. My friend Rolf and I are going to head over to

Flussrand in one, and you'll take the other. You *can* drive, right?" Sigrid nodded. "Good. Get dressed. We can't stick around here any longer than we have to." Sam turned toward the street-facing window. Several people outside had gathered and were pointing at the home. "The longer it takes them to get back to Flussrand, the more suspicious Eichler will be. Now, where can I find that dynamite?"

Sigrid's uniform didn't look half bad. She'd used some spare clothing to bulk up in the thighs and upper torso. This gave her a thick, muscular appearance under the fatigues, hiding the soft curvature Sam had become fond of. She tied her hair up neatly under the cap. The absence of makeup suggested a soft masculine face, rather than a feminine one. It wasn't perfect, but it would have to do.

"*Gruppenführer Schwarz,*" Sigrid said to Sam while standing at attention, a devious slant forming in her eyes. Sam analyzed her presentation up and down. She'd helped him blend in, and now he'd returned the favor. He didn't need to gauge the authenticity—they had that down since they'd pulled the uniform directly from the *Gruppenführer* himself. He looked for any indication she might not be a man.

"It'll have to do," Sam said. He'd changed into the clothing of one of the soldiers himself, sourcing the pants from one of the dead men upstairs and the shirt from the other who hadn't been bloodied. He also used a needle and thread he'd found in a drawer to sew the cyanide capsule into the new sleeve's cuff. The uniforms were a mismatch of sizes; many of the corresponding sister pieces had been covered with the evidence of the death in the form of red spotting. Blood on a uniform might not be a giveaway; many wounded soldiers were often forced to don the same fatigues they might have sustained injuries in if the military was in short supply. What worried Sam was that they didn't have the injuries to support the evidence, and the stains were still fresh and rosy, rather than the rust color dried blood evolved into. "I'm going to see about Rolf."

Sigrid tended to her own housekeeping. She retrieved some jewelry, not because it consisted of any real value, but because it had been sentimental: her mother's wedding ring, a watch that had belonged to her father and some photos of her childhood. She held no regrets about leaving the rest behind. Sam had reminded her that it was all just "stuff," much of which was replaceable. It was the irreplaceable things that she should take with her, most importantly the files that highlighted much of the information going to and from the ministry.

Once she was satisfied that she had packed her pockets with everything she could carry, and had found the relevant files pertaining to the project she'd hand over to the Americans, she took one last look at the room holding her valuables. This was the place she'd spent so much time in with her father, where'd she learned valuable tactics and obtained advice, all of which had come in to play in the last several days. She also stopped in the kitchen, where she'd been regaled by tales of her mother's own life, and where she'd learned how to be a cook, and a lady, and a daughter, and perhaps, someday, a wife and mother.

She arrived downstairs to say one last goodbye to Sam, but after calling his name out several times and receiving no answer other than the echo of her own voice, she suspected he had left. She found herself at the street-facing window on the second floor. Outside, several nosy neighbors were now discussing what they'd witnessed with a patrolman. Only one jeep sat idle in the street. Sam was *gone*.

What had she expected? One last passionate good-bye? A "thank you for everything?" It seemed foolish. They had not been kids on dates. They'd behaved in a cloak-and-a-dagger-fashion, and that was all there was left. Never mind the acute romance that had presented itself in the heat of certain death—those types of things were too good to be true, and if it seemed too good to be true, it probably was.

What plagued Sigrid was the thought of knowing what Sam was up against. Walking into Flussrand, she knew from experience, was a dangerous proposition—even for someone as adept as Sam. Eichler would protect his project at all costs, and Sigrid felt more firmly than ever that she would not see him again.

If she'd learned anything from him, though, it was to resist stewing in this torment and move on. If he could, *she* could, because that was what he'd expect of her. Her way out of this conundrum she'd brought upon herself was within reach, so she grabbed the keys Sam had taken from one of the soldier's bodies and made her way to the truck outside.

———

Sam spent the better part of the trip to Flussrand with his eyes on the rearview mirror. There'd be no sight-seeing of the *Schwarzwald*—he'd seen enough, anyway.

Rolf's nervous, shifty eyes reflected back at him in the glass. One might think Sam should be watching the young man's hands, but they'd be wrong. A man didn't watch another man's hands to know his intentions—eyes gave away far more. The hands would warn you of what he was currently doing, but the eyes, the precursor to actions, would tell you what he was *going* to do.

It helped that Rolf had kept one hand on the steering wheel and the other gripped on the shifter. It would take a considerable amount of time for him to attempt anything fishy, and Sam thought it unlikely he would try anything. He was a *kid*, after all. Even if Rolf did want to cause trouble, Sam held the gun's barrel against the back of Rolf's seat. One wrong move and Sam would put two in his back and go it on his own.

They traveled outside of Karlsruhe for some time, first along the rail line that Sam had taken to get there, then outside of the small city and on to newly constructed roads that stretched into farmland that made up the better part of the countryside. Rolf's gear change signaled that they'd met rising elevation. It wasn't long until they began to climb, and the roads curved up and along switchbacks that had been carved into the thickly wooded territory. The farther up they drove, the darker it got inside the truck. The Black Forest was aptly named—the abundance of trees populating the land painted the ground in perpetual shadow, and one might be led to believe the sun never shined there at all.

Fitting that Eichler would have chosen The Whispering Oak—the place the two had first met in the bowels of New York—to conduct his shady business dealings. Their first encounter's location mimicked its Bavarian cousin in many ways. Now Sam was here for real, preparing to see the massive super-weapon he'd uncovered amidst Eichler's presentation. Sigrid had warned that the man he'd bested would be there, but if Sam was any good at his job, they'd never see each other face to face. There'd been an aura about Eichler Sam particularly disliked—a conniving, snake-like quality that suggested Eichler was not to be trusted, perhaps even by his *own* people.

If he did meet Eichler, Sam was worried he'd be recognized, and he was sure Eichler wouldn't be so keen to let him walk *this* time. Be that as it may, if Sam did encounter him, he would be sure to be the one to deliver the bullet to the project manager's head. Men like Eichler deserved the bullet, not just because they were Nazis, but because they were warmongers and profiteers. Eichler wouldn't care *whom* his super-tank trampled, as long as he was collecting the medals at the award ceremony.

"*Da ist es,*" Rolf said, pointing through the windshield. Sam jerked his gun forward, agitated that Rolf had moved his hand abruptly off the shifter. "*Flussrand.*" Soon, however, his attention turned to the gap ahead at the peak of the mountain. The gargantuan pines parted to reveal a valley-like forest below. A sea of trees stretched as far as the eye could see, covering mostly flat land. At its center, the area had been manicured to accommodate the rectangular, fortress-like structure that stood among a plot of carved-out foliage. One long dirt-covered road led straight into the place, and Rolf was heading straight toward it.

"*Du weißt was zu tun ist,*" Sam said to Rolf.

Rolf's eyes met Sam's through the mirror. A

perplexed expression crossed his face before he asked, *"Du sprichst Deutsch?"*

"I'm full of surprises," Sam replied. Sam waved the gun and told Rolf to pull over. The truck stopped, and Sam instructed Rolf to open the back hatch. Inside, a large ammunition case rested in the otherwise empty compartment. Sam and Rolf removed the weapons cached inside—a multitude of rifles, grenades, ammunition, and sidearms. Then, Sam climbed inside the rear of the truck. He collected his thoughts for a moment, formulating his sentence before he spoke so his German came out properly, then said, *"Denken Sie daran, sie ist auf dem Weg nach München. Wenn mir etwas passiert…"* Sam trailed off and let Rolf fill in the blanks. The soldier understood the threat.

Sam climbed into the large case and shut the lid behind him. This was the second box he'd been stuffed in over the last week, but this one had been far less roomy than the last, and it stank of gunpowder and incendiary supplies. He tucked his limbs against his chest to accommodate his body, and hoped that clearing the perimeter and getting into the stronghold wouldn't take too long. The truck started up again, and soon they were moving.

He had no way of knowing whether or not Rolf was still playing ball. The sensation of traveling on a downgrade kept him calm, sure he was traveling toward his destination, but the sound inside the aluminum prison was muffled and lacked detail. Sam reasoned that Rolf was too scared to tell the soldiers standing guard that one of the spies they sought—the saboteur who'd actually come to finish the job—was hiding in the back of his truck and was going to be delivered right inside the castle. It was a Trojan horse built entirely out of Eichler's own actions. All Sam needed to do was get inside. Once there, he'd need to grab the dynamite. Sigrid had assured him that the supply room remained unlocked.

The trip became rocky and disorienting as the truck negotiated the uneven terrain leading to Flussrand, and Sam knocked his head against the top of the case several times. The air inside was growing stale and unusable. He opened the case briefly to exchange the bad air for some fresh oxygen, but the closer they got to their destination the riskier that would be. After one particularly jarring bang, which rattled Sam violently inside the steel coffin, the truck came to a halt. They'd arrived at the first checkpoint.

A flurry of exchanged words came from outside the truck, but Sam could make out few details. He heard Rolf speak, then another man answered, then Rolf again, and then finally the truck clicked into gear and started to move. Sam breathed a sigh of relief—both metaphorically, and physically—by opening the lid one last time to gather a clean gasp of air. He took a look out of the back window briefly; the tall perimeter fence was growing more distant through the glass, and the guards closing the gate behind them suspected nothing.

They doddered along the bumpy road for another few moments, and soon hit the second checkpoint with a rumbling halt. The same process was repeated: Rolf spoke, then one of the men standing guard, then Rolf again, but this time the truck didn't move right away. Now Sam could hear the sound of steps crunching against gravel tracking around the truck—first one set, then two, then a third.

Muffled German words surrounded him, but he

remained silent. The troops had encompassed the truck, and they were examining its interior. One of the men asked a question, and soon the back hatch squealed—they'd *opened* the truck.

"Jeder Moment, den Eichler wartet, ist gefährlicher," Rolf warned. He'd said it loudly enough that even Sam could hear the statement—he was warning them there was no time to be wasted. Sam pulled out his sidearm and pressed the barrel where the lid's seam met the edge of the case. It turned out he wouldn't need it. The door closed swiftly and soon the truck popped into gear once more. He was *in*.

He braced himself against the side of the case as the truck took a wide turn, and then the truck stopped and the engine went silent. Sam lifted the lid cautiously, his eyes first peering through the small crack to gather intel about his surroundings. Confident Rolf's arrival had garnered no further attention, Sam climbed from the case and tapped on the interior metal twice with the butt of the gun. Rolf hurried around to open the door, and Sam quickly grabbed him and spun him forcefully before pressing the gun against the small of his spine. The movement forced Rolf forward with an awkward lurch.

"Autsch!" Rolf hissed.

Sam pressed the gun harder yet, then said, "Quiet." He took inventory of his surroundings. Rolf had pulled up to the rear side of the mighty structure. The forest was quiet, the sound dampened by the high-reaching trees encircling the property. Only the conversations of twittering birds met Sam's ears, and he was thankful they didn't speak English or German.

The perimeter fence was at least twenty feet tall, and

if that wasn't bad enough, it had been decorated with barbed wire that spiraled at the top. Getting in had been relatively easy—it was getting out that had him concerned. There was no way he was just going to barrel through the two front checkpoints. He supposed he could steal one of the several trucks resting inside the property, but that would be reckless, and it would take only one well-placed bullet through a windshield to stop him.

He could negotiate barbed wire. A few bad slices were manageable. Though they were a deterrent to the average Joe, anybody with a set of balls could tackle the razors if they just pushed through and took their time. He'd hopped plenty a barbed wire fence as a child, although he'd been smaller and that had made things a bit easier. Rolf could get him out too, he suspected, but he wasn't so sure he could count on him now that he'd been put within reach of Eichler.

Rolf was his best bet. Sam cursed the dead SOE men, as well as his compassionate turn in Sigrid's favor. Their capture alone had sent red flags shooting up the mast, and now it was up to Sam to do what needed doing. His slapdash entry and exit was the best he was going to do. *Damnit, Sam. How do you get yourself into these pickles?*

Sam caught sight of a wandering guard outside the perimeter fence in the corner of his eye, then grabbed Rolf and tucked himself between *Erdschlag's* home and the truck in a crouching position. "Can you be quiet?" Sam asked. Rolf nodded. Sam pulled the gun from his prisoner's spine and kept it pointed at him. The spy massaged his chin between his thumb and forefinger while surveying the property. Stroking the stubble from his growing facial hair provided a sort of comfort in his deep thought as he contemplated his next move. Normally, a cigarette would have been recruited for that job, but Sam never smoked while in the heat of infiltration. He soon found what he was looking for: the door that would lead him inside the building was within reach. *"Sie werden her warten. Verstanden?"*

"Ja," Rolf answered.

"Gut," Sam said before rising and peering through the truck's windows. Whether or not Rolf would wait for him was up for debate, but Sam had to try. "Remember, *München, ja*?" Sam reminded Rolf. The best leverage he had was the threat of violence to Rolf's family, and he was going to get as much mileage out of it as he could. Sam searched the dense forest nearby, and when he was satisfied no one was watching, he crept swiftly along the side of the building.

Once at the door, he grabbed the handle and opened it softly. He surveyed first, and found no threats in the dark hall ahead. He closed the door with a feather-like finesse behind him, gripped his side arm tightly at his side, and jogged along the concrete structure's base floor with the elegance only a man who had no desire of being caught could display.

The hall was cold and unwelcoming, a characteristic he'd come to expect with all things Deutschland. *Why should their architecture be any different than their stoic personalities?* Not a single soul was present in the cavernous stretch of grey slabs, and one lone steel door built into the wall ahead called to him. He inched toward it quietly before arriving, and knew he'd found the right place when he read the sign on the door that said *"Nachschub."*

Sam opened the door and searched for the word "*Achtung.*" The room was a workshop full of all manner of supply and tools. Industrial-grade impact guns were hanging from heavy hooks along the wall. Crates were filled with items, and he rifled through them as he tore the lids off, discovering hard hats and tubs of lubricant, as well as wrench sets and hammers. Finally, he found a crate that intrigued him: on its side a multitude of hazardous warnings in universal symbology had been labeled, such as a skull and cross bones and an exclamation mark. *That's it.*

Sam grabbed a hammer nearby, dug its teeth under the lid, and pried with all his strength. Just as he'd hit his limit, the top cracked with a creaky wooden pop, and the dry wood sang the tune of success. There, resting in the box among a soft paper bedding, were the sticks of dynamite. How many had Sigrid said it would take? Just a few, he remembered, though he grabbed eight for good measure. When it came to destroying enemy tools, there was no such thing as "too much."

He handled the dynamite with care, gently resting it inside the satchel at his side and secured it with gobs of the paper bedding. Each stick needed to be finessed, and his movements from there forward required precision and care. He was familiar enough with the fickle nature of nitroglycerin, and God forbid any of the old, unused dynamite was sweating—if it was he'd be in for a bang of his own. The cold chill whistling through the hall gave him less worry. Sam secured the lid in case anyone came snooping. One of the rules of espionage was an emphasis on covering one's tracks—he'd learned that rule the hard way before.

Sam stepped back out into the hallway, now ready to

get on with the most dangerous phase of the mission, and reoriented himself away from the exit. Ahead, a faint red light bled onto the walls in front of him. The hall stretched deep along the length of the building, and the closer he got to the end of it, the more it felt like an ominous descent into hell itself.

21

An ominous droning tunneled through Sam's ears. Each of his steps returned echoing clacks as he continued through the corridor. There was no enemy at the end of the hall, only a gradient of bleeding red light that fell off into shadow and was exchanged with the darkness stretching toward him. He unsheathed his knife once more, keeping it at the ready with the blade protruding forward. That was his preferred method of wielding it—he thought many other styles clumsy and unmanageable, and his method allowed him to switch his striking stance at will if necessary.

His heart thumped steadily at over a hundred beats a minute, the perfect zone with which to move swiftly. Ahead, the cavernous howl of emptiness signaled he was close to his target. The room beyond was gargantuan—and a room that size could only house one thing. He proceeded with a few last skip-like steps, and met the edge of the small corridor. His face was bathed in the soft, rosy light as he crept beyond the wall. His jaw responded by slowly falling in awe of the machine that lay ahead.

His feet moved autonomously as he entered the massive room, his attention fixated on the mesmerizing feat of engineering towering above him. He continued forward, secluded in the shadow cast by the tank, a wide pool of darkness formed at its base. The barrel above his head, if vertical, would rival even some of New York's skyscrapers. The treads could crush a battalion of men, maybe even a fleet of smaller, lesser tanks. The steel casing looked as impenetrable as had been described, yet it bore no markings on the front of its prototype phase. It did not yet bear the insignia of its creators.

The two floodlights present at its front end—juxtaposed with the machine's facade—gave it a sort of sinister, anthropomorphized scowl that almost seemed to taunt Sam where he stood. It looked like a fierce bull ready to charge. If someone met the monstrosity face to face, they'd suffer the judgment of its menacing glare. A series of numbers printed under the headlights was the only thing convincing Sam that it wasn't in fact *alive*.

Sam surveyed the catwalks surrounding it on all sides and ensured there were no other soldiers nearby. He was confident he was *mostly* alone in the room, but he still needed to move stealthily. Eichler had likely dedicated all of his resources to the exterior perimeter of the facility, and because of that they'd left the egg all alone in the nest. Sam hoped that all of the resistance he might meet was behind him—at least until he got the explosive in place.

Now he was circling the tank, half of him admiring its construction and the other looking for an entrance point. The ladder he had been told was at the front side of the vehicle had been retracted. He wouldn't be getting in that way. The anti-aircraft artillery that had been built into the tank was terrifying in its own way. With the defenses normally reserved for a stationary base, the tank indeed had been accurately described as more of a mobile fortress than a moving weapon.

Now that Sam was able to see the vehicle in profile, he became aware of the long, finely machined rail that was present along the top of its barrel. It ran the entire length of the machine from front to back. This, he thought, was its method of launching a rocket. The machine had been retrofitted to fire not just a high-caliber shell but also a self-propelled missile that could travel between continents. The thought made his heart race just a little bit more. What kind of world was man entering when he could destroy a city from his dining room with a simple command?

Sam used the cover of the massive treads to his advantage as he sought his entry point. He arrived at the second ladder at the rear, then a soft clacking above alerted him to the presence of a guard. The guard had been entertaining himself with a low whistle, and thankfully he was unaware of Sam's presence. The spy preferred to keep it that way. He tucked himself between two of the treads while the soldier passed. The soldier bore an automatic rifle gripped in both hands. An exchange of fire wouldn't buy Sam the time he needed to get the job done and escape.

Sam didn't mind the challenge. The best tasks were the ones that required no loud weapons. Guns were effective, yet they were anything but efficient in scenarios of sabotage. Once satisfied that he was out of earshot of the guard, he moved swiftly forward and resumed his journey to the ladder at the rear. Once again, he found no luck. In the interest of time, he quickly shuffled to the tank's rear right side. Thankfully, that ladder was accessible, and allowed Sam to climb to the machine's second tier. He climbed rapidly up the ladder. The soldier standing guard had meandered toward the front of the structure, and now Sam felt more at ease to move freely around the machine's walkways once he arrived.

The relief was short lived. Soon another man approached on the walkway above him, and Sam halted his climb mid-step. The soldier's attention was more focused than his compatriot's, and his eyes trailed along the catwalk and searched the machine's base for signs of movement. Above Sam, a steel panel functioning as a shield for the ladder provided cover, and Sam bolted with a light step up into the cylindrical hiding place. The guard paused mid-step, but Sam held firm. Once Sam heard the sounds of the man's feet progress once more, he made his move for the second tier.

The steel under his feet was firm and unwavering. Sam followed the walkway, doubling back around the tank's rear. He attempted the rear entry point there, but the ladder remained inaccessible. *Damn.* If he was going to get in, it seemed like the powers that be were going to make him work for it.

He traveled along toward the front end, keeping his body tucked tightly against the machine's side in an effort to blend in with its dark exterior. The steel under his feet dampened the sound of his steps quite well. The next ladder to the third tier was visible—and deployed. Soon he'd be out of sight. He continued gracefully, and with each step he took, he employed the finesse of a ballerina's soft touch. Just navigating the mobile fortress had been an adventure all on its own.

When he arrived, he surveyed the walkways once more. He was closer to the soldiers now, and the threat of being seen increased. The first guard he'd noticed had made his way back around to Sam, and this time he wasn't so distracted; his eyes were fixed firmly on the length of the tank. Sam rapidly searched either side of himself. Against the broad side of the tank, he was clearly visible. He had nowhere to hide, and he'd be dead in the water if they spotted him. His attention turned to the hatch for one of the secondary artillery posts, and he ducked into a crouch and moved for it. He slipped into the small hole, using the gunnery's front-facing shields for cover. He watched through the small space above the gun's barrel as the guard wandered by. Though Sigrid had told Sam the hatch would be of no use to him, if something could be utilized, Sam Abel would find it.

When Sam was confident he could maneuver again, he ascended the final ladder with cat-like efficiency. He'd be in the open permanently once on top, and there'd be nowhere else to run. He paused on the ladder, only the tip of his head rising just above the machine's top floor. Confident with his maneuver, he crept on to the platform, satisfied he'd achieved a minor victory.

At the top, the door he sought stared back at him like a majestic prize. All he could do now was hope it was open. If it was locked, he'd be a failure on his way back to America. He wasted no time, moving for the door's sturdy handle and checking his surroundings before turning it. When he was sure there were no eyes upon him, Sam opened the door. The newly machined door moaned with only the slightest resistance, and Sam's eyes widened with excitement.

Sam shut the door quietly behind him and let loose a mighty sigh of relief. The interior was a dark, quiet room with two small corridors snaking away from it. On his left were two aluminum crates larger than grown men, and Sam moved over to one out of sheer curiosity. Wondering what was inside, he opened the lid. Cushioned in a custom frame built to keep it snug and secure was one of *Erdschlag's* fearsome shells. Sam felt minuscule in its company, as if he was living in some kind of science fiction story in which he'd been shrunken down with futuristic technology. It was the stuff of imaginative literature, the tank itself a fanciful feat.

The presence of the shell made him queasy, and he shut the lid before surveying the rest of the quartermaster's room. Shelves lined each of the walls flanking him, and each contained a variety of military-grade supplies such as rifles and pistols, with protective equipment available as well. A small army of its own could be deployed from the location.

He'd seen enough. His schedule had no time for distractions, and he didn't want to be inside of the monstrosity any longer than he had to. Just being around the behemoth made him uneasy. Sam continued past the wash closet and galley on either of his sides. If he hadn't seen the armory, the tank would have given him the impression he was in a hotel for soldiers traveling abroad rather than a war machine.

At the end of the dimly lit corridor, which had only been illuminated via infrequent bulbs, he found himself at the top of an aluminum staircase. He descended and found the real glory of the tank's controls. Surrounding Sam on all sides was a myriad of flickering and blinking instruments. Panels housed a series of small lights that looked like an industrial interpretation of a Christmas holiday decoration. There were levers and sticks of all variation and even a massive periscope centered in the room. Each wall of the interior screamed of technology. Sam, though he couldn't work any the tools, was positive they all represented some means of fine-tuned purpose. The tank surely needed precise navigational, radio, and assault controls. It was all quite *grotesque*.

Sam descended the last staircase, which would lead him to the situation room. When he entered through the aluminum door, the flavor of craftsmanship changed dramatically. The interior was warm and inviting—a far cry from the offensively industrial style of the rest of the vehicle. On the back wall, a massive party flag had been painted across the broad wooden panel, and under its insignia were two mounted, decorative rapiers, forming an "x." At the center of the room was an empty wooden table with seating for eight. There was even an offensively red carpet lining the floor that gave the room an intensity that made Sam squint. There was no time to be wasted.

Sam reached into his sack, pulled out the sticks of dynamite he'd been provided, and bunched them together. He retrieved the tape in the bottom of the sack and grabbed at it with his teeth, ripping it with a grunt to obtain a suitable strip, then wrapped the dynamite together as instructed. He retrieved the pencil detonator and jammed its end as best he could into the tip of one of the dynamite sticks. He hoped that the cupric chloride would be hungry enough to eat through the wire holding back the firing pin. Chemistry was not his expertise—he'd managed to get into the fortress and that was enough. He crushed the end of the detonator, then paused briefly.

Ten minutes, Sam said softly to himself. He'd love to see the look on Eichler's face when his mechanism went up in flames, but saboteurs were rarely granted those opportunities. He'd need every second he could get to reach safety, so he wasted no time leaping to his feet. His satisfaction was short lived—the door behind him opened.

Sam felt his stomach make an attempt to exit through his throat. Barring him from the door was not a man, but a *monster*. Bathed in shadow, the titan stepped through the doorway, though he had to duck his head to accommodate his height. Once through the opening, his torso blocked the exit point completely. The light in the room painted the body brightly: the man's muscles appeared unearthly and stone-like. Massive veins curled like spaghetti under his glistening skin, each carrying small rivers of blood.

The beast hadn't neglected a single part of his body. The thighs and calves rivaled small tree trunks, and they ended at a pair of black combat boots fit for a bear. The man said nothing, but a thin smile curled around the bottom of his face as he sized Sam up and down. Juxtaposed with the hulking colossus, Sam had been rendered a *child*. Each of the man's hands looked capable of snapping even the most solid of a grown man's bones with ease. He did not wear the uniform of any of the soldiers nearby, but only a pair of plain, black fatigues.

Sam was confident in his hand-to-hand skill, and yet he'd wished he'd slung one of the rifles from the armory over his shoulder. What could have been a quick, painless fight, was now sure to turn into a test of endurance. The man extended his fingers into long, sausage-like rods. He stomped forward, and with every step he took, the room trembled under his weight. In that moment, Sam desperately hoped he'd live to see the error of the machine's only piece of flimsy construction.

The man thrust an arm forward like a battering ram, and Sam leapt back to dodge the blow. The other arm came fast, hooking across Sam's chest, and Sam parried that attempt too. To Sam's surprise, the man was not just a blunt attacking weapon, but also quite swift and spry. Each attack came with speed to rival even a prizefighter, and Sam was convinced brute force would not aid him in this fight. The beast lunged forward once more, and Sam found his back against the wooden conference table. Sam jerked back, lifting his feet and using the barrier to his advantage as he sprawled himself on to its surface, but the monstrosity brought both fists crashing down like sledgehammers, the fingers clasped together to maximize the area of attack. The table cracked and splintered under the impact. Sam tumbled toward the base of the mammoth's feet, dropping his knife in the process, and found a bulky head looking down at him as if he were an insect.

Next, the combat boot rose high, obscuring the light of the room like a planetary eclipse, but Sam rolled clear with every bit of strength he had as the boot crashed down next to his ear. The thud sounded like the drop of an anvil. Just one connection with the man's foot would send the soft tissues inside Sam's skull oozing through every orifice.

One of the collapsed table's severed legs rested beside

Sam's head. He gripped it between his fingers and sent the jagged end surging up toward the man's gut. Before the spear end reached the mighty torso, the man stopped it with the palm of his hand. The splintered wood pierced his skin, and blood leaked from the wound, but the man didn't even flinch when his thick fingers curled around the wooden leg. He pulled the sharp end from his palm with a grotesque squish, and sent the blunt end crashing forward and into Sam's face. The blow brought tears streaming from Sam's eyes, and he attempted to rise to his feet amidst the disorientation, but the man grabbed him by the thick swath of hair at the top of Sam's head and brought Sam's face to meet his own.

The monster delivered a swift punch to Sam's gut that forced a gasp for air. Sam choked for oxygen, and a panic set in that he might suffocate. That might be the more pleasant way to go—if there was one—because Sam believed the ogre might pummel him to death slowly if given the chance. Sam, recognizing his inability to win through force, targeted the man's throat and delivered a lightning-quick fist directly to his trachea. This prompted the man to drop Sam, and the gargantuan mass tumbled backwards while tripping over his own feet. Sam collapsed on to the floor, and finally caught a bit of air as he regained his composure.

How much time had he wasted? He couldn't keep this up much longer if he was going to get out of this alive. He'd still need to get clear of the blast zone, and tussling with the beast in front of him was killing his chances. Sam managed to stand up, and the man, now red-faced and enraged, steamrolled toward him like an avalanche. The next fist came quickly, and though his ribs absorbed most of the blow, Sam was rocketed backward against the back wall that bore the Nazi flag.

The leviathan trucked forward like a freight train, lifted Sam once more with a firm grip on his neck, and slammed him against the wall like a rag doll. Every bone in Sam's spine ached under the blow, and now the grizzly bear of a man wrapped both mitt-sized hands around Sam's throat. Sam felt his eyes bulge, and the sensation of choking as the man squeezed his neck with a guttural growl. Only a few more moments of this and Sam would either choke to death or suffer a crushed trachea.

Sam struggled, desperately seeking a way to break free, but the beast only pressed *harder*. Sam felt the pressure of every finger wrapped around his throat, each of them squeezing with the force of a group of anacondas suffocating their prey. He kicked his feet against the man's chest, but the monster didn't budge. Sam swung his arms, hitting the man's skull with balled fists—still nothing. Not only was the man powerful, he was nearly immune to the pain from Sam's attacks, caught in a blind rage of red sight rivaled only by the rosy color of his face.

Sam struggled once more, swinging his arms and feet in an attempt to land just *one* good attack, but he was losing steam. With every attempt to free himself, Sam found less gas in the tank. His consciousness was fading quickly. He kicked his feet once more as the man gave one more firm press on his neck, and Sam started to see stars. Luckily, Sam's hearing was unaltered, because he caught the jingling sound of metal shaking above his head—the rapiers.

Almost completely depleted of energy, Sam made a

desperate attempt to reach above his head, and he felt the handles of each of the rapiers in his hands. The monstrosity looked up, registering what Sam was doing, and his eyes grew wide with surprise. Before he could remove his hands, Sam ripped both rapiers from their hanging hooks, brought them down in front of his face, and sliced down diagonally with all the force he could muster. The swords met in the middle and crossed with a metallic scream, and the titan's neck was caught between the razor-like scissor formed by them.

His gaze, now one of utter confusion, returned back to Sam. The fingers around Sam's neck loosened, the muscles of the beast slackened, and then the blood started to flow from the wound. The fluid came cascading down the front of his massive chest like a fountain, and after a moment of wobbling on the tree trunks he called legs, the man's body crashed down to the knees, then collapsed backward under his weight.

Sam watched as the blood pooled around the dead man. He knew that a human adult housed one and a half gallons of blood in the body, but judging by the small pond forming at his feet, Sam wagered this man was holding closer to three. Even against the bold red fabric of the carpet, the blood glistened in the bright light of the room. Sam massaged his neck—which he was sure had turned purple—and allowed himself to regain his breath. As he gagged and coughed, for possibly the first time in his life, the last thing he wanted was a cigarette.

The bomb, Sam thought. *How much time have I wasted?* Without hesitation, he barreled out of the doorway and back up the steps to the tank's second floor, passing the control room once more and taking the next staircase two and three steps at a time. He arrived back in the quartermaster's room, and cursed himself for not taking a gun below. That would have made his previous fight easier. He'd dropped a considerable amount of weight by ditching the explosives, and now the priority was getting as far away from the blast zone as possible.

Sam quietly opened the door to the third tier, thrilled to be free of the tank, and stepped toward the ladder that would get him back to the ground floor. He prayed no one had heard the sounds of combat. The clatter of a hundred boots surrounded him, and he froze in his tracks. Staring back at him were the many faces of a small army of men, each of their barrels fixed directly on him. He ducked for cover immediately, and retreated behind the machine's shell loader. He'd been found, and now he was *surrounded.*

22

The haunting room's silence was interrupted by the rhythmic approach of boots. Sam followed the sounds of the steps, peeking through a small gap in the machine's construction until finally witnessing the tall figure brushing past each of his subordinates. He arrived at a small catwalk that jutted out toward the machine, raised a hand to the soldiers to signal a hold-fire, then stopped and tucked both hands behind his back. *Eichler.*

Sam's rival craned his neck, scrutinizing the nooks and crannies of the tank before calling out, *"Du bist gefangen!"* The words reverberated off of the aluminum walls, leaving distant echoes of the last syllables tapering off slowly. *"Bitte kommen Sie unbewaffnet heraus."* Eichler held for a response; Sam offered none. *"Es muss nicht chaotisch sein. Sie erhalten ein faires Verfahren, oder wenn Sie tatsächlich ein feindlicher Eindringling sind, werden Sie in ein Militärgefängnis gebracht. Ich werde Ihnen diese Höflichkeit anbieten, wenn Sie dasselbe tun würden.*" The words rang against the cave-like room once more as Eichler let Sam contemplate them.

Sam searched his surroundings. The only two ways out were the ladder in the rear—which was currently not deployed—and the one he'd utilized to get up to the third floor. Neither would do. If he tried to go down the accessible one, he'd be captured, and if he made an attempt at the rear, he'd suffer the same outcome.

"Very well," Eichler called out. "Perhaps you don't understand, so I will offer the same conditions in English." He cleared his throat, then said, "We cornered you. Please come out unarmed. It doesn't have to be messy. You will be given a fair trial, or if you are indeed a hostile invader you will be taken to a military prison. I will offer you this courtesy if you come willingly." The English was brisk and proper, as was to be expected from a man who had attempted to entice American industrialists toward his project the last time Sam had met him.

Sam looked to his pistol—it was pointless. Even the sharpest shot in the world stood no chance against the sheer number of guns drawn against him. The automatic rifles nearby wouldn't help him either. He could climb back in the tank, but hiding would be useless. They'd smoke him out, sure enough, and he'd be right back where he started, or worse, die in the blast. The best hope he had would be to negotiate, and if captured, take it from there.

Sam rose slowly, both of his hands held up in submission, and revealed only the top of his torso. He kept the better part of his body covered with the steel barrier meant to shield the door from enemy fire. If he revealed himself, perhaps he could buy himself some time. Eichler's head tilted slightly, and his interest level appeared to grow. He stepped forward cautiously, and his eyes squinted to survey Sam more clearly, then he paused mid-step when the realization set in.

"*You,*" Eichler snarled. The details of his face sharpened and became stone-like where the skeletal cheeks pressed against the skin.

"Hallo, Herr Eichler," Sam called out. "Good to see you again."

"There is a special place for people like you," Eichler growled. "One way or another, you will see it. I'm going to kindly suggest that you step down and come quietly. I don't want to have to damage my machine."

Sam made a fist and rapped his knuckles against the thick steel. "Looks pretty sturdy to me. German engineering, eh?"

"Perhaps you would prefer to die quickly," Eichler replied. "If I capture you alive, you can be sure I'll force you to talk." Eichler paused, then said to his men, "Kill him."

The bullets flew quickly, an onslaught of gunfire that pinged against every surface. The acoustics of the room amplified the sounds ten-fold, making it sound like he'd been trapped in a war zone. He ducked for cover, each bit of shrapnel ricocheting around his body and just barely missing his limbs. He tucked his feet up to his chest, minimizing the surface area his body covered as the sound of metal on metal sang around him. He surveyed the catwalk through a small gap behind his shoulder—the soldiers were on the move and descending the staircase to mount the tank. Sam wouldn't have cover much longer.

A bullet crashed against the surface near Sam's head. He cupped his ear reactively, and the impact caused a vicious ringing inside his head. With no fear of damaging the well-manufactured machine, the attack from his enemies came with extreme prejudice. Another several bullets banged across the floor at his feet, nearly ripping a series of holes right through his leg. He had to think, and *fast*. He searched frantically, his head pivoting around his surroundings with almost manic attention.

And then he saw it; the shell loader directly across from him was open and ready to receive the enormous ammunition. The barrel, which must have been hollow on its way to the end, had not been blocked by the mammoth firing pin that was currently retracted. What lay at the end of the barrel? Surely it was a long fall to the ground floor, though Sam didn't have time to consider the dangers—it was a way out. He scrambled across the tank's third floor, his body pressed low to the ground, and dove into the colossal cylindrical barrel of the tank's primary weapon.

It was dark inside, but there was only one direction Sam was concerned with: forward. A bleak light at the end of the metal tunnel promised a viable exit. Sam continued into the barrel with haste. The barrel was not wide enough to stand up straight in, though it was large enough that he could squeeze through quickly via crouching.

He moved through the barrel like a snake seeking a burrowing prey. With every step forward, the gunfire ringing behind him became muffled and distant. The rate of fire became less frequent and was soon replaced by a clamoring of boots. Each came with a tinny clanging as his pursuers rushed up the ladders and around the walkways of the machine. The light ahead became more bright, now fully reflecting the red emergency lighting around the curvature of the barrel's edge. He was getting closer, and yet he'd already felt the fatigue a wide receiver sprinting a glory-play might. How much farther would it be? All that mattered was that he was less close to the barrage of projectiles that had nearly torn through him only seconds earlier.

Had they arrived yet to his original hiding place? Had they deduced what he'd done? If he didn't reach the lip of the barrel in time, one single well-placed shot would stop him where he crouched. Perhaps if the bomb didn't work, his body would wind up in London, scraped along the barrel and forced through the hole alongside one of the tank's massive shells. He kept his feet moving; the calf muscles were screaming with every thrust forward.

And what would he find when he got to the end? He foresaw his body plummeting and hitting concrete. He could only pray there would be something there to aid his escape. As it was, he saw *nothing*.

He was close enough now to the exit that the reverberating echoes of yelling troops were closer ahead than to his rear. German syllables reverberated like ghostly wails against the thick metal. Had the enemy gathered where Sam planned to exit? It didn't matter—there was only one way out and that would have to be good enough. Perhaps the bomb would go off while he was still inside. That wouldn't be all that bad. He probably wouldn't feel much—the force of the explosion would make his death quick—and at least he would have succeeded. He subdued the thought and proceeded more quickly.

Now his thighs were crying, begging him to take a

break. The awkward position he'd contorted himself into was testing muscles he hadn't used in quite some time. Ahead he saw nothing but the reflection of the structure's interior wall. It was getting brighter; he could see the red luminance on the fabric of his fatigues. *Not much further, Sam.*

The gunfire ceased—what did that mean? They'd likely arrived on the third floor of the tank, and it wouldn't be long before the jig was up. Perhaps Eichler would send them right in behind him. Could they see his tiny silhouette against the far end of the barrel? He hoped not.

Now Sam's legs were losing steam. With every command he gave his legs to propel him forward, they argued back. He was approaching the point where the muscles would become rubbery and unusable, the stage when marathoners get clumsy and fall and athletes make mistakes. The only thing keeping him standing and pushing forward was the cool draft hitting his skin where the exit waited.

A guttural yell—the abrasive kind that only comes from an aggressive German—traveled from the far end of the barrel and met his ears. Sam paused and turned to look back over his shoulder. He saw blurry, indiscernible motion ahead. They'd figured him out. He paid no mind to the commotion that continued behind him, focusing only on the growing circular hole ahead. *Almost there.*

Every muscle in his legs thanked him for the momentary break, but he begged them for one final push. He breathed heavily and forced every bit of oxygen he took in to fill his diaphragm completely. It was a trick he utilized if ever he felt winded. The muscles were asking for more blood, and specifically more oxygen. The key to good circulation was proper breathing. As he sprinted forward, Sam wondered if surviving this ordeal might be enough to get him to kick his smoking habit.

He turned back once more to search for his enemies. They were gaining—it didn't matter. Sam stopped completely, and found himself now stalled at the barrel's circular edge. He glanced outward, and seeing where he was in relation to the second-floor catwalk, realized that the barrel had been tilted slightly upward. He'd been running on an *incline*.

There were no men ahead. Could he leap for the catwalk? Surely not. It was a good forty-foot diagonal drop, and even if he *did* make it, the gap looked like a recipe for two broken legs and perhaps a broken wrist as well. *Damn.* Sam cursed himself momentarily. *Act first, think later.* Sam's motto often got him into trouble, but was standing here, alive and able to criticize his old adage.

He edged his feet closer to the lip then surveyed what lay below. There were crates present, and though the room was unacceptably dark to be sure of their material, Sam guessed they were wooden. How many were there? There were several piled on top of each other in various spaces, some columns stacked higher than others. It was still a far fall, but he reasoned that perhaps if he landed on one and allowed himself to roll to those below it, he might just manage the fall—maybe a sprained ankle, perhaps a broken clavicle. Those he could manage.

He took one more look at the catwalk—now he was second-guessing himself. There was no time for that, and then a loud crack from his rear made sure to remind him. Several more followed from an automatic weapon, and two bullets ricocheted off the interior of the barrel, spraying sparks in his face. There was no more time to think. He had to make the leap of faith.

He positioned himself at the edge, took inventory of the boxes below, and honed in on one group of crates in particular that had formed a large—and hopefully reachable—column. Flanking it was one that had been stacked only three crates high, and next to it one more crate that might just help break the last fall. The final one would be a doozie, especially after the two initial impacts, but he had no choice. Three more bullets whizzed by his ear, and he was thankful that the mirage-like quality he'd experienced earlier was now working its magic on the pursuing men.

Now or never. Sam crouched low, lunged forward, and felt the whistle of wind howl in his ears as gravity did the rest. He bent his knees loosely, placed his hands forward, and smacked the first column of crates with a heavy crack. Had something snapped? He couldn't be sure, but he hoped with every ounce of his being it had only been the wood under his body. He channeled the momentum into a roll as planned, and then his body slammed on to the next crate down. That impact rocked his shoulder, and might have injured his clavicle as predicted. Without hesitation, he tumbled forward once more, preparing himself for the final fall—which would be double the height of the last—and landed with a dull thud onto the wooden top. The weakened crate collapsed under the impact, and he was happy to find that the final leg of his journey had been the least painful.

With no time to waste, and no moments to spare to

consider the pain he felt in nearly every limb, he clawed out from the crate and leapt forward without looking. His escape was short-lived. A grouping of men had him cornered, each with a rifle drawn to his face. He was yet again surrounded completely.

"He went that way!" Sam yelled, extending his arm and pointing toward the dark corridor opposite him. No one laughed. There was no way out of this one, and Sam slowly raised his hands on either side of his head.

One of the soldiers dropped his firearm, and ordered the two flanking him with a flick of his finger. *"Über-prüfe ihn."* The two soldiers rushed from his sides, one grabbing both of Sam's wrists forcefully and the other running his paws along Sam's torso. The ferocious treatment they handled him with was a painful reminder of every spot on his body that had taken damage from the fall. They removed the dagger from his waist, seized his firearm from its holster, then vigorously checked every pocket on his uniform.

The lead man who'd been giving the orders strode up to Sam's face, ripped the *Wermacht* patches from his uniform, and pocketed them. He glowered at Sam for a moment, his nose only inches from Sam's. Sam could sense the man wanted to hit him, perhaps even spit in his face, but he suspected Herr Eichler had made it clear that if anyone was going to rough the spy up, it was going to be *him*.

Where was Eichler? He'd probably sent his lackeys to do his dirty work. Sam suspected Eichler was no soldier. He was an opportunist looking to get his brass and rub elbows with the party leaders—just another sycophant looking to grab a seat at the Eagle's Nest in Berchtesgaden and pat themselves on the back for the genocidal disarray they'd plunged the world into.

"*Warte auf Eichler*," the man in charge requested.

How long had it been? Sam wondered. Eight minutes? Nine? He didn't need an answer. It came quickly in the form of a muffled blast. The sound captured the attention of all of the soldiers nearby, and a brief silence followed.

Is that it? Sam was displeased. But it wasn't the end —far from it. The next boom blew any door that wasn't fixed securely to the tank off its hinges, and then a series of concussive blasts spewed fire indiscriminately as every segment of the machine's gas reservoir felt the heat from its neighboring tank.

The bursting flames caused a panic, and soon the massive fortress displayed the fireworks show Sam had hoped to see, albeit far closer than he had planned for. The soldiers scattered, and the flames shot out of every one of the machine's orifices like an unruly dragon had erupted from the inside out. The abundance of oxygen in the large room fed each of the flames, and now panels of all manner were shooting from the tank's exterior.

One panel flew forward, prompting Sam to dive to the floor. The large piece of debris hit Sam's captor in the back and incapacitated him. Each soldier beside him had fallen over from the blast, and Sam watched his gun clatter against the concrete floor. He grabbed it, then searched frantically for the dagger. The fire roared, and the intense light from the bursting flames reflected the glint of the blade's hilt in his eye. Sam crawled toward that weapon as well, retrieved it, then rose on his aching feet. The remaining soldiers who'd been brave enough to keep their firearms trained on Sam fired in unison, and he took cover behind the crates, which had now saved his life for a second time.

The tank erupted in yet another massive fireball, this one more impressive than the last, and the housing was engulfed in flame. The fire rolled like a carpet of thunder clouds, engulfing the room and filling it with a magnificent orange glow. Screams emanated from all directions behind the crates, and Sam was confident he'd taken the majority of men out with the blast. He peeked his head out from behind the crate cover and watched as the sides of the tank spewed flames from its weak points. The soldiers nearby, many caught in the fire and flailing wildly, scattered about the room.

The fire, still raging, curled up the tank's exterior in terrifying tufts. Smoke billowed into the room. The byproduct of the flames was thick and black, so Sam's next priority was to get clear before he suffocated inside the burning structure. He'd already felt a tickle growing in the black of his throat, and he checked his ammunition before searching for his exit route.

Debris had spilled into the corridor Sam had entered in, covering the exit in smoldering, mangled metal. A bullet cracked against a crate, splintering thin, razor-like pieces of wood against his face. He ducked for cover once more, tucking his back against the crate, then lurched his head around the box and hit the soldier between the eyes with one well-placed shot. Now he'd daresay say he *liked* the O and W 40. The soldier fell quickly, but another took aim. Sam redirected his weapon to the soldier's leg, then fired, and the bullet struck the man once in the knee. The injury sent him collapsing on to the weak leg. He sprayed gunfire blindly at Sam as the injury registered, which forced

Sam to retreat. Sam emptied two more rounds into him, silencing him quickly.

Sam took inventory of his options. There was another corridor opposite the entry point, but he was confident—as per the geographical layout he'd been made privy to—that it would not yield an exit. There were, however, a set of steps leading up to the catwalk. Sure this would help him find his way to safety—a door, or at least a window—Sam begged his legs one last time to show up for work.

Sam took one good breath, preparing himself for the toxic smoke on the second floor, and made his move for the staircase. The soldiers were scattered, barking commands and yelling above the screaming fire and moving about the room in a frenzied manner. Because of his uniform, Sam thought he might blend in amidst the chaos. He made it to the foot of the steel set of steps, but then a yell from his right drew his attention.

Three riflemen took aim, and Sam took to the staircase without pause. A storm of bullets sprayed the railing at his side, causing an onslaught of sparks that obscured his view as he tore up each step. With the amount of adrenaline flowing through him, he doubted he would have felt a hit if he had taken one. At the top of the staircase, a soldier who'd been unscathed by the explosion took aim. He fired, and the bullet clanked against the railing near his face, but Sam shielded his eyes with his elbow. Luckily the foe had been a poor shot—something Sam was *not*. Sam drew his firearm, put two bullets into the man's chest, and rolled forward onto the catwalk.

Now the elevation was on his side, and none of the gunfire from the men below had any chance of contact.

He tucked his torso tightly against the wall, keeping low and maneuvering for the small hall to his left. He finally took a breath and felt the sting deep inside his lungs. The smoke was becoming incredibly thick in the room. Pillars of black tornados reached from the tank toward the ceiling. The scratch at the back of Sam's throat had morphed into a full-blown cough with each exhalation. Even the heat on the second-floor catwalk was beginning to become unbearable. Sweat from his scalp trailed down his temples and flowed down to his chin.

Sam took cover in the hall and was thrilled to be momentarily clear of both natural and enemy fire. The walls were yet another tunnel of concrete enclosure, but the air was cool and quiet. Ahead rested one lone aluminum door with a glass panel on its face. A locked door was problematic, but glass was good—it was *break-able*. Sam sprinted forward, confident there wasn't much left in between him and a good gasp of fresh air. He arrived at the door and saw a wooden plaque below the glass panel that had been etched with golden letters that read "Eichler, L."

He grabbed the door handle, twisted quietly, and burst into the room with his eye placed level with the gun's sight, drawing the pistol around the dark space. To the left, an office had been constructed separate from the room, and at the far end a large wall-to-wall shelving unit housed files. A door ahead was the last obstacle to freedom that stood in front of Sam; he'd seen the staircase leading to the ground level when scouting the property. How many soldiers would still be outside? He'd hoped he'd taken a good number out with his little pyrotechnic demonstration.

He made for the door, pausing only momentarily at

a desk beside him that caught his attention. This desk bore a small placard too, and on its face had been written: Lang, S. *Sigrid,* Sam said softly to himself. Had she gotten to safety? He could only hope, and if he could stop getting distracted and beat his damn feet, he might be lucky enough to meet her there.

Sam bolted through the gloomy room and to the aluminum door at its far end, swung the handle forward, and took a strong breath of fresh air. The deciduous, cool breeze of the forest's abundance of plant life was welcome. The overwhelming sensation of pine and evergreen had never smelled so good. Outside, the property was quiet. No soldiers or guards were present. An eagle soaring above the property caught Sam's attention. The bird was gliding on its majestic wings and circling Flussrand in the sky.

It was time for Sam to make his move. He wasted no time, but barely made it a step forward before feeling a flash of intense pain. The blow came hard—a smack to the base of the skull with a hard object that vibrated his brain with a sickening rattle. He felt the sensation of falling, the stomach-churning notion of a loss of control, and saw the staircase below coming at him—closer, and closer, until there was *nothing*.

23

———

Sam came to in a black cement cube. A fixture hanging above his head droned with a soft buzz, which seemed to be in sync with the one emanating at the back of his skull. Behind him, there was a consistent tapping. A rogue crack in the ceiling leaked water, sustaining a dripping sound that began a subtle torture before anyone had even entered the room. It ticked with a soft patter like a stopwatch counting down to impending doom.

He felt the crusted blood below his nostrils, a dried mustache that reeked of iron. His hands had been bound with rope behind his back and were also tied to the wooden bar that braced the chair. The threads were tight, and left little to no give where they met his skin. He attempted rocking himself over to break the wood, but before he could take much action, the door ahead screeched.

A tall figure lingered in a silhouette at the entrance to the room. Sam didn't need to see the face to recognize his visitor—the height told him everything. The door closed, and the man was left in shadow. He stepped forward slowly, casually, in front of Sam, still obscured in grim darkness by the single light source above his head. He paused there, his head tilted slightly, analyzing the defeated captive.

"I don't like torture," Eichler said. His words were calm, and one might even say warm, yet he towered above Sam like a disappointed parent who took no pleasure shaming their child. Sam lifted his head, ensuring whatever Eichler did next, he'd have to look his prey in the eye. Sam's vision adjusted, refocusing on the details of Eichler's face. It had been months since their last meeting. Eichler looked different now than the last time Sam had met him—worried and sickly and beaten down. His skin had become pasty, his face unshaved, and his eyes were sunken and hollow.

Eichler stepped to his side, leaving Sam's peripheral, and began to circle him. "It's barbaric, truly. I think of myself as *better* than one who needs to toy with an enemy who has no ability to defend itself. The lion does not slash at the prey—it clamps down on the throat. Even the venomous snakes of the world send their prey into instant paralysis—a courtesy, really. I'm not fond of the idea of drawing this out with you. Simply put: it's unfair."

Eichler maneuvered behind Sam. His boots landed on the cement floor with heavy thuds and a slow, calculated pace. They were alone, and his voice echoed against the cold walls with a haunting reverberation. "However, I need to know *who* you are. I also need to know *what* you know. You have jeopardized my intentions—*twice now*, I might add. You have become more than a thorn in my side." He'd navigated to Sam's right side now, almost completing the full rotation around him. He leaned in and spoke softly, but sternly, into Sam's ear. "You have become glass in my foot, a rotten tooth that needs to be extracted. Well, I'll be extracting the rotten out of you, my friend, even if I have to take several other teeth with me. It is clear to me now that you are a spy— a *saboteur*—and, I admit, a *good* one. Good spies, I understand, are notable for their abilities to withstand pressure. We will see just how long you can manage."

Eichler continued his pacing, then stopped again in front of Sam. "Or, you can tell me what I want to know, and I will do you the favor of making your death quick and painless. There are other ways of causing you pain, my friend, ways that don't require I lay a finger on you."

Sam's head rose swiftly. *Sigrid.*

Eichler smiled. "I think we understand each other. *She's* not a trained spy. She will not last long, but I can make it last as long as it needs to, and you will *watch*. You will know that the pain she feels will be *your* fault, and you will feel it just the same." Eichler let the words hang, then rose again to stand tall. "We will start with you first, though. If you don't talk, we'll alternate with her. We'll go on like that—back and forth, *back and forth*—until one of you decides you can't take any more. The question is, who will crack first? I would place my bet on her, but then again, she's shown bravery."

Anticipation hung thick in the air. Eichler gave Sam a moment of respite before the games began, but a disappointed frown crossed his face when Sam offered nothing. If he was going to get information, Sam was going to make him work for it.

"Have you ever seen an eagle hunt?" Sam didn't

answer. His eyes remained on Eichler's, but he offered no sign of interest. Eichler began to pace again, and Sam feared—more than he feared torture—that he was about to be subjected to the diatribe of a man who was fond of his own voice. He was correct.

"We have had an abundance of birds of prey in the area since we began the project at Flussrand. That's not a complaint. I see it as a divine sign of things to come. It is a response, though, to a greater problem. This project has had to accommodate a great number of men to see it through to completion, and that, as you could imagine, creates a lot of waste. We've had a *terrifying* amount of waste since the project began, and so we've altered the ecosystem to a degree with our presence. The rodents, of course, are attracted to the waste. They see an opportunity to eat, and so, they wiggle out of their little holes in search of food. They're quite good at it. They have an exceptional sense of smell that directs them toward meals, and they share the news with their little friends. Soon they've created an infestation. This is a problem."

Eichler's eyes followed the walls as he continued to circle Sam. He was locked in a state of reminiscence. Sam half-wished he'd get on with the torture, because listening to the madman was almost as bad.

"When I was a child my mother would scold me if I left any breakfast or dinner out after eating. This would attract pests, and once they'd figured out where the bread was buttered, they were incredibly difficult to get rid of. They just *kept coming back*." Eichler paused, and turned his head to face Sam. "So you need a predator. We, at the time, recruited a feline. It worked out quite well. She would hunt—very adept at it. Soon they took the hint, and poof!" Eichler arched his hands as if performing a magician's trick. "No more rodents. We don't have that luxury here. We can't have cats running around Flussrand, and so the birds of prey have answered the call. They linger in the sky, watching patiently for the rodents to reveal themselves—and they *always* do. They sneak from hole to hole, squirming and wriggling and darting. After some time, though, the eagle finds her prey. Sometimes, she loses the chase, and the mice scurry back into the shadows, but sometimes she wins, and when she does, the mice change their behavior. She is faster than they are, more swift and agile. They possess a craftiness, but she possesses *might*. This reward is two-fold; she feeds, and we have less pests. Her efforts serve as a warning to the rest of the rodent's company: don't sneak around where you don't belong."

Sam licked his dry, chapped lips. Not only had his thirst done a number on him, but the cold had as well. "You got any cigarettes?"

Eichler frowned. He leaned in once more, looking over his shoulder before speaking quietly into Sam's face. "I am trying to save you from what *they* will do to you. The people I work for, they're not going to afford you the same luxuries I will. I am doing you a favor, whether you realize it or not. You see," Eichler dropped his voice even lower, now speaking in a barely audible whisper, "the difference between us is that *I* know what self-preservation looks like. I, too, can be a mouse, flittering about from hole to hole and stealing morsels while the eagle soars above. The smart mouse knows what the eagle looks like, and so he adapts to blend in with the forest floor."

Sam didn't speak. Momentarily, he considered spitting in Eichler's face—a low blow if there ever was one—but he resolved that it would be an indignant action. Sam might be a killer, but he had class, if there was such a thing. Eichler's words had caused him some confusion.

"I see the gears turning in your head," Eichler said with a grinning purr. "Now you are questioning just what it is I'm referring to. I am not mad you've destroyed my work. I don't *care* about the machine. I'm not an engineer or a tinkerer, I'm..." Eichler paused and thought about it. "I'm an opportunist. What I'm mad about is that you've set me back considerably. I can't come back to my people empty-handed. I'll need something to show for this setback, something to absolve me of my sin. I need to make this right and get back on track. If you won't talk, then I'll have no choice but to hand you over for questioning, and I promise you, they will not stop until they get what they want. They won't kill you though—not *yet*. They'll ensure they pull every thread until you're down to just one, and then they'll sew you back together. After that, when the time is right, they'll pull it all back apart again. I can save you from that. Consider it a favor." Eichler was right, and Sam knew it. Eichler said, "What I don't have is *time*, and neither do you."

"Reach into my pocket," Sam said.

His opponent's face twisted into a strange manner of confusion. "Excuse me?"

"This one," Sam said, nodding with his chin to the breast pocket stitched against his heart. "Reach in there for me." Eichler hesitated, then forcefully dug his hand into the pocket. His fingers grasped something, then he pulled it from Sam's pocket. In his hand rested the watch Sigrid had given Sam the day before. Eichler examined the watch's face. "Is it still ticking?"

Eichler listen for a moment, looked curiously at Sam, then answered, *"Ja."*

"What time is it?" Sam asked.

"It's a quarter to five," Eichler answered. His face crunched at the seams.

"Well," Sam said before snorting up a wad of blood that had been dangling from his nose. "Then *I've* still got time."

Eichler balled a fist around the time piece that turned his knuckles white, then drove his mallet-like hand directly into Sam's cheek. The impact caused Sam's head to bob around his shoulders like some type of carnival game. Sam spat the blood out on to the concrete floor, then straightened himself up. This only caused Eichler more frustration, and he repeated the attack, pounding the same place further until Sam's cheek split under the pressure. Blood trickled down his jaw.

Eichler grabbed Sam's scalp, taking a full clump of Sam's thick locks with his hand. "Don't play these games," Eichler said. He was nearly foaming at the mouth with a seething rage. "The pain will only get worse."

"You'll get tired before I do," Sam said with a sneer. "After all, I'm the one who traveled halfway across the world to meet you."

"I'll save my energy," Eichler replied contemptuously as he put the watch back into Sam's pocket. "Oh, and by the way," Eichler said, then reached into his own pocket.

"I found this." Eichler held out the small cyanide capsule that Sam had been given.

God damnit. The sentiment came out vocally in the form of a low grunt.

"Can't have you *dying* on us now, can we?" Eichler pressed two fingers in his mouth, and let out a whistle that could likely be heard even outside of the concrete prison. Two soldiers, not nearly as big as the monstrosity Sam had faced inside *Erdschlag* but intimidating in their own right, entered. Eichler extended a warning finger to both of the soldiers, then said *"Töte ihn nicht."* Eichler took one more disapproving glance at Sam, then stormed out of the room.

The man on Sam's left popped his knuckles, pressing each curled finger inside a cupped hand and going through the entire family of digits with a series of cracks. The man to his left rolled his neck around his shoulders. Sam clenched his teeth tightly, took a deep, preparatory breathe, then closed his eyes and let it out with a slow, prolonged exhale. An attack far greater than the storm of bullets he'd endured earlier was fast approaching, and unlike the last scenario, this time he had *nowhere* to run. Would it be as bad as the last time, as bad as the time he *should* have been taken to Pforzheim?

The first attack came from the knuckle-cracking man. Sam thought it likely the force of the shot had managed to dislocate his jaw. Then the other man stepped up to bat and took a swing, and his attack met the brow of Sam's right eye like a rogue fastball pitch.

They went at him like that for three minutes, but to Sam, it felt like hours. When one knows the pain is coming, it's hard to prepare for it. After a few more good knocks from the man on the right, Sam's cheek bone—

the one that had already been injured—cracked under the pressure. The room began to spin, only adding further to the dizzying nature of the torture. His brain rattled around inside his skull.

They hadn't gone easy on him, and yet he knew that this wouldn't be the worst of it. He'd been close to the limit he could tolerate before, but lived long enough to tell the tale. Now here he was, ready to be tested *again*. Worse, his backup plan—the capsule—was no longer an option. He feared what would come next: if he was handed over to the *Gestapo,* the *Abwehr,* or the *SS,* he might wind up in one of the camps the world had been murmuring about in low whispers.

The man on his left cupped a hand around Sam's chin and tilted it up toward his own face. Sam looked lazily into his eyes. The face was indiscernible, a mass of flesh obscured by a hazy fog. Sam's own face had become a puffed mess of swollen skin. "OK," the man said, and nodded to the other soldier before letting Sam's head fall down against his chest. Both exited, and Sam let out a bloody, frothy sigh.

He struggled against the knots binding his wrists, but it was pointless. Not only did he not have the strength, he found it difficult to even focus. He felt an overwhelming dizziness, so he allowed himself to slip off into a void where consciousness was fleeting.

Some time had passed, though his brain had difficulty figuring out just how much. The sensation was that of a fever dream, where a man's temperature had risen so high that his sense of time was toyed with. Sam's level of alertness was tottering. It wasn't just the beating that had broken him, but the lack of consistent sleep and sharp focus needed ever since he'd landed in Germany. It was all adding up fast.

The door opened once more, and Sam lifted his head slightly to see who'd come to pay him a visit this time. A set of black combat boots shuffled hastily into the room. Once again the lone incandescent bulb buzzing in the fixture above obscured the face of the next person who'd do a number on him. He surveyed the uniform—standard-issue *Wermacht* fatigues—but this visitor did not have the stature of the previous ones. They'd sent someone else in to have at him.

"Sam," a soft voice said. The change in tenor was angelic. The voice belonged to a *woman*. She stepped forward—now with urgency—and crouched at his knees. She lifted his face with a warm hand that felt boiling against his cool skin. Her fingers massaged his injuries. "Sam, wake up!" she cried. The demand was a high, desperate whisper. She looked over her shoulder. A set of boots clomped by before passing into inaudible territory. "Sam!" The woman removed the cap from her head, under which luscious blonde hair had been matted. She gripped his face between her hands and forced him to look into her eyes.

It was Sigrid. He *was* dreaming. *How beautiful that my mind in its state of pain would grant me a last visit from the ghostly specter of the woman I've shared a fleeting romance with. I've been awarded a wonderful dream to compensate for this nightmare.*

"How's... how's America?" Sam stuttered.

"I'm here, Sam!" Sigrid argued.

"I know," Sam replied with a drunken slur. "Stay with me."

"We have to *leave*," Sigrid demanded, the whisper

now rising with her pleading. She pulled a blade from her hip and moved alongside the back of the chair. He felt her pulling at the knots, heard the sawing sounds of knife against thread, and then he lifted his head more alertly. He turned to watch her, his consciousness now taking acute interest in what she was doing. He was reminded of the pain in his body, and the realization that she *was* there set in.

"Sigrid?" Sam asked with a lazy stupor.

"Quiet!" Sigrid barked.

"What are you doing?" Sam asked.

She sawed feverishly at the bindings. "I'm getting you out of here!"

"But you're supposed to be on the freighter," Sam replied in confusion. The threads of the ropes securing his hands to the chair popped with a release that sent his battered limbs wobbling. Sigrid jammed the knife back into its leather sheath and climbed to her feet.

"Stop talking," she said, and then she pressed her warm lips against his. She held them there, letting them linger on his bottom lip for a moment. The feeling sent a reinvigorating jolt through his body like that of a stimulant. "Can you walk?"

Sam nodded, then straightened himself and rose to his feet. He winced when he put weight on his limbs. The pain radiated from his skull and worked its way through the upper torso where his body had taken the brunt of the fall, but he was able to move, and that was all that mattered.

"Where to?" Sam asked.

"*Amerika,*" Sigrid replied with a smile.

24

Sigrid stealthily surveyed each hall beside the cell door. No one was keeping watch of the high-value prisoner—or locked his door—likely because no one expected Sam to free himself from his bindings. Concrete tunnels stretched like long rock tubes on either side of her. Moisture had gathered inside of the structure, forming streaks of mold that dripped down the walls and gave off the foul odor of decaying things.

"Where are we?" Sam asked.

Sigrid waved him on and stepped out into the hall. "The guard's post at the front of Flussrand."

"How did you get in?" Sam asked.

"There was barely any security," Sigrid replied. "I expected to meet quite some resistance. Imagine my surprise when I found I could drive right up without incident."

Sam manifested a smile through the blood-crusted face. "They were all at the fireworks."

Sigrid smiled back at him. "You can see the smoke from several kilometers away. Come."

Sigrid led the way through the hall, her body pressed tight against the wall of the corridor and her eyes set on the light pooling at the end of its mouth. She was on the hunt for dancing shadows that would signal the arrival of troops. All they needed was a clean break for the truck.

"Eichler's still here," Sam warned. "Along with the two guards who gave me this makeover."

"Alright," Sigrid said after pausing her progress. "You can tell me all about your adventure later. Keep quiet."

Both escapees lingered at the corner where the hall made a right angle. Cool air whisked toward them like a welcoming hand—the door that led to the exit had been left ajar. "There," Sigrid said after pointing to the exit.

She hustled forward, pressed her face to the crack in the door, and surveyed the broad patch of land beyond the gate. The gate was also open, and beyond that, the dirt road stretched near infinitely. "Look," Sigrid pointed. "The truck is about one hundred meters from the gate, tucked beyond a series of clustered trees. I rolled it down the hill in neutral to keep quiet. I don't think anyone saw me, otherwise we likely wouldn't be having this conversation."

"Smart," Sam replied. "What time is it?"

Sigrid checked the watch on her wrist. "About six."

"We've got to move," Sam replied. "We're going to miss the pickup if we can't get to the container soon."

"Can you run?" Sigrid asked.

"I'll make do."

"You go first," Sigrid said. She cupped his face between her hands, gripped the cheeks tightly against her fingers, and gave him the kiss she thought she'd never get again. They were almost home free. She opened the door slowly, careful not to let it produce any more noise than was necessary, and turned back to Sam. "Run like *hell*."

"Ladies go first—"

"Quiet," Sigrid snapped. "This is not the time to debate the strengths and weaknesses of men and women. I'm the one who got you free, yes?"

"Yes, ma'am," Sam replied, and he took off from the doorway. He hadn't sustained any leg injuries, but his muscles screamed. He felt a clumsiness in his otherwise spry body. When his adrenaline began to pump, his vision became almost tunnel-like. The effect was amplified by the abundant trees hugging the road on either side of the cleared path. They embraced the dirt roadway from high above and blocked the little light from the moon penetrating through the canopy. The darkness would aid the heroes in their escape, and Sam was thankful for the *Schwarzwald's* namesake.

Sam, now attempting his best sprint, turned to look over his shoulder. He'd focused harder on trucking through the pain than watching for Sigrid—she was right on his tail. He waited for the shouts of the guards, but they never came. No one had seen them leave, and as soon as they made it to the truck, they'd be free and clear. Traveling by night would be best anyway, and the pick-up point was not far.

They cleared the gate that separated the tall fencing wrapped around the property. There was no guard at the post. Sam thought it likely they had been barbecued in the explosion. The soft crunch of frosty grass under his feet turned to the hard, unforgiving sturdiness of dirt. Now they were on the road.

"Just up ahead!" Sigrid called out from behind him, and Sam saw the faint glint of the truck's exterior shell in the moonlight. She'd ditched it behind a large tree trunk that obscured most of its body, and the dark olive paint only made it that much more camouflaged. He pushed harder, and moved toward the truck like a runner ready to steal second base.

A deafening crack rippled through the forest like a rogue thundercloud. Sam knew instantly what it was: the sound of high-caliber rifle fire. Sam stopped, sliding through the cold dirt and looking toward Sigrid. She'd fallen, tumbling onto the road while clutching her gut.

Her eyes met his, and they were wide and glistening and full of surprise and horror. She rose to a knee, looked down at her abdomen, and saw blood spreading out like a morbid flower against her uniform. "Sam?" she said.

Was it a question? Sam didn't know. It was more like a statement of desperation. Sam, what do I do? Sam, what's happening? Sam, am I going to be okay? Sam, please don't leave me.

He ran toward her and lifted her to her staggering, unsteady feet, while saying, "Sigrid, look at me. Stand up, damnit." He urged her to move now not with the warmth of a lover, but the commanding tone of a superior officer. He wasn't asking her, he was *warning* her.

The next shot followed, and this one, now that it had his full attention, seemed louder. He saw the muzzle flare from the roof of the structure beyond, a tiny flicker of light that gave away the shooter's position. Within a fraction of a second, the bullet tore through her throat, ripping her from his supporting arms as if to say, "you can't have her." She collapsed on the floor once more.

Before the echo of the previous attack had subsided, another shot came, and this one missed Sam by only inches. Sam instinctively dove for the cover of a nearby tree. Another bullet came for him, this one splitting the bark against his ear into wooden confetti.

He crouched low and looked to Sigrid. She was lying on her side, her face contorted into a petrified gasp. Her hand was clutched tightly to her neck. Blood gushed between her fingers. Her face had already begun to lose its color, the rose cheeks now cool and blue. Her mouth opened and closed like a beached fish begging for oxygen. She was frightened, yet Sam could do nothing for her. The woman who'd so impressed him with her brash and unwavering resolve now looked quite like a *girl*—a scared, defeated girl who just wanted comfort.

He couldn't give it to her. She was bait now. He watched as the life left her eyes. He'd known better than to do that—that was how a man became haunted. His inability to act thrust him into a spiral of debate as he stared at her.

Her confusion and fear were quickly becoming shock; in front of her neck the blood had ceased seeping into the dirt and began to pool. He wanted nothing more than to run to her, to lift her up and carry her to safety, but he knew that even if he did retrieve her, there was no chance she wouldn't bleed out. If the first shot had missed vital organs, the second had drained her of blood.

"I'm sorry," Sam said with a shaky whisper. It was all he could think *to* say. She let out a deflating sigh, and then her body relaxed. Sigrid's head fell to the dirt and the muscles in her face all eased in one final release. The stupor remained locked in her eyes, a permanent display of confusion. She was gone.

The forest was silent. The shooter was waiting for Sam to make his move. He imagined the sniper's finger resting on the trigger, his eye pressed to the scope. Sam couldn't wait—too long and Eichler would send the remaining troops his way. He took one last look at Sigrid, whose lifeless body rested in a cold shock. She deserved a proper burial—if there was such a thing.

Sam Abel wasn't stupid enough to take the bait. If the man in the distance with the long barrel drawn on him thought otherwise, he'd be waiting well into the night. Sam, on the other hand, was running out of time. He lurched forward, searched for the truck, and caught a glimpse of the tire tucked behind the trees ahead. He could make it, but *would* he make it? It was a shot in the dark, but he had no choice.

A soft crunching echoed through the wooded area. The oh-so-familiar steps were slow and casual. They stopped just short of Sam's position, and Sam pressed his back against the tree to hide. Only the spectral sound of air circulating through the endless forest whistled in between the maze of trees. Then, the man lurking spoke. "She was warned." It was Eichler. Sam searched the dark patches and pockets. The voice seemed to travel in a whirlwind, reflecting and snaking through the environment and making Eichler feel *everywhere*. Eichler clicked his tongue, "Tisk, tisk." Now, Sam knew he was hovering above her body.

"Brave, though—to come back for you like that. You've shown me that not one, but *two* of my dogs were disloyal." Sam's thoughts shifted to the last time one of

Eichler's own had defected—the German Shepherd, Tutu, who'd saved Sam's life in New York. Eichler sat in the silence, waiting for a retort from Sam. "Nothing snappy to say this time?" He waited for a response, only interrupted by the hoot of an owl off in the distance. "By now you know that you are currently centered in the crosshairs of a man just up there on the roof. He's very good, as you saw. So, if you're going to do something, you'd better be quick."

Sam wasted no time making his move. He catapulted his body from the tree, first diverting immediately to his left and using the sporadically grown trees as his cover. A shot cleared the air, ricocheting off a limb just to his rear and filling the air with shards of bark. Sam switched positions like a runner in a pickle between bases. A zig-zagging movement would be his best bet, and now he was heading back toward the road. Another crack of gunfire sounded from his flank, and this one passed just in front of his face, splitting the very air he was breathing. The shooter was leading him now.

Sam turned once more—if the shooter was going to nab him, the man was going to have to work for it. Sam got a moment's respite and cleared some land. The shooter had likely been reloading, though Sam couldn't be sure. And where was Eichler? Sam had heard him but never *seen* him. Sam paused once more behind a large tree. Maybe the shooter had lost him during the reload.

There was the truck, angled in such a way that it was ready for an escape. Sam only needed to make one last go at it, one good sprint that would get him to the escape vehicle. He leapt once more from the tree and summoned whatever energy he had left. His feet tore through the dirt floor with fierce propulsion.

Sam flung himself at the vehicle and pulled the door open. One more bullet roared from his rear. It struck the metal edge of the door with a screeching *ping*. Sam froze —if he hadn't pulled the door in front of him open, the bullet likely would have ripped through his shoulder. Judging by the work it had done to the door, the high-caliber ammunition might have torn his arm from his body completely.

Sam climbed into the truck, and now he had the cover of the tree behind which Sigrid had ditched the vehicle. He dug around the dark interior of the truck, searching frantically for the ignition. The keys had been left in it—one last piece of support from the woman lying dead in the road. He started the truck, jammed the stick into the reverse position, and hurled the truck backward in a semi-circle.

He slammed the brakes once he'd straightened it out toward the road ahead. Something in the rearview caught his eye: a shadowy figure stood dead-center in the road. The coat, reminiscent of the long, flowing leather that SS party leaders were so fond of, billowed in the breeze. But Lothar Eichler was no party leader; he was a minion looking to squirm his way into a position of power. His tall figure glowed in the soft glare of the brake lights, reddening his face and painting it in a sheen that made the man look even more sinister than he'd looked earlier.

Sam wanted to leap from the car and grab Eichler's throat. He wanted to beat the man's face until the bones crumpled beneath the skin, until Lothar Eichler was a no-longer recognizable mangled mass of flesh and blood and bone. Sam clenched his teeth tightly and waited as if begging Eichler to just give him one reason to meet him face to face once more. *My hands aren't tied any longer, Lothar. Let's settle this like men do, without your soldiers and tanks and snipers. Let's settle it with knuckles and blood.* Eichler stood waiting calmly as if to coax his enemy to do so.

What had Sigrid died for then? To send Sam right back into the mess? No, she'd come back to see him escape, to see him live to fight another day. If he walked back down that road to face Eichler now, he'd likely catch a bullet almost immediately.

"Next time," Sam said aloud. Whether a reassurance to himself, or a warning to the man staring him down in the rearview, the words he spoke felt like they sizzled when they left his mouth. He threw the truck into first gear with a hard smack and the rod clicked into place. The tires spun through the dirt until finally they caught a good grip and the truck powered forward. The glowing man in his rear slowly darkened until only his silhouette remained on the empty road.

Sam worked his way through each of the truck's gears without once looking back at Flussrand. The chassis rattled on the tormentingly bumpy road. He'd cared nothing for the speed limit, or the dangers, and he'd gotten the engine up to its speed limit in short time. He'd remained in the truck's fifth—and highest— gear for the better length of the road. He'd maxed out the tachometer, the needle bouncing somewhere between five thousand and six thousand RPMs, and he cursed whatever governor had been installed to limit the machine's tolerance for punishment.

Sam's vision was sub-par, and his face swelled worse with every passing minute. His right eye was pulsating in the socket, and a crunching sensation behind the cheek assured him something in there was broken. The adrenaline pumping through his blood was beginning to wane, and with that came the return of the pain encompassing every inch of his body. Every touch of the clutch reminded him of the energy required during his ascension through *Erdschlag's* barrel.

To add insult to injury, his skin was becoming cool. He'd been stripped of all warm layers of his clothing down to only the boots, pants, and a thin undershirt. Blood loss wasn't helping regulate his temperature. The thought that he could freeze to death in his return container lingered, but with no other options to find safety, it would have to do. He only hoped that the shipment would get where it was going—back to the burned man, back to the freighter, and ultimately America. Eichler had likely put the military on high alert; they'd surely be on the hunt for him now. It wouldn't just be the *Wermacht* that was looking for him any longer, it would be the SS. The value of the American spy would be priceless.

When the long road finally curved left, Sam took the turn with a skidding slide. If the road had been wet, he would have rolled the vehicle. He took every turn along the mountain climb away from Flussrand with disregard for his own safety, only focused on getting as far away as possible quickly. The depot wasn't far, but if he didn't make good time, there'd be trucks at his back. The soldiers wouldn't know where he was going, which at the moment was the only thing working in his favor.

He pictured the trucks rolling out of Flussrand, tumbling unceremoniously over Sigrid's body. Had Eichler even had the decency to move it? She'd have been branded as a traitor—a *spion*, just like himself—

and the worry of just where Sigrid's body would rot made his stomach churn.

When the incline became steeper, Sam threw the truck into a lower gear. The engine groaned under the stress, but it made negotiating the sharp switchbacks more manageable. The final turn at the top of the mountain came up fast, and when he passed around it to see the other side, a truck much like his own brushed past him. The tires screeched just before the turn, and Sam grasped what was happening in his rearview. The truck had done a sloppy u-turn, and now headlights were shining brightly through his rear window.

Sam put the truck into a higher gear and slammed the pedal to the floor. The next mile or so ahead was a straightaway. The enemy truck closed the gap quickly, and by the time he'd hit the end of the narrow road at the mountain's highest point, it was right up against him. The lights in the depot twinkled in the valley below —safety was in sight.

The truck lurched forward, and Sam heard the violent scrape of his pursuer's bumper against his own. The hit sent the truck swerving, and Sam gripped the wheel and turned to compensate. Another impact followed, and now the truck was *pushing* him downhill.

The glass in his rear window shattered without warning. They'd fired on him. He swerved ungracefully in an attempt to make their job harder. How many were there? He couldn't see past the two blinding lights obscuring his vision. Several more bullets followed. One hit the seat next to him, ripping through the fabric in an explosion of cotton. Another shot came, and this time it struck the windshield in front of him, forcing a spiderweb of crackling through the glass. Sam swerved once more, this time against the unguarded edge of the cliff before turning into the bend that would lead him back down the opposite side of the mountain.

Sam glimpsed the sharp edge of the road beside him; one wrong turn and he'd plummet down the mountainside. A fall like that with a full tank of gas would undoubtedly end in a fireball. He cleared the turn and accelerated once more. His pursuers took the bend more gracefully than he. Why wouldn't they? This was *their* territory, and he didn't know the roads like they did.

Sam, always one for pushing the limit, floored the truck until he felt the pedal touch the floor below. The other truck closed the distance once more with little effort—what kind of motor did they have that he didn't? The driver clipped Sam's bumper again, sending Sam into a tailspin. Sam corrected it, then noticed there was another bend ahead.

He was beginning to feel like a race-car driver navigating an unregulated course, except his competition wasn't trying to beat him, they were trying to *kill* him. Sam took the turn with too much force, skidding into it and slamming the truck against the natural rock wall against the driver's side. Though it was an unskilled move, it reoriented the truck. The driver behind him was more prepared, and took the turn with finesse. He was right on Sam's tail, and Sam knew he'd have to do something drastic if he was going to win.

Sam threw caution to the wind, pinned the tachometer to its highest point, and flew down the next long stretch of switchback. He accelerated with no regard for what lay ahead, but the headlights soon fell off into a gradient of dark emptiness, and he knew yet another dangerous curve with no barrier was fast approaching. The truck behind roared with a diesel growl, and just before Sam met the dangerous turn, he slammed the brakes.

The tires clung to the asphalt, leaving in their wake an alley of smoke and burned rubber. The driver behind him attempted to do the same, but, likely out of fear of hitting Sam, swerved just before making contact. The truck zigged, then zagged, then slid perpendicular to the road and into the harsh edge. The enemy truck's inertia was unstoppable. There was no way in hell the driver was going to correct his course with that much momentum.

Sam caught a glimpse of the man behind the wheel briefly through the driver's side. His eyes were full of surprise and his mouth circled into a large "o" that was the visual representation of his error. Sam, now paused and watching the show, displayed a smirk as the driver struggled with the wheel. It didn't work; the truck slid off the edge of the cliff, now going into a barrel roll and flying through the air.

There was silence as the mass moved through the open blackness, and then came the grotesque crunching sound of a frame buckling under deadly force. A series of screeches, clangs, and scrapes echoed through the valley, until finally the truck pounded against a burly tree and stopped its death roll in an instant. The explosion never came, but Sam wasn't dissatisfied. He'd seen enough things go boom during his time in Pforzheim. Sam slammed his foot on the pedal once more and continued down the mountain.

When he arrived at the depot, Sam met no resistance. He did what he was best at, keeping to the shadows until he finally arrived at the home-bound container. There were no soldiers present, which he was thankful for. He wasn't sure that he had the energy to put up another fight, and more importantly, he was unarmed.

Sam shut the cargo container door behind him, pulled out his cigarette tin, and collapsed into the corner. He had one smoke left. He barely had the energy to hold the damn cigarette, but the tobacco was calling. It trembled between his fingers when he struck the match to light it. He savored it, concentrating on and enjoying each puff, until finally the cherry burned the knuckles on his fingers.

Sam tamped the cigarette out, then curled up against the boxes in the rear. The contents in the container he'd arrived with had been exchanged with others during his absence. Sleep would be the last enemy he'd have to fight until he was sure he was safe. He slapped himself a couple times on the cheek—each impact a reminder of his injuries—in an effort to stay alert. After some time, the sound of a motor approached. The container lifted into the air, was loaded onto a truck, and Sam allowed himself to ease up. He thought of Sigrid, and the pain of her loss eventually tired him more than he could fight. He finally fell into the sleep he so desperately needed.

25

hy, was the only word that repeated *ad nauseam* in Sam's head. *Why?*

The door to the shipping container opened just in time. Sam was closer to death than he'd ever felt before. He'd shivered involuntarily for several hours, possibly from loss of blood or concussion, but more likely from the low temperature. Both the burned man and Newton were glad to see him. The former did display some confusion about Sigrid's absence, but that vanished quickly when they'd pulled Sam from the container. Sigrid had left folders inside of it that Sam had not seen. She still had tricks up her sleeve.

The freighter hummed along with a deep drone. The large craft cut through the waves, and each lapped against the hull with a defeated splash. Though the ocean was strong, the machine fought back against the current, pushing along with little regard for whatever nature would throw at it. The air was cool and the smell of saltwater wafting toward Sam was a welcome change from the leaves of the Black Forest and the lingering odor of gunpowder and explosives. It smelled less like death.

The trip home would be much more calm than the storm they'd encountered on their way out. They were safe in international waters, but Sam was not confident he'd actually get a good night's sleep. He was on his way back home, but what had it cost to get there?

They carried Sam back to the infirmary under the deck, and there his wounds were tended to by the doctor who'd cleared him for the trip. They'd also cranked the heat up to an unbearable eighty degrees, but for Sam it felt just fine. He'd suffered some of the fractured bones he'd feared, as well as the sprained wrist. A mild concussion made him temporarily sensitive to light, but the rest of the damage would heal. Some bandages and a handful of stitches here and there on the face were nothing to write home about, not that he *had* anyone to write to.

It took nearly three days to get back to D.C., and once he'd arrived, Sam continued to rest in another infirmary with a view of the nation's Capitol. The burned man had not debriefed Sam yet, which he was thankful for. Sam speculated his superior had been far too busy transcribing and poring over the documents Sigrid had left behind.

Sam lay in the bed, sick with grief—a grief unlike any he'd experienced prior. He'd seen men die, but it had been the first time he'd seen someone with a vested interest in *him* die. Her death, he felt, had been a direct result of his actions. He kept seeing her eyes, and the terrified expression that had been frozen in them, during the trip back to the freighter.

He suspected the burned man might still be disappointed. *Erdschlag* had been destroyed, and that mattered, but he'd failed in successfully helping the defector escape. Any information that had been stored in her head and not written down was now lost to time. The only thing keeping Sam from not running right back into enemy territory was that her sacrifice had not been in vain. If she hadn't returned, the Germans would probably still be pulling teeth from his mouth, but at least *Erdschlag* wouldn't be pointed at London.

God damnit, Sigrid. Why did you have to come back? Sam wondered if he would have made the same choice if he'd been in her position. Of course he would, because that was what guys like him did. Sigrid, it seemed, was just as nuts as he was. She would have made a great team member. Sam vowed to make Eichler pay when they saw each other again, and he knew they *would*. Sam knew that as things ramped up and American boots found German soil, he'd be back soon enough. The question was, would Sam be returning of his own volition, or be sent by the burned man?

After several days passed, Sam felt better. The warmth of the sun melted the icicles draped from the windowsill outside his room. Spring had arrived. Sam had finally been able to sit up when the nurse tended to him, and she likely took that as the cue that he was ready to talk. Soon after, even before his superior walked into the room, Sam caught a whiff of the pipe tobacco stench. The burned man knocked on the door, to which Sam didn't respond, though the man allowed himself entry anyway.

The burned man tapped his pipe into a glass ashtray, switched out his charred tobacco for some that was fresh, and lit it with the touch of a match. He surveyed Sam, and their eyes locked momentarily. The burned man squinted lightly with the inhalation of his pipe. He took a seat opposite the hospital bed, the scarred portion of his face favoring the shadows the sun didn't touch.

Sam wanted to tell the man to take a hike. He wasn't in the mood to talk or share war stories. He also wasn't in the mind space to replay the events in his head. He saw one thing and one thing only: the cold, dead eyes of Sigrid staring back at him. He couldn't shake the image of her bleeding out on the dirt road where her enemies had left her. He kept reliving a terrible visual of the trucks leaving Flussrand and running over her corpse. The image would be frozen in his mind for some time.

There the burned man was, comfy and sucking on his pipe and ready to bark his orders. He'd probably never lost a night's sleep. Why should he? He was like the queen bee, sending out her soldiers to go sting at will, all while she stayed plump and content in her hive.

"There's something different about your eyes," the burned man said. Sam was caught off guard by the comment. What the hell did that mean? "You've got those callous eyes. I noticed them the first time we met." He pointed the pipe toward Sam. "I know, because I've been told the same thing. You and I have something *missing* from our eyes—though not in that unhinged, mad fella sort of way. Our eyes say, 'I'll ruin your day.' " He bit the pipe once more, now talking through his teeth as he said, "See, most people got a little *light* in their eyes. It's like a tiny little bulb that says, "I ain't ever seen nothin' too violent, nothin' *too* scary. I've never seen a man kill another man. I've never seen a tragedy. I grew up nice." The burned man inhaled from his piped thoughtfully. "We *had* it, both you and I. Everybody starts with it. The reason I bring it up is because somehow, and I'm at a loss as to *how*, you seem to have got it back."

Sam didn't reply. Instead, he did what he always did and removed a cigarette from his tin. He wished he'd had a mirror so he could see just what the hell the burned man was talking about. The old man's pipe flared, and Sam saw the tiny flicker of the burning tobacco reflected in his own pair of black spheres. There was the light in his eyes, and it was twisted in a poetic way.

"So what was it?" the burned man asked.

Sam exhaled with a long sigh. His eyes fell to the cigarette burning in his hand. The smoke curled up the fingers, snaking up the knuckles and rising slowly toward his face until finally hitting his nose and filling his senses. He thought he could use a break from the smell of things smoldering. Sam looked to the burned man. "A lot of bad things had to happen for me to get the job done."

The burned man sat on the comment, then nodded his head in understanding. He leaned back in the chair, fixed his gaze on the pipe, and slipped deep into thought. He took Sam's meaning without further prodding. He said, "I wasn't always this pretty, you know." He inhaled once more from the pipe, then tilted his head back and directed his view to the wall above Sam as if his mind had begun its own projection. "And I'm no stranger to the way these things go." He shifted in his seat, settling in for a good story. Sam's attention darted momentarily to the mangled flesh that covered the side of his boss's face. "Back in '18 we were charging ahead at full steam. We were moving toward Metz. Sometimes we'd lose so many guys in one day that the puddles that formed would make a man think it rained blood. If that wasn't bad enough, the flu had been running rampant through our teams, so if our guys weren't injured by opposing fire they were throwing up their guts. We captured Buzancy. Sometimes I wonder just *how* the hell we did it."

The burned man looked at Sam, bit his pipe, and focused on Sam's eyes to make sure he'd gotten his subordinate's attention. "The 23rd was tired. We'd lost a lot of guys pushing on. I was in charge of resupplying when necessary, and for the better part of those terrible hundred days I'd managed to keep my ass out of the line of fire. The supply depot we'd propped up caught a shell, and since I knew my guys wouldn't do much good running out on the front line with nothing but knives, I carried as many supplies to safety as I could. Well, eventually the cache caught in such a way that it triggered a nasty explosion which sent most of our equipment flying. I had a buddy over there, Murphy, and we'd always promised to cover each other's asses. One of our men was prepping a grenade when the boom hit, and he'd pulled that pin at just the wrong moment. I'd tried to tell him to hold off and get clear of the munitions, but when the shit goes like that, well you just can't hear much of anything over a shelling. I couldn't hear a God-damned thing myself, and all of sudden, I see Murphy yelling at me…"

The burned man trailed off for a moment. There was conflict, a war waging in his eyes with his own history—perhaps regarding how he remembered it. Sam wondered if the old man had truly reconciled it. His gaze wandered again, now focused on the pipe in his hand that had ceased burning. Only charred black flakes remained in the bowl. He twirled it between his fingers before continuing. "I can see him still; he's still yelling and pointing, but I don't hear anything. He's coming toward me and he's pointing, but I'm just kind of caught there, frozen in the moment because I can't hear a God-damned thing and I'm trying to read his lips. He's pointing to my feet and running toward me. I look down, and there's a grenade just sort of wobbling on its side, rocking back and forth before it idles there for a moment. I couldn't even see whether the pin had been pulled yet or not. I don't got that much time to figure it out. The next thing I know I feel this impact on my chest that throws me for a loop. It hit me so hard all I saw that moment was the grey sky above me. I think to myself, 'Well, it wasn't a bad run. This is a shitty way to end it, but at least I had some fun.' The only thing I could see in that moment was this girl I'd been with before I left—Betsy Dean. I told her I'd marry her when I came back. Boy, oh boy, *Betsy Dean*. If there was ever such a thing as *too much* woman, it was Betsy Dean." The burned man smiled with the warmth of nostalgia. He shook his head back and forth as his reminiscence segued to Betsy Dean before resuming the story.

"Anyway, I'm on my back, thinking I'm about to float right up ahead to meet my maker, but then the *real* crack comes—and this one made the first feel like a walk in the park. Everything goes silent, and there's a ringing. Then another comes from behind—a concussion—and soon my face feels like the devil himself is poking it with his spear. I leap up to my feet—thankful that I still got 'em, mind you—and the next thing I remember is the God-awful smell of burned man. You ever smell a man on fire?" He didn't wait for Sam to answer. "You don't want to. My face is burning like all get out, and I'm patting at it and running in circles like some kind of fool. That's when I see Murphy—not in one place, but a few. I'm trying to get my damn shirt off and rolling around on the ground, screaming like some kind of banshee, and when I finally figure I've extinguished the fire well enough, I realize just what the hell it is Murphy's done. The son of a bitch dove on the grenade and took the impact."

The burned man frowned, and the creases in his tobacco-battered skin became deep folds of shadow, valleys in which the dark recesses of his past remained visible. "I was laid up in the field hospital for weeks, my damned face wrapped to high hell in bandages while they stick needles in my arm to counteract the pain— and I've never had pain like *that*. One day young boys from a unit came in celebrating and cheering like kids who'd found the candy stash. They're raving about how the end is in sight, but you know what? It don't mean nothin' to me. Part of me wished the damned war never ended, just so I could get back out there and knock around some more Kraut heads myself. What's worse than losin' your best man is seeing him in the mirror every day staring back at you."

The burned man smoothed his tie, crossed his legs, and sat up in his chair. He pointed the pipe toward Sam once again, extending the tip toward him as he spoke. "So what I suppose I'm saying is, Murphy didn't get caught in the crossfire because I made a poor choice. We all signed up knowing what it was we were doing, and he made *his* choice. To this day I consider him the bravest son of a bitch I've ever met, and that's *real* bravery. The shit we do, well that's just akin to having a good set of swinging balls, but a man like Murphy, looking death in the face while spitting back at it—that's the real mettle to test a man. He knew what came next and the damn fool did it anyway… and now, well, I'm here sharing a pipe with you. I often wonder, had I been given the same choice, would I have done the same thing? A man can say he will. Talk is cheap, but when the reaper's right there in front of you, baring his bony grin and swingin' that scythe, do *you* still make the same choice? I supposed I would, and that's what got me out of that hospital bed." The burned man paused, let his eyes wander to the window that displayed the city abroad, then said, "And that's that."

Sam pulled on the cigarette, but the cherry singed his fingers. He'd been so enamored with the story that the cigarette had lost his attention and found its way to the end before he'd even gotten a chance to smoke it proper. It had been the first—and only—thing he'd ever learned about the burned man. He still didn't even know his real name.

"What about Betsy Dean?" Sam asked in an attempt to lighten the mood.

"She married some shmuck car salesman while I'd been gone," the burned man replied. "I seen her once back at home, but I hid behind a market aisle for fear she'd see me… you know, like *this*. I'd considered trying to go back to her, trying to get back a piece of me that

I'd hung on to while I was over there." He shook his head from side to side shamefully. "There's no place for a man that looks like me in the world of a lady like Betsy Dean. Not because of this..." He pointed to his scarred face. "But, you know. I might say the same could be said for a man like *you*. Men like you and me..." The burned man paused, then packed his pipe once more. "We're made of a different material than God intended. That don't mean he don't want any part of us—it's the contrary, I think. He made men like us so the better part of 'em could do, well, whatever it is that men *not* like us do. Perhaps," the burned man said before pulling on the pipe with a strong inhalation. He let it out with a long sigh that filled the room with smoke, then said, "so they could make girls like Betsy Dean wives and mothers."

The old man leaned forward, rested both elbows on the desk, and directed the stem end of the pipe at Sam in the same way he always did. "You did a good thing over there, son. No matter what it cost, the return was greater. She left us with a hell of a nest egg. The boys in Washington are doing cartwheels. *She* knew that. Do *you*?"

The assumption piqued Sam's attention. He'd never said a word about Sigrid, but the old man somehow knew. Perhaps, Sam thought, it was in the eyes.

The burned man stood. "Get some rest. I'm not saying you're going to sleep—very hard to do that after these kinds of things. Rest, however, ain't always about sleep—it's about clarity. We'll talk soon." Just before he turned to exit, the phone beside Sam's bed rang. "You might want to get that." He smiled deviously. "Tell him I said 'hello.' "

"I don't even know your name," Sam called out.

The burned man paused in the doorway, then said, "Brandt. Hank Brandt."

Sam reached for the phone as Brandt left, though his body begged him to leave it be and relax. When the door closed, Sam pressed the phone to his ear. "Yea," Sam responded with a lack of interest.

"I'm told I'm in your debt," the man on the other end of the phone said. He spoke a fine, proper British accent used by those in the upper echelon of society. "That I, and those I represent, owe you a great deal of gratitude." The "r's" in his speech pattern rolled with authority. The voice was nasal, but *powerful*—a commanding force even via phone. Sam heard the soft exhalation of smoke on the other end of the line.

"I just did what any other man would have done," Sam replied.

"Lesser men than yourself have 'done what needed doing,' " the man responded. "Men that go beyond the call of duty are the ones who stand out as exceptional. I'm told two individuals tasked with running a particular errand were unable to do so and that you filled that void."

"You can sleep peacefully," Sam replied. "Tonight, at least."

"I don't sleep much at all these days," the man replied regretfully. "Be that as it may, should you ever find yourself in London, the least I can do is offer you good company and a cigar. Perhaps you can regale me with the story of your efforts."

"I'd rather not relive it," Sam said.

"Well, then," the man said, a hint of deflation in his voice, "just the cigar. I tip my hat to you—what did you say your name was?"

"I didn't," Sam replied.

"Probably better that way," the man said. "Thank you for being a light in this dark time. Right now, my little island is very dark, and we will only see the shadows if we have light."

ACKNOWLEDGMENTS

Thank you for reading *The Shadows of Might*. If you'd like to go on more adventures with Sam Abel—and there will be more—you can continue with *Everywhere and Nowhere*, in ebook, paperback, or hardcover formats wherever books are sold. This is the third of many books I have planned for release. I'll be offering both stand-alone novels for those like me who like contained reads, as well as series for those who like to stick with a longer story . If you're enjoying my books, feel free to leave a review wherever you review books.

After Pam (the Black Mouth Cur) inspired me to finish *A Whisper in the Oaks*, I knew that Sam was going to need a proper adventure to go on. I knew only three things when I started the story: that Sam was going to infiltrate Germany, that he was going to fall for a defector, and that he would meet Lothar Eichler once more. Despite the fact that I had spent three weeks in Germany touring my family's home, I knew that to write a period piece was going to require a ton of research. I've always had interest in World War 2, specifically in the field of espionage, but there was still a lot I needed to learn.

I was inspired by my grandmother's memories of Pforzheim, and was lucky enough to visit the same streets she grew up on with her several years ago. The *Schwarzwald* was my main inspiration for this story. There's something very mystifying about that area of Germany, something fantastical and romantic, and yet, something brooding and intimidating. Perhaps it's the abundance of trees and the otherworldly feel it offers when one is deep in its forests. Even on a bright day, the sun's rays have a tough time reaching the forest floor, and that gives it a unique identity as one caught between light and shadow.

After doing my due diligence to write the best story I could when I set out to create *The Shadows of Might*, I began to expand that research considerably to continue to develop Sam's stories and adventures. I began to read more non-fiction than fiction to gather as many details about the war as I could, particularly when they pertained to espionage. What I found were thrilling stories of secret meetings and information gathering that lead to Allied advantages, as well as mythic tales of infiltration and defection.

As I continued to outline the story, I knew that I would be focusing on the morbid repercussions of these tales, the uncelebrated heroes, and the consequences of participating in the transfer of information of value to undermine the enemy. Those who took major risks to turn the tide of the war are often unknown. Perhaps the nature of operating in the shadows bring with it an anonymity that never reveals the identities of those heroes and villains. Often those who receive glory are few, and standing in their shadows are lines of aids and supporters, the names of whom are lost to time.

During Sam's adventures, I will always try to explore the nature of war, espionage, and the grey areas wedged between the black and the white—somewhere in between the light and the shadow.

You can look for updates (and join my mailing list) at www.clarkemayer.com

ABOUT THE AUTHOR

Clarke Mayer is a filmmaker, photographer, and writer from New Jersey. Most of his day is dominated by a Black Mouth Cur named Pam who doesn't ever run out of energy. He likes to write, hike, and run, but most of all he likes to read and watch crime, spy, horror, and thriller stories.